LUCID DESIGN

BOOK ONE OF THE DESIGNED SERIES

LUCID DESIGN

BOOK ONE OF THE DESIGNED SERIES

KATE TAILOR

FIFE
PRESS

an imprint of

YOUNG DRAGONS PRESS

OGHMA

C R E A T I V E   M E D I A

Bentonville, Arkansas • Los Angeles, California

www.oghmacreative.com

Library of Congress Cataloging-in-Publication Data

Names: Tailor, Kate, author
Title: Lucid Design/Kate Tailor | Designed #1
Description:First Edition | Bentonville: Fife, 2020
Identifiers: LCCN: 2019946954 | ISBN: 978-1-63373-542-2 (hardcover) |
ISBN: 978-1-63373-543-9 (trade paperback) | ISBN: 978-1-63373-544-6 (eBook)
BISAC: YOUNG ADULT FICTION/Science Fiction |
YOUNG ADULT FICTION/Loners & Outcasts |
YOUNG ADULT FICTION/Action & Adventure
LC record available at: https://lccn.loc.gov/2019946954

Fife Press hardcover edition February, 2020

Cover & Interior Design by Casey W. Cowan
Editing by Gordon Bonnet, Linda Knight & Amy Cowan

Published by Fife Press, an imprint of Young Dragons Press, a subsidiary of The Oghma Book Group.

To my only slightly evil twin.

ACKNOWLEDGEMENTS

THIS BOOK IS POSSIBLE because of a group of speculators, an accountant, a podiatrist, a Belgian, a set of crazy aunts and their husbands, two lovable children, a father, a missed mother, an extra mother, and a great group of Oghmaniacs.

LUCID DESIGN

CHAPTER
01

PAIN PULSED THROUGH Raleigh's leg with each beat of her heart, startling her back to consciousness. Asphalt bit into her cheek, and her metal bike-frame tethered her to the ground. The metallic odor of dirt and mud overtook the lingering smell of morning dew. She'd blacked out, again, the fourth time this week.

It wasn't her first episode on a bike, there was a reason she'd never been handed the keys to the car, but it was the first time she'd awoken on this stretch of path. A creek rushed in the distance, and a cement underpass lay ahead. It came back to her, she'd been on her way home from Emily's house.

She had to get up. Her leg covered in warm blood was the worst of the wounds. If the accident was bad enough, her mother would use this as more reason to have her stay home. Raleigh couldn't let a scratch hold her back, couldn't let the blackouts hold her back. Not anymore.

"Are you all right?" A man in cycling shorts stopped his bike and crouched down near her. His hands opened in a gesture of help, but his face held the open-mouthed expression of not knowing what to do.

"Fine." She caught her reflection in his wrap-around sunglasses. Her hair poked out of her helmet.

"That was a bad fall. Is there something I can do?"

"No, I'm fine."

"Your leg." The man pointed to her calf.

Raleigh winced as she shoved the bike to the side and got a look at her left leg, or at least tried to look at it. Blood ran down her skin, dripping onto the concrete and staining it red. A deep cut, but still just a cut. Not a broken bone or a concussion. This scar would add to the collection she already had going. The bruises from two days ago were a deep purple.

Home was a thirty-minute ride away. Not that she'd be riding in this condition. Closing her eyes, she mapped out the city behind her eyelids. There should be a hospital a few blocks away.

The man had his phone out. "I'll call an ambulance."

"No, don't. It's not that bad. I'm fine. You can go." Raleigh grabbed her sleepover clothes from her pack. She compressed the nightshirt over the cut, gritting her teeth through the pain. Then she tied the two arms together. It worked just well enough to stop the bleeding, or at least mask it.

She lifted her bike up and limped in the direction of the hospital. He pocketed his phone, and after another head-to-toe glance, picked up his own bike, mounted in one fluid motion, and was off.

With him gone she had no reason to appear strong. She crumpled against the bike, a painful wheeze strangling in her throat. She hurt, but at least her bike wasn't broken, and neither was she. This wasn't her first fall. The most important thing was to get back up again, not stay down. Her condition could only defeat her if she let it, and today was not that day.

Ten minutes later she'd dragged herself the four blocks to the hospital. It would be another Sunday morning spent in the emergency room. The automatic doors opened for Raleigh, and the tart odor of disinfectant stung her nose. She wobbled in, the gash on her left leg seeping with each step. The shirt no longer masked the blood, only sopped it up. With only a few open seats in the waiting area, she wouldn't be getting out of here anytime soon.

Second in line, Raleigh waited behind a family with an infant. His wails cut the air, and she instinctually gripped her ears, the blood from her hand wetting her hair before she could think better of it. Over the mother's shoulder peeked a beet-red face, but it was more than a fever. Raleigh sensed the blood throbbing painfully through each ear. Every scream threated to pierce the inflamed eardrums. Raleigh clenched her teeth, trying to ignore his pain, wishing she could block him out. Instead she waited uncomfortably until they stepped away, and the distance eased the intensity.

The receptionist peered over her desk, frowning at the trail of blood Raleigh left in her wake. "I need a mop," she called over her shoulder. Then, to Raleigh, "Have you been here before?"

"Once a few years ago, I should be in your system." A fair bet, Raleigh was in all of them. "My name is Raleigh Groves."

"Are your parents here?"

"I'm eighteen."

"Then take these forms, fill them out, and we'll get to you as soon as we can." She handed Raleigh a towel then craned her neck to speak around her. "Next in line."

Raleigh winced to the side as a man with a mop appeared. Reaching down, she pressed the soft white cotton on top of her dirtied shirt. The only open seat in the room was beside a woman wearing a mask and gripping her stomach.

"I might have the stomach flu," the woman warned.

Raleigh needed to rest her leg and took the seat anyway. Her own stomach turned as she sensed a wave of nausea roll through the woman. That wasn't the flu. A tiny heartbeat fluttered away low in the woman's abdomen. The fetus couldn't have been more than eight weeks old. His kicks were too light to bother his mother, but he was human enough for Raleigh to sense. Obviously, the woman didn't know, and Raleigh didn't want to risk her secret by telling.

After returning the form to the receptionist, she sat and waited. She let the stinging pain of her leg distract her from the infant's ears and the woman's nausea and the rest of the ailments in the waiting room. Then an older couple entered, and she fought the urge to grab her head. The older man's head felt as though it were cleaved in two.

"Donna, let's go back, it's too busy. I'll take another aspirin," the old man said. His wife ignored him and spoke to the receptionist.

How could he think with pain that bad? His left hand moved toward the bridge of his nose as if he had to feel his way. Funny, he was usually right-handed.

He was having a stroke.

The man took a seat in the corner with his wife. Raleigh couldn't stay silent about this. "Excuse me, this man is having a stroke!" She used the tone of voice her uncle Patrick, a physician, used. No one moved, instead a hush fell over the room. "Look, he's favoring his left side."

The receptionist moved quickly from behind the desk, her white sneakers squeaking on the clean floor. She crouched down to his level and studied his eyes. "Get the nurses, his pupils aren't the same size."

Raleigh crept back to her seat, careful to keep out of the way as a pair of nurses rushed over with a wheelchair. They loaded him up and moved quickly through the heavy doors to the exam rooms. The attention of the room went with them. Only the receptionist kept her eyes on Raleigh. "You're an observant girl," she said as she walked back to her desk.

Raleigh shrugged. Hopefully no other urgent problems walked through the door. Catching one ailment could be overlooked, but two would draw suspicion. Not that those suspicions ever went anywhere. She'd referred a great number of people to Uncle Patrick and his colleagues. Always grateful, the physicians had come to trust her, despite no one knowing how her ability worked. Raleigh held a place alongside unexplained medical phenomena like dogs who smelled cancer.

Eventually, a nurse dressed in panda bear scrubs escorted her through the double doors to a wide hallway flanked by exam rooms. "It says here you fell off your bike?" The nurse flipped through her questionnaire.

"Yeah."

"Was a car involved?"

Raleigh took a deep breath. "No car. I blacked out."

"Fainted? Please step onto the scale."

She didn't bother slipping out of her shoes. "It happens all the time."

"Did you eat breakfast this morning?"

Thankfully the nurse didn't immediately try to tease out if she was doing drugs. "Yes. It happens a lot. I just need a few stitches." These questions weren't necessary, all she wanted was to be fixed up and on her way.

"Have you been to see a doctor about it?" The nurse led Raleigh into an exam room with a bed on wheels. Cries and talking echoed through the glass wall. The curtains didn't keep out the shadows of the other patients walking to their rooms.

Raleigh sat down on the solitary bed, the plastic lining under the sheets crumpling under her movement. "Many. I'm only here for the shin."

"Okay. Doctor Ng will be in to see you shortly."

Dr. Ng entered before the nurse finished saying his name. He grabbed a pair of gloves, and the nurse stood in the doorway ready to help.

"She fell off her bike," the nurse said. "Blacked out."

Dr. Ng sat on the stool and slid over to Raleigh. Delicately, he unwrapped her leg revealing the peeled back skin and cut that had begun to clot. "Good idea, using the shirt. This looks pretty deep. You'll need stitches, but you knew that, and that's why you're here."

He pulled a small tray over, and the nurse handed him some thread. The disinfectant stung as he cleaned the cut.

"What caused the blackout?"

"No one knows. But I get a few a week. I wear protective pads when I cycle, but every now and then I fall on something sharp. I'm not sure what cut me this time. When I woke up on the bike path, I wasn't far from your hospital, so I walked."

"Brave girl," Dr. Ng said.

There were two types of doctors. The first didn't want to delve into her problems, and the second liked the challenge of her mystery illness. Dr. Ng's face grew contemplative, and she feared he was more of the latter.

"Have you been tested by a neurologist?" he asked, as if he was the first to consider it.

"Lots. It's not seizures or anything with the vasomotor system."

"Big word for an eighteen-year-old. Is it hormonal?"

"We don't know what it is. It started when I was seven, before puberty. So, they don't think it's that. And it's not cancer, before you ask."

"I don't normally ask that. I'd presume that you would've mentioned it on your form... if you knew you had cancer."

"I'm one of those medical mysteries."

"You know, I've heard about a girl around your age who's supposed to solve those."

She fought the urge to shift in her seat. For a moment she wondered if he knew, but his smile indicated it was an off-the-cuff comment. He, like many doctors in the area, had probably just heard of her in passing. Most of them didn't put too much stock in her legend, unless they saw her at work. Ironically, she could diagnose everyone else's illnesses, but not her own.

"All done." Dr. Ng patted her good knee. "You're good to go. Hope they find out what's causing those blackouts."

"Me, too." She wondered if he was going to offer her a sucker.

The nurse told her to stay put for a moment and came back with a printout of what they'd done, when to follow up with her primary, and a little information on scar care. Raleigh thanked her and was on her way.

———————

"I'VE BEEN WORRIED about you," Raleigh's mother, Beth, said at the sound of the mudroom door opening.

This didn't come as a surprise. Her mother constantly worried, and with Raleigh's condition, she was a good candidate for that concern. Raleigh put down her helmet and pads, then stood in the mudroom for a few moments readying herself before heading into the kitchen.

"I tried calling your phone." Beth stood near the stove, her doughy hands on her hips. A yeasty odor lingered in the air. When she was stressed, Beth baked. Currently the countertops were over-run with cookies and breads.

"The screen broke, so I couldn't answer it."

"Did you fall again?" Beth inspected her daughter, homing in on her shin. "When did you get that?"

"This morning, on the way home from Emily's house."

"I told you she lived too far away for you to ride your bike."

"It's a forty-minute bike ride... usually."

"Emily should have driven you."

Raleigh sighed. "I could just as easily have fallen a few blocks away. The distance has nothing to do with it."

Raleigh's dad stepped into the kitchen and headed straight for the coffee pot. "Raleigh, you're home. See, Beth? I told you she was fine."

"Theodore, she has been to the ER."

Theo swept his eyes over his daughter. "At least it's not her head. You were wearing your helmet?"

Of course, she'd worn her helmet, and the pads, and the ugly reflective jacket so people could spot her better. She bit down the snarky comment that burned in her chest. Over the years she'd given them too much grief. "I wore my helmet."

"Mail came for you yesterday." He handed her a packet off the counter. "It looks important."

The seal of the University of Colorado adorned the corner of the thick white envelope. So far, she'd managed to intercept all university-mail before her parents saw it, which meant stopping at home before going to after-school activities. She didn't expect the registration packet for another week. How often were people ahead of schedule? Better yet, how often did it ruin everything?

"What is it?" Her mother reached out her hand.

Raleigh grabbed the envelope before her mother could take it. She had a speech prepared to tell her parents. One that she'd been revising since last December when she'd been accepted. The timing was never right. Of all the moments though, this seemed the worst. The thick envelope weighted heavy on her hand and conscience. She had to come clean. "I've been accepted to the university."

Her father smiled, and her mother said, "Online university! I'm so glad you decided that's best."

"No. University, university, in Boulder. I want to become a doctor, and the best way to do that is by taking pre-med classes there."

Her mother's face fell slack. While her mother stood at a loss for words, Raleigh indulged in what this scene would look like in a normal household, or hers if she were a normal girl. The college-bound child announcing to their parents that they'd been accepted and given a full scholarship. A scholarship earned with a 4.0 GPA. After the announcement, they'd pick out duvet covers for the extra-long twin bed in the dorm room. There might be some fussing over the class schedule but nothing troubling. One thing was for sure, there'd be smiles and congratulations. Unfortunately, Raleigh wasn't that girl.

Her father clasped her shoulder. "Congratulations, Raleigh." The small statement aligned him with her against her mother. Raleigh's father might've been the lawyer in the family, but her mother was far better at debating. She also usually got her way, at least when it came to Raleigh.

Her mother's brow furrowed, and Raleigh could imagine the arguments brewing. The frustration on her mother's face gave way to confidence and a bit of a warm mother-knows-best smile. "Honey, we haven't budgeted the money for college. Don't forget I just opened the flower shop. You'll dig yourself into debt. And with your health situation, you might never be able to work it off."

"I earned a full scholarship."

Her father let out his breath, and she could feel his chest loosen. It occurred to Raleigh that he may've scraped together the funds and gone against her mother. Now he didn't have to spend the money.

"That's quite an accomplishment." His eyes communicated an effort toward diplomacy.

Beth let the talk of money die there. If it wasn't going to help her, it wasn't worth discussing. "You're simply too sick to go."

"I'm going to be sick no matter where I am."

"Yes, but here you're safe."

"No safer than anywhere else. And being there might be a little safer. I can probably walk everywhere."

"People don't know about you. You'll cause a fuss."

Raleigh anticipated this argument. People who didn't know that she blacked out tended to be upset upon seeing her unconscious on the ground. They generally called 9-1-1 and attempted to resuscitate her—even though she never stopped breathing. One odd woman once pulled her tongue for fear that she was choking on it. Often in the heat of the moment, people overlooked the medical bracelet on her wrist. "I'll wear a sign." She winced at the embarrassment of the idea.

Her mother's brow line softened, and her eyes grew glossy. While good at arguing, she was a master at guilting. "Let's not give up hope for a treatment." Beth used the word treatment because a cure was less likely. Usually she spoke of cures, but she pulled out all the stops now.

"There's never going to be a treatment! No one knows what this is. The answer isn't going to magically show up one day. This is what my life looks like."

"Raleigh," her father said, his eyes soft.

"No, Dad. I've had the advantage of you two helping me exhaust all options in my search. Now, when I go out, I don't need to hold on to the hope. I know there is none. It's not that bad. My illness could be a lot worse. I could look different and have to worry about discrimination. You guys were against me riding my bike, and yes, I get a few scrapes, like today. But look how well I've managed getting around. I'm going to continue doing that, getting around. And college is the next step." Raleigh's back stood straighter after the speech. For too long she'd let hope bury the truth.

Her mother wrung her hands around a dishtowel and stared down at the checked pattern. "No matter where you go in life, Raleigh June Groves, you never give up hope. We'll discuss this later."

For now Raleigh had won, and she hadn't needed to use the big guns—that she was eighteen and they had no right to tell her what to do. She'd only use that argument as a last resort.

Leaving the tension in the kitchen, she headed up the stairs to her bedroom. She shut the door and ripped open the thick packet. It contained her dorm assignment, roommate's name, and class registration information. Hope looked different to her than it did to her mother. Hope was freedom. Hope was leaving. Hope was in that heavy week-early envelope.

CHAPTER
02

"NO AMOUNT OF laundry is going to make her forgive you." Thalia, Raleigh's younger sister, leaned against the dryer twirling her nose ring with her finger. And Thalia would know. She'd been testing her mother's limit with her punk appearance and loose grades for a while.

"It can't hurt." Even if Thalia was right, Raleigh was still going to try. A week had passed since the college confrontation, and since then she'd cleaned the kitchen, the bathrooms, and the garage. Now she tackled the laundry. After that, she'd sort the boxes in the basement. As Raleigh worked through the mountain of housework, her mother held steadfast to her grudge, like a sea captain enduring a maelstrom.

"I still think it's great that you're going." Thalia hopped onto the dryer and started folding a shirt.

Raleigh smiled. "Why are you helping all of a sudden? Are you in trouble or something?"

"Going to be. Alec Quick asked me out."

"The kid whose pants fell down in gym last year?"

Alec was the guy to date in Thalia's small group at school, a crowd that colored their hair and smoked near the front parking lot. Despite their appearances, none of them got into any real trouble, there was no cutting class. Thalia merely tested her parents' patience but didn't break it. Amethyst hair could only do so much.

"It doesn't make him any less cool. I'd think you'd have more sympathy, with your fainting and all."

"I blackout. I do not accidentally lose my pants in front of two gym classes. He's going to be a senior, isn't he?"

"Yeah, but I'll be a junior."

"Tell him to take out his eyebrow ring before he meets mom."

"She might not notice him with all the sulking she's doing about you leaving. I always thought Lana and Ben would leave me, but never you."

A pang filled Raleigh's chest. Everyone in her family had made sacrifices on her behalf. Raleigh always sucked up attention like a vacuum. Maybe Thalia was punk to stand out against Raleigh, not to anger their parents.

"What are these ribbons for?" Raleigh lifted two peach silk ribbons off the dryer. They looked like they belonged in a Louisa May Alcott book or on the head of a kindergartener.

Thalia tugged them away. "Mom says I have to wear my hair in a braid for Uncle Patrick's party tonight. These are to tone down the purple."

Raleigh smirked. "That's going to look good."

"Yeah, I know, but mom's been so pissed about your college news that I'm not going to fight her about it." Thalia slid off the dryer and shoved her hands into her pockets, wrinkling the ribbons in the process.

SWEAT SUCTIONED RALEIGH'S legs to the leather car seat. The itchy nylons her mother made her wear already had a tear near the ankle, and she resisted the urge to move and rip them further. She wished for tights but reconsidered when she glanced at Thalia. Her sister looked like a prairie girl from a bygone era, as long as you ignored the purple braids. Two years separated the girls in age, but Raleigh, with her neatly-styled brown hair and lavender cocktail gown, appeared much older. It helped that her back stood a little taller since the college confrontation with her mother.

Thalia flashed Raleigh a strained look. In that glance, Raleigh recognized the resemblance she had to her sister. A similarity that went beyond their hazel eyes, small noses, and freckles. They both dreaded things like this, social situations that their mother thrived on. They were their father's daughters.

Gravel pinged at the wheel wells of the car as they drove up the pebbled path to the mansion. Family birthdays usually consisted of a few scoops of ice cream, not rented venues, and certainly not valets.

Raleigh's family got out of the car, handed over the keys, and gawked at the house before them. If the building could speak, it would scoff at Uncle Patrick's mere fifty years. Its red bricks and iron gates boasted permanence. Raleigh followed her mother up the front steps. They'd put a hold on the conflict that simmered between them so they could celebrate tonight, but the truce wasn't loose enough to accommodate chitchat, and the silences sat crisp in the cool air.

"Are you with the Emerson Birthday?" a young doorman asked.

"Yes," Beth answered for her husband and children.

"Right through here." He ushered them through two large wooden doors. The early summer breeze drifted in with them prompting Raleigh to rub her chilled elbows. The young man deposited them in a grand entryway that opened into a vaulted ballroom.

At least a hundred people crowded together in groupings of three and four. Fancy dresses sparkled under the chandelier overhead. A quartet played in the corner, a pleasing background to the laughing and mingling.

"He's only turning fifty." Theo laughed at the spectacle of it all. "This is more befitting someone who's reached the big one hundred."

"Shannon likes parties." Beth's voice held a clear warning for him to behave.

Theo could be charming when he wanted. Being a lawyer, the suit he donned now was everyday wear. Still, he much preferred jeans and a t-shirt to this sort of thing. He gave Beth a wink—a promise that he wasn't going to comment again about the overdone venue.

"Would you like a glass of sparkling wine?" A petite woman approached them carrying a tray of champagne flutes. The bubbles knocked against the glass catching the light.

Theo took one. Beth held up her hand, refusing. The woman inched the tray closer to Raleigh. "I'm not old enough."

"You're such a square." Thalia rolled her eyes. "Don't turn it down at college."

Raleigh and her mother stiffened at the mention of college. Raleigh sensed the muscles in her mother's jaw tighten and then relax. Beth motioned to the crowd. "Why don't you girls go find your cousins?"

That was one order Thalia didn't hesitate to obey. Raleigh stepped away slowly, her eyes searching the room, finding familiar faces in unfamiliar clothes. Her gaze caught on Keith Moore, one of her classmates. Former classmate, as they'd both graduated.

Keith stood next to an older woman deep in conversation. With each word a dimple in his cheek faded and reappeared.

"You could talk to him," a voice said from behind.

Raleigh didn't need to turn around to know the speaker. If she hadn't recognized his voice, she would've known him by the pain in his arm caused from years of pitching baseball in college.

"I don't know what you're talking about." Warmth crept up her neck, and she could only hope it didn't show on her face. She turned toward Dr. Moore, father of the boy he'd caught her staring at.

"My son is a nice kid. He could use an influence like you."

Dr. Moore spoke as though Keith was some sort of vagrant who needed good influences. They both knew that wasn't the case. He was in almost every sport, and, like Raleigh, he graduated last semester with straight As. Undoubtedly, he was going to attend a prestigious college next fall, but she wasn't sure which one.

"I think he's doing fine without me," she said.

"Tim, you found her!" Raleigh's uncle rushed up and gave them each a warm pat on the back. His heart tapped anxiously in his chest, which surprised her, as her uncle normally had an even demeanor.

"Pat, what do you think of your niece and my son?" Dr. Moore asked.

Patrick looked at Keith and then to Raleigh. "I think she's too good for him."

Dr. Moore's smile waned a little. "In all honesty, I think you're right. Don't you worry, Raleigh, you'll find the right guy someday, and he'll be special."

"Yeah, he's going to have to be really good at baby-proofing the house and catching me when I fall." Raleigh meant it as a joke, but as the words slipped out of her mouth, she knew they were true. She'd spent more time in doctor offices than on dates and had more conversations about illnesses than cute boys. She snuck another peek at Keith, once again her peers moved forward without her. An ache blossomed in her chest. The thought of college squelched her self-pity.

"You are so much more than your illness." Dr. Moore, an oncologist, was accustomed to talking people through overwhelming obstacles. He walked the line of optimist and realist well.

Patrick gave Dr. Moore a pointed look. There was a secret.

"What are you hiding?" she asked.

Patrick tapped his nose. "I've never been able to keep a secret very long around you."

She shrugged. "You're excited about something. It wasn't hard to guess."

"When you turn twenty-one, we're taking you to Vegas," Dr. Moore teased. "But in all honesty, we wanted to discuss that talent of yours."

"You have a patient you need me to look at?" Cancer had a unique quality to it, out of control, sloppy, and reckless. Dr. Moore's patients were uncomfortable to be around.

"Not a patient." Patrick's eyes scanned the room. "It's about you. But we shouldn't talk about it here." He led them towards a room near the gardens. On the way over, more than one guest nodded his way or flagged him down. In return he gave friendly smiles but didn't allow any of them to detour them.

Patrick held open the tall door. Raleigh entered first. In the grand room her heels made small clacks on the polished wood floor, here a wool rug ate up any noise. The books along the wall gave off a dusty smell, and that coupled with the stiff odor of the leather furniture gave the room a stately presence. Dr. Moore shut the door behind him, and the voices from the party became a muffled din.

"Are we allowed in here?" Raleigh asked. The sofas and desk sat untouched. Most of the house masqueraded well as a wedding venue. This room had touches of personality that reminded her that it had once been a home.

Patrick glanced around. "Yeah, it's included in the rental. It's where the groom gets ready if there's a wedding. Or it can be a place for the guest of honor to escape when he doesn't want yet another person to remind him that he's half a century old."

"Or for a young lady to find out the truth." Dr. Moore's eyes twinkled in the dim light.

Her stomach did flips in anticipation. Memories of being young and hiding in her father's office added to the excitement. "The truth about what?"

Patrick's face transformed to the stoic one he used with his patients. "Tim and I have been doing a lot of research... to learn about your blackouts."

Raleigh's stomach knotted. Whatever they knew caused her uncle to be giddy. They had an answer. Doubt tempered her own eagerness. This wasn't the first time someone had claimed to know something. "You know? Like really know?"

"We think we do." Patrick put a hand on her shoulder.

"There is a story," Dr. Moore interrupted. "This is the most magnificent medical thing I've ever come across. We're going to walk you through it."

Patrick nodded. "Tim, you do it. I've never been a storyteller."

Dr. Moore took one of the chairs and motioned for them to sit on the sofa. "This all started when I stopped focusing on your main symptom, which is blacking out, and started investigating the other one."

"There is no other one. I don't get an aura, headache, or seizures. You know all this." In the past both men had tested her countless times. They knew the aspects of her riddle as well as she did.

Dr. Moore leaned back in his seat. "Your ability to sense disease, Raleigh. I didn't look in to it because it took me so long to understand what you do. At first, I thought you were observant or following a hunch. It took me a while to understand that you actually feel the disease."

"I thought you believed me about that a long time ago."

"I had faith in you. But I didn't understand precisely what you meant."

"It is a hard thing to believe," said Patrick. "Even with all the evidence, your mother still refuses to acknowledge it."

Dr. Moore resumed telling his story. "A year ago, I thought, why not follow that? And I did. I learned about an obscure group of scientists in the nineties who researched this exact sort of thing. The idea that some people can feel the ailments of others. History is littered with stories of people who can do it. Some thought they were inspired by God, some were undoubtedly fakes, and others charlatans. However, some of them were probably real, discounted for the same reasons people will want to discount you."

"Other people have been like me?" Little good it did Raleigh now. If only they could go back in time and Dr. Moore could tell the therapist who insisted that she was delusional.

"Yes, but probably not as good. These scientists in the nineties not only looked in to who could do it but how. They discovered a whole tribe of people with your skill. When a townsperson fell sick, the healers would drink a potion that helped them 'speak to the spirit' of the person afflicted. They put a religious bent on it, but it is the same thing you do."

"I don't drink anything." The mystical leaning made her question if it was the same as her affliction.

"No, you don't. Most of the people could only sense disease when they drank this potion and were in distress. You said that your ability enhances when you're nervous, such as during public speaking."

"Yes. I can pick up on people farther away when I'm scared or stressed."

"So, like them, you have increased abilities during these times."

"But...."

Patrick put up his hand. "Let Tim finish."

"The scientists found that these people had a hormone in their system, and they named it Lucidin. When enough of this hormone was present, it allowed the person to sense someone else. The drink caused the body to produce more Lucidin, as did stress."

"So, you think I have this Lucidin in my system?"

"You do." Guilt riddled Patrick's face, and he bit his lip. "That's what I checked your blood for two weeks ago."

"You didn't want to get my hopes up." Raleigh barely remembered giving him the blood. Two weeks ago, he'd requested some, saying it was for yet another routine test.

"The results came in too late last night, or I would've told you." Joy radiated from him, Raleigh could feel it building in his chest.

No not yet, she wouldn't get excited until she was sure. "The results came in from where?"

"From Doctor Orman, a Lucidin expert," Dr. Moore said. "She's flying in to do more tests with you."

Patrick put his hand on Raleigh's shoulder. "It's a formality. She's confident the Lucidin is causing your blackouts."

Of all the theories and misdiagnoses that Raleigh had endured, this was the most outlandish. If she didn't trust these two men so much, she would've assumed it was some kind of joke.

"Is there a cure?"

"We'll have to talk to Doctor Orman," said Patrick. "Don't tell your mother—not yet. Let's be sure before we say anything."

"That shouldn't be a problem. Mom isn't talking to me much these days."

"Come by the hospital Monday. You can meet Doctor Orman, and we can establish where we're going from there," said Dr. Moore.

The conversation ended, and they sat in silence. For so long they'd searched for answers, and now one could be days away.

CHAPTER
03

TWO DAYS LATER Raleigh sat on the exam table. Across from her hung a picture of a tree in all its autumn grace. With her numerous trips to doctors over the years, she'd become an exam room art aficionado. Most practitioners and institutions chose landscapes like the one on this wall. Others were more adventurous and went with impressionists. Raleigh's neurologist was obsessed with babies dressed in costumes. The tree across the way appeared happy despite being on the verge of losing its leaves.

A long dormant emotion crept up her spine—hope. It had been absent so long that she'd forgotten the way it fluttered in her stomach and lightened her shoulders. When she was young and her issues fresh, hope was always with her. It made her eager to go to the doctors and willing to complete any tests or labs they wanted. Over the years that hope had gradually been replaced by cynicism. The trips became yet another doctor's appointment—a formality of being sick rather than an opportunity to get better. She hadn't fully realized the extent of her disillusionment until now, when hope niggled the back of her mind.

What if?

Two quick raps on the door drew her from her musings. Dr. Moore, Uncle Patrick, and a slip of a woman entered the room. The lady, who couldn't have been much more than five feet, was dwarfed by the two men. Her rapid heartbeats, thin fingers, and delicate cheeks likened her to a fledgling bird. Thin gray hairs escaped matching clips over her ears.

"Raleigh?" The woman's French accent came as a surprise. "I'm Doctor Sabine Orman."

"Nice to meet you, Dr. Orman."

"Please call me Sabine." She placed a small case on the side counter and opened the twin clasps. "It is so nice to finally meet you. I've been talking with your uncle and friend. We were discussing how much Lucidin we found in your blood. Did they tell you what Lucidin is?"

"Yes. It's what lets me understand people better than most. It's why I can tell you have hypothyroidism and your treatment dose is perhaps a little too high."

Sabine looked at Dr. Moore. "She is skilled, as you said."

"You should see how well she can detect cancer." Dr. Moore spoke with all the pride of a father. "Her early detection has already saved a lot of lives. When I think of the career that she has ahead of her...."

Sabine's face remained unaffected. Inside, however, the doctor wasn't placid. Dr. Moore's words caused her shoulders to tighten and her stomach to churn. Hallmarks of worry, but the reason behind the concern remained elusive.

"There are tests that my uncle said you could perform," Raleigh said.

"Yes. The blood work that your uncle provided showed that you create Lucidin. It's the rare person who does that, and even then they make very little, much less than what we've seen with you. I believe it is the abundance of the Lucidin that is problematic. It will depend on the number of receptors you have in your brain. If my theory is correct, you have many receptors and they're overloading with Lucidin. Think of it like a circuit with too many appliances attached. If there's a surge of electricity from the demand, it will cause them all to overload. In short, that's what I think's happening, a high number of receptors overloading on Lucidin causing a surge and then a blackout."

Raleigh hadn't ever thought of herself in that way, overloading, but it fit. "Has this happened to other people you know?"

"No. No one else I've known has made so much that it overwhelms them. A few have made a lot, but it didn't have the same consequences. That's why the receptor volume is important. I've brought along a marker that will bind to them and give us an idea of how many you have, and if that is indeed causing your problem."

"Sabine gave me the marker and ran the test earlier," Dr. Moore told Raleigh. "I was interested to see how many receptors I have and didn't want your uncle to accuse me of making you a guinea pig. So, I figured I'd go first. It didn't hurt at all."

Pain didn't concern Raleigh. Over the years she'd been picked and prodded enough that she was numb to it. She turned over her arm, exposing the crisscross of veins.

It didn't take long for Sabine to inject the marker. "We'll have to wait a half hour for the marker to circulate to your brain."

"Sabine and I will commandeer the imaging equipment. We'll meet you down in imaging." Dr. Moore and Sabine took their leave.

Raleigh and Patrick waited alone in the room. Her eyes rested on the painting of the tree, while his searched her face. "You don't seem as excited as I thought you'd be. I thought you'd be thrilled about figuring this out... after going so long without any answers."

Her uncle was right, but she couldn't let her hope rise only to have it fall. "I am excited, but she didn't mention a cure."

"One thing at a time."

"I think Sabine is scared of something."

"I didn't get that impression."

"Her body tensed up while we were discussing Lucidin."

"Perhaps because it's making you sick. As she said, you're the first person she knows that it makes ill."

Her illness didn't make doctors that uneasy. She didn't talk to her uncle about it further. Instead, they anxiously watched seconds tick pass on the clock until it was time to go to the imaging room.

Forty minutes and one imaging session later, Raleigh and the doctors crowded into Dr. Moore's office. She'd spent time in here before, meeting people who had the unfortunate need to become Dr. Moore's patients. Everyone held their breath, a silence settled in around them. These doctors could train their faces to hide emotions, but their bodies betrayed them.

Sabine put three scans on Dr. Moore's board. The marker lit up the three different brains with varying amounts of fluorescent green. The first had a spattering, the second a decent amount, and the third looked as though someone had let a highlighter bleed out on it.

"This first scan is Dr. Moore." Sabine traced her fingers along the green pattern. "Half the population doesn't have any receptors to speak of. This many would put him in the sixty-seventh percentile."

"Half the population?" Dr. Moore asked. "But I don't have any of Raleigh's skills."

Sabine nodded. "You have receptors, but you do not create Lucidin. This scan beside yours is from someone who falls in the eightieth percentile. They also didn't make Lucidin, so, like you, they are unaffected. This last scan is Raleigh's. I think we can safely say that the high receptor volume and the overproduction of Lucidin in her system is causing her blackouts."

It was an answer, a solid answer after all this time. Raleigh let go of the breath she'd been holding.

"If I took Lucidin, could I sense people?" Dr. Moore asked.

Sabine shook her head. "It might give you better awareness of your own body."

Patrick pointed to the brain scan in the middle. "Could that person use Lucidin the way Raleigh does?"

Sabine paused, and her shoulders once again tightened. "Our initial research hoped to allow people to use Lucidin diagnostically. Unfortunately, Lucidin is very rare, and it's harmful for people to take. Only people like Raleigh, who make it on their own, benefit from it. In her case, I wouldn't call it a benefit if she's blacking out."

"That brings us to our next question," Patrick said. "Is there a treatment?"

"To study Lucidin, a device was made that can extract it from the body. If she extracts it, then it should decrease, if not completely eliminate, the blackouts."

"I could go to college and be normal." There would be no ugly reflective vests or signs strapped to her back to set her apart.

Dr. Moore rubbed his hands together. "How do we get hold of one of these machines?"

The side of Sabine's mouth dipped down. "I have one, but it's large and bulky. Eventually, I might be able to get my hands on something smaller and portable, but that may take months, if not years. Until then, I can happily invite Raleigh to use mine."

"Great. That's great," Raleigh said. Maybe she could keep it on campus. It didn't really matter, without blackouts she could learn to drive. "Can I keep it in my dorm?"

"I'm sorry, no. It's much too large for that. I'm suggesting that you come with me to my home and receive treatment there. The machine is old and can't be moved, especially not across the Atlantic."

"Are you from France?"

"No, Liege, Belgium."

Raleigh shouldn't have been surprised that her home was in Europe. Patrick let out a long whistle—no doubt thinking of the long argument that his sister would put up if Raleigh asked to go.

Reality always had a way of knocking Raleigh down. "That's too far, and there's no way I could afford to live there."

"My sister-in-law owns a bakery there, and they could use another set of hands. The work would cover your room and board," Sabine offered.

"Or we could wait for a portable machine, and you could go to college here." Patrick made the suggestion, but he didn't look happy with it.

Dr. Moore snapped his fingers. "Or we could build one! If she'll need treatment for the foreseeable future, it would be worth it."

Sabine flinched at that solution. "To do that we would have to dismantle the one we have, to see how it works. All the schematics were destroyed when people stopped studying Lucidin. I'm not sure we could ever get the device back together if we take it apart. I think that she should come to Liege for treatment. The sooner, the better. The falls are a danger to her."

"Only if she lands wrong," said Patrick.

"I promise to take good care of her. Why don't we see if we can give her a chance at a normal life, free of this condition?"

Patrick exchanged a look with Raleigh. Her mother would fight this. The question now was, did it matter? That maturity Raleigh had gained a few days ago made her think not.

Patrick shook Sabine's hand. "We are so thankful that you've discovered the cause of Raleigh's blackouts. The offer you're making for treatment is very generous. But we'll have to discuss it with her parents before a decision can be made."

"Of course," Sabine said. "Raleigh, I hope you'll come, and I look forward to treating you. Please take your time and let me know your decision."

Patrick and Raleigh followed Sabine out of the office. Raleigh watched as the small woman walked down the hall, her steps soft. Then she turned to her uncle. They had a lot to discuss.

PATRICK DROVE SILENTLY, tapping the steering wheel every so often to the music. The tires broke through puddles. It rained during the brain scan, and the smell lingered in the air. Raleigh stared out the window. "She's not going to believe me."

"Who's not going to believe you?"

"Mom."

Patrick took a side road, detouring from her house. He pulled into the ice cream parlor parking lot. "Let's talk about what you want and what exactly we're going to say to your mother."

The clock on the dash showed that dinner was in an hour, and Beth would scold her if she filled up on ice cream. Another small hit. Raleigh climbed out of the car.

Old ladies sat on a bench outside, their cones dripping onto their liver-spotted hands. Patrick held open the door for his niece, and she stepped inside. The sweet smell of waffle cones brought a smile to her lips. Inside, children bounced on the balls of their feet trying to see the options.

With teenagers pulling crumpled dollars from their shorts and whispering about the other classmates in line, Raleigh easily fit in.

She glanced at the different flavors under the glass in half-full tubs. Uncle Patrick would get what he always got—butter pecan. Patrick had been bringing her here since she was too young to remember. Back then her older sister, Lana, would often order for her, and her older brother, Ben, would finish the cone when she was full.

Patrick treated Raleigh. As her tongue made its first trip around the scoop, she wondered if this was to celebrate learning about Lucidin or to soften the very serious discussion that lay ahead. Probably a little of both.

Customers brushed by them filing into line. Patrick motioned to the door. "Let's go outside. Better not to have this talk in public."

Patrick and Raleigh headed across the parking lot into the nearby neighborhood. They passed by the houses, avoiding the cracks in the sidewalk. Music echoed from a car driving by. Kids played on lawns, their skin tan even though school had only been out two weeks. This was her first summer vacation when the next year hadn't been plotted out. If she elected to skip college, then she'd be venturing out into adult life, a life she hadn't considered before. In that moment she was older, even with the chocolate ice cream in her hand.

"We shouldn't tell your mom the details about Lucidin." Patrick's steps fell into an easy rhythm. "She's never believed that you can feel illness. If we use that as evidence that we've solved your problem, she'll discount it. Instead, we'll say that you have a rare hormonal imbalance."

"It's not a lie. And you're right. She thinks I'm crazy when I bring up sensing people, so that's not a good place to start."

"Those stupid doctors have her believing you're making it up as a coping mechanism for your own illness. It makes you wonder how many things we ought to believe but don't. How many things do we discount because they're scary or fantastical?"

Raleigh stopped him from going off on one of his tangents. "Should I go to Belgium?"

"I'm not sure. If you didn't already have plans for college, the obvious answer is yes. To put your college plans on hold, I'm not sure it's worth it."

She couldn't discount college. Registration for classes began in two weeks. Her mother couldn't stop her. All her efforts would be wasted if she simply picked up and moved to Belgium.

"It would be a treatment," Patrick said.

The word hung on the air mingling with the smell of grass. Long ago she'd given up wishing for a treatment, and now one had arrived. It didn't come packaged the way she expected. She'd imagined it would be a pill. Maybe she'd have some nausea or other side effect, but she'd already decided that a treatment was worth a whole lot to her. Was it worth postponing college?

"It's not like I would never go to school. I would defer for a year or two. That was the plan before now, my mom's anyways. She wanted me to hold off until I got better. I guess she'll be getting her way."

Patrick crunched on the last bit of his cone and dusted his hands together scattering the crumbs. "I think that you should refrain from putting it like that. I doubt your mother will want you to go to Belgium, treatment or not. It's going to be an interesting debate, and you know how my sister loves those. Would you keep your scholarships? I'd imagine those would go away if you defer."

"I don't know. I could check. I suppose that would be another downside." Raleigh's wants shifted from college to the prospect of getting well. If it worked, when she did go to college, she wouldn't have to wear a sign around her neck. She wouldn't have to be known as the sick girl. She could have a normal life. "I want to go to Belgium."

"You don't have to decide now."

"I do, though. I have a deadline for registration and my tuition. If I'm going to go to Belgium, I need to decide now."

"We just found out. Sometimes it's good to sleep on it. And we don't really know Doctor Orman."

"You didn't look into her?"

"I did, and her professional résumé is impressive. Not only is she a physician, but for a number of years she taught at an orphanage. But I know nothing about Liege and her life there."

"You know my mother. The moment she learns of the treatment, of Belgium, and the rest of it, she's going to plan out exactly what I should do. If I go to her without a firm plan of my own, I'll end up like Lana. Remember how she ended up in a major she hated freshman year because Mom insisted?"

"We can hold off on telling her while you make sure this is the right choice."

Raleigh absently kicked a rock on the sidewalk and watched it skitter to the gutter. "She's not going to be happy that we've kept this from her. Don't say she won't know, she figures out everything."

"It just seems like a hasty decision. I know how much you want answers, but I don't want you to feel pressured to leave in an attempt to find them."

"I can always come back. Sure, it's across the world, but there are planes. Some of my classmates are taking a year off to find themselves. That's what we'll call this."

During their talk they'd circled the block and had made their way back to the parking lot. With the ice cream eaten, they were ready to leave. Patrick unlocked his door. "I guess, then, it's time to go home and tell your mother the good news."

CHAPTER
04

THE AROMA OF Beth's lasagna greeted Raleigh and Patrick when they entered the house. Raleigh's father muttered to himself in his study, something about paperwork and unrealistic deadlines. An otherwise average day, if it wasn't for her extraordinary news. Anticipation gripped her stomach. Going to Europe wasn't anything like college. There wouldn't be weekend visits to do laundry, and her parents couldn't stop by for lunch.

"Dad?" Raleigh said, peering into his study.

Theo flipped through a small mountain of paper on his desk. "I'm busy, Raleigh. I'm hoping to get a few more emails sent out before dinner."

"It's important."

He looked up, his shoulders sinking. "Is this about your mother not wanting you to go to college? You should go."

"It's a bit more complicated than that," Patrick said, walking in behind Raleigh.

"Patrick?" Theo left his papers. "Are you staying for dinner? Maybe we can watch some of the game."

"That'd be great."

"Let me get you a beer." Theo led them into the kitchen. "Beth, your brother is here."

Beth removed the lasagna from the oven and pressed a finger on the melted cheese. "Patrick, are you staying for dinner? We have enough for your whole family. Should I call Shannon?"

"No. I'll stay, but I don't think you're going to want a crowd."

Beth pushed a lock of red hair behind her ear. She raised an eyebrow at her brother's physician voice and scrutinized his face. "What is it, Patrick?"

"Mom, we know what's making me sick," Raleigh said.

Beth's oven-mittened hand flew to her chest. She looked at Raleigh, then at her brother, and lastly her husband. "What?"

"We figured it out today. Uncle Patrick had a specialist come and analyze me, and she solved it."

"What!" Beth gulped down a sob. "Are you going to be all right?"

"Better than all right!" Raleigh hugged her mom and took in the flour, cheese, and all the other wonderful smells associated with her. "There's a treatment and everything."

Beth's eyes grew glossy. "I knew. I told you. Didn't I? I told you that we'd figure it out. Now we have. What is it?"

"A hormone." Patrick didn't include the name. "I sent the specialist, Doctor Orman, the blood work last week. We got confirmation that the hormone is the likely culprit behind the blackouts."

"It's a miracle." Beth grasped Raleigh's hands. "And the treatment, is it a medication? We'll have to start her on it immediately."

Raleigh's mother had none of her daughter's reservations about hope. Raleigh capitalized on that. "That's the most important thing, right? That I get better?"

Her father must have heard her apprehension. "Yes. That is what matters most. If you're worried about the cost, we'll find a way to afford it."

"Is it expensive?" Beth asked. "It doesn't matter. We'll work with the insurance."

"It's free." Raleigh glanced to Patrick. The bad news had to be delivered at the perfect moment.

"Well, that's even better!" Beth beamed. "To think, when we woke up this morning it was a perfectly normal day. Patrick, thank you so much." She embraced her brother. "How soon can she start? Of course, I'll want to see all the research on the treatment, but I can tell you're confident."

Patrick grimaced at Raleigh. "There is a treatment, and it is free. But it involves an extraction of the hormone from Raleigh's blood."

"That sounds serious," Theo said.

Patrick shrugged. "Doctor Orman didn't imply that it's anything to be nervous about."

"Is it like dialysis?" Beth was familiar with the process because of her father's kidney disease years ago.

"Similar," Patrick said. "Only it can't be done at one of the local centers. It requires a special machine. Doctor Orman's is old and difficult to move, so Raleigh will have to go to her for treatment."

"Well, we can make arrangements to drive her to the treatments. I don't want her moving to downtown Denver." Beth tucked a strand of hair behind her daughter's ear.

Raleigh inched back from her mother. "Dr. Orman doesn't live in Denver. She lives in Liege, Belgium." Confusion crossed her mom's face. "It's the tiny country north of France. Waterloo." That was the extent of the information Raleigh knew.

Beth looked back and forth between Raleigh and Patrick. "I know where Belgium is."

Patrick spoke again, heading off the argument. "In a year or two, the doctor thinks she'll be able to provide Raleigh a portable version. Until then, the large one in Belgium is the only option."

Beth's face grew pensive, and Raleigh sensed her pulse slow and her breathing steady. "Then Raleigh will have to wait a year or two."

Patrick pressed his lips together and looked to Raleigh. "If she stays, she'll likely be a sophomore when the machine comes."

"She's not going to college," Beth said.

Raleigh let out an exasperated sigh, she'd had enough. "So, let me get this straight. You aren't going to let me go to college because I'm sick, but you aren't going to let me go to Belgium to get better."

"You can't go to college while you're ill because you could get hurt. The school is so large and people won't be familiar with your condition." Beth stood rigid. She wouldn't back down. "We've had this conversation enough times. There is no way I'm allowing you to go to Belgium. We don't know if this treatment will work. I admit, I'm excited that you two are so on-board with whatever Doctor Orman told you, but I haven't met the woman. How many doctors thought that they'd solved your problem only to do nothing? Living abroad is challenging, and you might still be sick. Even if you get better, it's going to be hard. You're only eighteen. We'll wait, get the portable machine when the time comes, and then, if you're healthy, you'll go to college. This is a wonderful development. You said you wanted to go to college and couldn't wait for a treatment. Now you have a timetable. You need a bit more patience, but I know you have it in you."

It figured that her mother had a third option. On the way over she assumed she'd push for her to go to college over Belgium. The idea of sitting and waiting hadn't crossed her mind. Waiting was like being in a stalled-out car while the rest of the cars breezed by on the freeway. She was all too familiar with it.

"I need to try this treatment," Raleigh said. Her mother had hit on a sore point. The Lucidin removal might not stop the blackouts. Unfulfilled promises of the past haunted her. What made this different was that it explained the sensing. Raleigh considered telling her mother that piece but left it out, knowing it would invalidate the diagnosis in Beth's mind.

"I want it to work." Beth squeezed Raleigh's arm. "But going away is out of the question right now."

Raleigh tugged away from her. "I'm sorry. I'm going. To Belgium, not college."

Beth frowned and narrowed her eyes. "We won't fund it." This argument hadn't panned out with college, but she was going to try it again with Belgium.

Raleigh had some money. Last summer she'd worked at a bookshop and saved every penny, in the event that her scholarships didn't come through. She'd have enough for a ticket there and enough to scrape by for a while. The bakery job Dr. Orman offered probably didn't pay well. There was also the whole issue of working internationally that she didn't pretend to know the logistics of. Still, if she lived frugally, she'd have enough to figure it out. Worst-case scenario was she ended up flying back in a few months.

"I don't need your money," Raleigh said. "And I'm eighteen."

"I forbid you to go." Beth turned away.

"Don't you want me to get better?"

"I do." Beth removed the plates from the cabinet, clanging them together purposefully. "But it can't be done hastily."

"Could you accompany Raleigh?" Patrick wondered aloud.

Hot mortification blazed Raleigh's cheeks. Her mother would fuss over her every inch of the way.

Beth swept her arm out. "I can't. I just opened the flower shop. Leaving now would sink the whole venture. I've waited years for this, not to mention the investment. I'm committed to it. Theo can't take leave from his work. He's taken too much as it is, over the years. Could you take her, Patrick?"

"I can't leave my practice, or Shannon and the kids. Raleigh might be gone months."

"Just long enough to set her up?"

Patrick rubbed the back of his neck and exhaled. "In two months, I can check-in."

"I can go for the holidays," Theo said. "We'll take turns."

Beth turned to Raleigh. "Can you wait until your uncle goes?"

A month or two? Would it become three of four? "I'm going to go now." Raleigh wouldn't compromise. Patrick might become a part of a study, or one of his kids could have summer camp, or any number of things could arise. It had been too many years, too much waiting, to put it off any longer. She couldn't let this opportunity slip away.

Beth pursed her lips. "Raleigh, you don't know how very large and cruel this world can be. I've sheltered you too much."

She couldn't deny part of that statement was true. At the same time, she knew a lot more about the world than her mother gave her credit for. Raleigh knew about pain and suffering. Through other people, she'd experienced depression and anxiety. People said that she had an old soul, and she did because hers had been soaking up the knowledge of so many around her.

"Please don't be mad about it," Raleigh said, sensing her mother's teeth grind. It amazed her that the woman had any molars left at this point.

"I'm not going to support you in this," Beth said and stormed out of the kitchen. Dinner sat on the counter near the plates. None of them moved to eat.

"I'll help you buy a ticket." Her father yet again took her side.

"Thanks." Raleigh hugged him.

With Patrick, they went to the study to buy the ticket. This treatment needed to work, otherwise she'd be crossing her mother in vain.

CHAPTER
05

SAYING SHE WAS going to Belgium was one thing, standing in line at customs she realized that going was another. The long flight left her tired and achy, but she wasn't the only one. Most of the other people waiting in the queue had the same soreness. Those that weren't stifling yawns had caffeine racking their nerves.

The singsong language of French kept begging her attention. Some of the familiar syllables tricked her ears into thinking they might be understood, only to be unrecognizable in the end. Despite not knowing the words, they still had meaning, with each conversation that passed they spoke to her about how she didn't belong, how her mother might have been right. The farthest she'd traveled before this was California, and she stood grossly unprepared for a journey this far.

Eventually, a customs officer checked her passport and ushered her into the terminal. With a good tug, her heavy bag lurched forward. People flooded around her, their suitcases and bags brushing her sides. A woman's roller suitcase clipped the edge of her toe. Ignoring the pain in her foot, Raleigh trudged down the hallway to the terminal.

The frantic terminal made her stop short, and her bag ran into the back of her calves. A man skirted around her and over to a little girl who he bent down to hug. Another set of passengers spoke loudly as they sat down at a small table. With so much going on, it would have been easy to get lost, then she spotted the row of people holding signs. Exotic names she couldn't pronounce scrolled across them, Groves stood out amongst the foreign monikers.

Tightening her hand on her bag, Raleigh approached the woman holding her name. This had to be Sabine's sister, but they had little in common besides their age. For starters, the lady was tall, heavy-set, and had dark thick hair wrapped up into a bun on her head. Her knees, hidden beneath a floral print skirt, had arthritis.

The woman searched the arrivals, pausing when she reached Raleigh. "Are you Raleigh?" she asked, her accent stiff and British, not French.

"That's right. You're Sabine's sister?"

"Sister-in-law. My name is Maggie. I live with Sabine and my brother. We'll head off to home if you don't have anything you need to do first."

"I'm ready to go."

"Great. We have a car at home, but the trains are much easier. Come this way."

They descended underground in a crammed elevator. Here in the underbelly of the airport the air tasted stale and thick. The cavernous tunnels captured the sounds of the trains and passenger commotion and echoed them away. Signs explained destinations and towns that she'd never learned of in school. Raleigh kept in step behind Maggie catching wafts of her perfume as she followed her to the platform. Maggie's manicured hands held a pair of train tickets.

While they waited, Maggie curiously looking her up and down. "Are you any good with baking?"

Raleigh shook her head. The kitchen with its burners and sharp edges had been off limits. Laundry and cleaning were safer. "No. My mom kept me out of the kitchen."

"You're going to learn, and I bet you'll love it. Sabine said you'd help me in the bakery. It will be nice having you. Sabine always says she will help once she retires, but she loves her work."

"What kind of doctor is she?" Raleigh didn't bring up the Lucidin. Presumably, Sabine had moved on from it.

"Family practice. She has considerably fewer patients than she used to. It's good news for you, otherwise she might recruit you for filing. That is very dull work."

"Then, thanks for the job." It was nice that they offered her a place to stay and she wasn't about to complain about the tasks they gave her. Baking and filing were both better than a slew of other jobs.

A gust of hot air arrived with the train. The door opened, and they navigated the metal steps. Raleigh's bag scraped the narrow passageway. Once in, she had to wrangle it into place alongside the other suitcases. Due to the humidity, beads of sweat formed on her brow. She wiped them away with the back of her hand before entering the train car.

She sat down across from Maggie and found the coarse fabric of the seat similar to the buses back home. The jolt of the train moving rocked her back into her seat. Slowly the platform faded from view, the train picking up speed.

"Is it far?" After the flight her legs wanted nothing more than to walk.

"Less than an hour. You will love Belgium."

Before Raleigh could ask why, Maggie delved into a complete history lesson on the small country. Every town they passed had some unique fact that Maggie offered up, often with large swooping hand gestures. They settled into an easy acquaintance, Maggie contrasted the hesitant nature of her sister-in-law.

Outside the window, Belgium rushed by in greens and grays. Towns and farms dotted the fields. At every stop Raleigh observed the people, wondering what their lives consisted of. Were they like her? Did they have warm families tucked away in the quaint cottages?

"This is us." Maggie stood.

Raleigh rose out of her seat, swaying as the train slowed and shook to a stop. By their stop most of the people had already gone, making the task of getting her bag easier. Tugging it down the steps she stood on the concrete platform, finally in Liege.

White pillars wove up in clean lines giving the impression of a large ribcage, the trains resting at the heart of the station. Overhead the clouds hung low in the dewy air. Stone-colored buildings melded with the sky. In the right light, it looked cozy, in some of the shadows, it took on a dreary tone.

"We'll walk, if you don't mind," Maggie said.

Even with the bag Raleigh wouldn't have turned down a walk, but she worried about Maggie's knees, a concern that Maggie herself didn't seem to have. She set a brisk pace, murmuring something about beating the rain.

It was hard going. The uneven stone sidewalk trapped the bag's wheels. Small cars flew down the tiny streets passing dangerously close to them. The uphill and thin path proved difficult to navigate. Still, at the lower altitude Raleigh's lungs languished in the abundant oxygen. Although cumbersome, this trek had nothing on her mountain hikes.

Row houses hugged the curves of the street, and parked cars

took over chunks of the already tight walkways. The city was designed before automobiles, and it showed. Hints of the past mingled flawlessly with the new. Lace curtains and old knockers sat alongside modern numbering and sleek windows.

Maggie stopped half way up a particularly steep incline. From her pocket she withdrew a heavy set of metal keys. She inserted the tiniest one, and the lock opened. "This is home."

They entered a tidy living room with a stiff-looking blue sofa and two white chairs. A modest wooden table sat a little further in and beyond that a sliver of a kitchen. Flanking the rooms on the right side was a stairwell with a worn wood banister. Sabine's birdlike presence announced her to Raleigh before she entered the room. There was also a tidy man who closely resembled Maggie.

Sabine walked over and kissed both of her cheeks. "I hope that your journey was safe."

"It was a long flight." Raleigh rubbed the bridge of her nose aware of the bags beneath her eyes.

"You've met Maggie, and this is my husband, Henry."

Henry's large hand delicately shook hers. "I've made lunch. You must be hungry." He scurried to the kitchen and returned with a tray of cheese, bread, and fruit.

"It looks great. Sabine, what about the treatment?" Raleigh whispered the last part quietly wondering how much Maggie knew about her. Surely, she wouldn't think that a teenager would travel across the world to help in a bakery.

Maggie's face didn't change, but Sabine's did. "So soon? Wouldn't you rather eat and be settled first? It's physically draining."

"I'm due for a blackout. I really want to know if it works." Every inch of distance she'd crossed had been in anticipation of getting better. Now she had to find out if it had been in vain.

"All right, then." Sabine motioned to her husband and then

the bag. "We'll take your luggage up to your room, and I'll get you started."

Maggie pulled a chair out from the small table and unfolded a napkin. "I'll start on lunch, if you don't mind."

Raleigh gripped the banister and followed Sabine up the thin steep stairwell. Not far behind, Henry struggled with the suitcase. Raleigh turned to assist, but upon seeing his warm face, she knew that he wouldn't allow it.

"This floor has Henry and my bedroom, our study, and a bathroom." Sabine pointed at the various doors before continuing to the next level. The third story had the same hallway and door configuration as the floor below. Sabine opened the first room revealing a tiny sink, toilet, and tub. "This is your bathroom. Next over is Maggie's room, and the last door is yours."

Sabine stopped in the stairwell, but Henry lumbered on to Raleigh's room. She followed, glancing inside at her first room away from home. White curtains hung half way up the window letting the afternoon sun filter in the top. The bed had a homemade quilt and an armoire. Simple but sufficient, she gave one full turn around the room before joining Henry at the stairwell.

Placing her feet carefully, Raleigh climbed the askew steps to the topmost story. The stairs creaked beneath the three as they ascended. Dust tickled her nose and drifted through the sunlight of the attic. Boxes sat neatly organized along one wall and filing cabinets along the other. Logically, Raleigh knew that this story was the same size as the lower lever, but the slanted ceilings and sloping walls gave it the impression of being smaller. In many ways it resembled Raleigh's basement back home, save one notable difference, a cot and large refrigerator-sized box in the corner.

"That machine is for the extractions." Sabine went over to the massive box and ran her hand along the side, etching fingerprints into the settled dust. "Now you understand why moving it would be difficult. Bringing it up four stories was challenging." Sabine motioned for Raleigh to sit on the cot. "The machine works by filtering the hormone from your blood. If it's all right with you, I'd like to install a port in your arm. Henry, please get my medical bag."

Henry disappeared and returned a minute later huffing. He placed a stiff leather bag next to his wife and then disappeared back down the steps as Sabine began to ready the installation. The latex gloves caught on Sabine's fingertips as she tugged them on. She hunched over Raleigh's arm and inspected where she would insert the port. Her quick fingers nimbly moved Raleigh's inner elbow. A nasty pinch made Raleigh wince, and she turned her face away from the abrasive sting of the antiseptic. When Sabine finished, thin tubes ran under Raleigh's skin, making her vein accessible. An angry red blotch swelled up at the site of the port. Discreet attachments reminded Raleigh of her grandfather's dialysis port, but hers weren't as obvious.

"Once the swelling goes down it won't look so noticeable. This tube will draw blood out of your body into the machine, and this line will deliver it back." Sabine attached the piping to the machine and flipped a switch on the side. The large machine awoke to life with a few uneven thumps and then a whizzing, like a dishwasher set on high. "We'll put it on full extraction, the highest setting. If you feel lightheaded, we'll decrease the rate."

"How long will it take?"

"Twenty minutes." Sabine checked her watch and took a seat across the cramped room. She was near enough to be of help but far enough away that Raleigh had her space.

Pressure built under her skin as the blood left and returned to the port. Her free hand instinctually wanted to scratch free the lines, but she didn't. Besides that discomfort, nothing happened.

She half expected a tingle or head rush to prove the process worked. The feel of Sabine's rapid heartbeat became less pronounced. Instead of heavy beat, it felt more like a dull pattering. It was akin to seeing underwater—it was difficult to see far and things were muted. Otherwise she remained unchanged. All fears of the process were soon replaced by boredom.

A picture on the machine caught her attention. She tilted her head trying to make sense of the sun-bleached images. The first was of forty or so boys all in uniforms. They smiled the awkward smiles of youth, with lots of teeth and squinted eyes. Adults flanked them, Sabine and Henry being two. The second photo was of two boys in their early teens, one blond with eyes so green they looked unnatural, the other was darker with a slight curl to his hair. The light-haired one's arm was slung around the neck of the dark-haired boy. They weren't Sabine's children. There was no resemblance. Both donned the same uniforms as in the other picture, and Raleigh pegged them as students. Patrick mentioned that Sabine had been a teacher.

Soft fingers touched Raleigh's shoulder, startling her. Sabine gave her a small grin then turned off the machine and unhooked her.

"I didn't feel you coming." Raleigh glanced to the far side of the room where Sabine had been sitting. It was rare that Raleigh didn't have forewarning of someone's arrival. Now she understood how people could be caught off guard. Her mother always complained about her lurking around the house.

"The Lucidin will slowly accumulate in your system. The feeling of isolation will last a half hour or so."

"You're sure it will come back? How do you know? I thought people didn't make as much as me."

"It's better if you don't ask questions about that."

"Who needed this machine?"

"No one in a long time." The dust on the top proved her point.

Sabine pulled a vial from the machine and held it up to the light. Rolling it in her fingers the light reflected off the clear liquid inside. After inspecting it, Sabine clasped it in her hand, hiding it from view.

"What will you do with that?"

"Dispose of it properly."

"And you're sure that other people can't use it? It seems a waste to throw it out."

"I, as much as anyone, wish that Lucidin could be used. That wasn't how it worked out. It's better to put it in the trash. It is also important that you do not tell people what you can do. I know back home you are used to referring patients to your uncle, but here you must keep quiet."

"But what if I sense something bad?"

"Then you can tell me. But you mustn't let on that you have Lucidin in your system."

"Why would anyone care? I thought that it couldn't be used."

"It's better to keep it a secret. I need you to trust me, and my experience, with this. You can't tell anyone."

Raleigh diverted her eyes to the machine. Something had happened in the past. Sabine had a reason she didn't want Raleigh to pursue Lucidin.

"Raleigh, I can make you well. But you must promise me that you won't say anything."

"I won't tell a soul." She first had to see if the extractions would work. Then she had to get better before she could consider helping everyone else.

––––––––––––––

A MONTH WENT by with Raleigh extracting daily for twenty minutes before bed, which effectively put an end to the blackouts. For thirty days Raleigh had been living the life of a normal teenage girl. The bruises from past spills healed, and the scars took on a glossy white tinge in the humid Belgian climate. She'd adapted to not living in fear of falls. The worries of before gave way to more trivial thoughts.

Raleigh awoke before sunrise, while the rest of the city slept. She untangled the sheet from her legs and padded down the hall to the bathroom. The mirror was misty from Maggie's shower. Quickly she washed, dressed, and tied her hair up into a knot on her head. With her eyes barely open she went downstairs to meet the day. The sound of Maggie's teacup clinking against the side of the sink met her when she reached the main floor.

"Ready to go?" Maggie approached with a bounce in her step.

Raleigh nodded and followed her out of the house onto the deserted street, the streetlights illuminating their path. At this hour, the world existed only for her. The silence gave her thoughts plenty of room to breathe. Ten minutes later they arrived at the bakery.

Maggie unlocked the back of the shop, and they stepped into the cold shadowed kitchen. First, Maggie fired up the dormant ovens, and Raleigh washed her hands. They had to make bread in time for the customers.

Raleigh loaded the industrial mixer with the ingredients for the dough. In no time she was covered in a thin layer of flour. Once the bread was baked, the pastries folded, and the custard made, the shop was opened, and the day officially began.

Simplicity characterized these days. Baking gave Raleigh a chance to work with her hands and reflect. Timed slowed without school and doctor appointments. Her thoughts allowed for loneliness to creep in. Back home there were family and friends vying for her free time. Here she had yet to make any friends. Now she understood why Maggie spoke to her so much—very few people spoke English. Maggie's French was superior to Raleigh's, but she had a thick accent that most of the locals struggled to understand. Teresa, one of the girls who worked the register, knew a few words of English, but a deep friendship between her and Raleigh failed to bloom.

Three o'clock signaled the end of Maggie and Raleigh's shift. Belgium's northern latitude meant the summer hours stretched out longer than the ones in Colorado. A whole day sat out before Raleigh when she left. Many of them she explored the city, others she hiked in the nearby forests. Today though, it was drizzly and miserable, the kind of day better spent indoors. Both she and Maggie went home.

Maggie shut the front door and slipped off her shoes. "I'm going to get a small nap in before dinner. I'm sure you'll find some mischief to get into."

Their ongoing joke was that there didn't seem to be any trouble around for Raleigh to find. "Not sure what I'll do."

"You could still catch that movie at the theater."

Raleigh went to the movies every Friday. The theater mostly showed American films dubbed into French. On the weekends they showed them in English with French subtitles. At first it was a comforting reminder of home. Now it made her feel homesick. One look out the windows at the weather and she lost the motivation to go. "I'll probably hang around here."

"Suit yourself." Maggie disappeared up the steps.

Raleigh went to her computer in the living room and video-called home.

Her father answered. *"Raleigh!"* His face came in too close and dominated the screen. Raleigh didn't know if he'd ever get used to using the computer to communicate. But it was what they had.

"Hi Dad. How's everything in Colorado?"

"Early." He glanced to the corner of his monitor at the clock. *"How are you doing? How are the treatments?"*

"Still working. And Mom, how's she?"

"Fine, but she still has to cart your sister to summer camp every day. School starts in a few weeks."

Everything in Colorado managed to go on seamlessly without her. Not that she wanted it to fall apart, but it was odd how normal her house seemed, how her father hadn't changed at all.

"Theo? Is that Raleigh?" Beth appeared in her bathrobe as she pulled the device away from her husband. *"I'm coming to see you in October. I bought the ticket yesterday. That is, if you're still living there then."* Her mother never missed a chance to mention the prospect of Raleigh coming home.

"I think you'll like Liege." She could picture her mother in the bakery. "When I get back, I have some recipes to teach you."

"Any cute boys?" Thalia yelled from behind her mother.

"None that speak English."

"They don't have to be able to speak!"

Beth shoved the computer to her husband. In the background Raleigh could see her mother chasing her sister up the stairs saying, *"Did you finish cleaning your room?"*

Theo watched them go. *"I should probably get to work. Love you. Take care, and call in a few days?"*

"Yeah, and I love you, too." The line went dead, and her computer background came up. It was a picture of their trip to the Grand Canyon a few years ago. Her fingers traced the faces of her family.

Raleigh tucked the computer away and went to the bookshelf. She grabbed one of the many mysteries that occupied Maggie's section. Flopping into a chair she read a few chapters. She stayed engrossed until Henry's heavy footsteps interrupted her reading. Accompanying the thuds were softer steps, Sabine's. Raleigh marked her place and went to help make dinner. She was becoming as skilled at cooking as she was at baking.

Raleigh slid the peeler across the top of a carrot and then diced the onion. The burner warmed her side nearest it. Sabine had a skillet simmering. During the month, Raleigh had found a place here, but it would never be home. She belonged back in Colorado and in college. It was a feeling she couldn't shake. Friends back home were fussing over roommates and looking forward to classes. She should be, too.

"Something on your mind?" Sabine added some white wine to the base of the sauce.

"College. If I go back to the States by November, I can enroll in the spring semester."

Sabine put the bottled down and picked up the spoon to stir. "It will happen for you one day. Someday you will look back on this time fondly."

"I will. I am enjoying myself here." Raleigh didn't want Sabine to think she was ungrateful.

Sabine smiled and then laughed. "The students Henry and I taught at the orphanage always had the same look in their eyes when leaving. The world seems like such a big place at your age."

Raleigh enjoyed hearing Sabine talk about the years she and Henry taught at the boys' orphanage. It must've been shortly after their years researching Lucidin. Raleigh once asked how they ended up working at the school. Sabine said it was fate's gift to her. Childless due to infertility, she said that those boys were the children she never had. Unfortunately, the only two pictures that accompanied the stories were on the extraction machine. Like the machine, all the parts of their past were tucked away in the attic.

Raleigh pushed thoughts of college out of her mind and went back to cooking. In two months she'd have to decide which was worse—treading water in Belgium or blacking out at home. Neither one seemed ideal.

CHAPTER
06

THUD. THUD. THUD. The heavy knocks sounded like someone was trying to break the door down. It drew Raleigh out of her musings on leaving and startled Sabine.

"Sabine!" The roaring voice from outside echoed through the small house.

Sabine paled and nearly knocked over the skillet. With four long strides, she left the kitchen. Raleigh sensed three people at the door—a strong man carrying something heavy, an asthmatic who'd let out the tortured cry, and a third with a faint heart beat who was dying. It was good Sabine was a doctor.

Raleigh rushed to the living room in time to watch the three men she'd sense fill the doorway. Panic filled them. Their wide pupils, racing hearts, and tight lungs made the hairs on the back of Raleigh's neck prickle. The strong blond man held the dying one in his arms. These men ran from something, and her own body urged her to get away, even if she didn't know the threat.

"Sabine, he's dying." The asthmatic strangled breaths stuttered the words. "We didn't know where to go."

Henry ran forward. "You came to the right place."

"We need to find Kappa." The strong one moved further in so Henry could shut the door. "Only his brother can save him now. They've drained him. We need to find him and soon."

"He's dying. He doesn't have time for that." All eyes turned to Raleigh with that admission. She hung near the dining room table, out of the way. "Sabine, his heart's going to stop. It's weak. We should get him to a hospital."

"Raleigh." Sabine's ashen face regained a hit of red. She took Raleigh's arm and led into the kitchen. "I hoped to shield you from this."

"From that boy dying?" Raleigh wanted to correct herself. He wasn't a boy, he was likely only a few years older than her. His fragility gave him that tinge, but he was a man, a young one.

"From the world he lives in. He's like a son to me. I need your help. He'll die without it." Sabine's thin fingers clutched Raleigh's arm digging into her skin.

Raleigh didn't know what to say. Sabine, of all people, never wanted her to use her gifts. "Me? I never worked on patients with Uncle Patrick and Dr. Moore. I just helped them figure out what's wrong. All I can tell you is that his heart isn't good. None of him is, really. He's in a lot of pain. I'm not sure what's causing it."

"He's like you. And he's been drained of his Lucidin. Can you give him some of yours?"

"What do you mean, drained? I thought people like me are rare."

Regaining some of her composure, Sabine released Raleigh's arm. "They are, extremely. He's similar to you in that he creates Lucidin. He, like you, is reliant on it. When too much is removed, the body recoils and ails. People who take it can be weaned off. But people who make large quantities die when too much is taken."

Raleigh rubbed her port. "I extract daily."

"They've taken much more than that." Turning her head, Sabine observed the three.

"Who? Who took it?"

Sabine returned her gaze to Raleigh. "I don't know. But he needs your help. Will you help him?"

Questions about Lucidin piled up. Ones she'd need an answer to. Now was not the time. First, they had to help the man. "He can have as much of mine as he needs."

Lifting up on her toes, Sabine threw her arms around Raleigh. "Thank you." They returned to the others in the living room. Waving her hand, Sabine directed them towards the stairs. "Take him up to the attic. We'll tend to him there."

The asthmatic didn't move, only sobbed lightly. "What about Kappa? Do you have Kappa's number? You can't save him. We've already given him two vials... and he's still dying."

Sabine went over to him. "Trevor, a few vials won't work. What he needs is a continual infusion. We understand that."

Already at the stairwell, Henry thundered, "Young man, take him up to the attic!"

The strong one sprang into action. His long legs took the steps two at a time, he moved faster than the rest, despite the load he carried. He cared about the man in his arms, and even though he wasn't crying like the asthmatic, Raleigh sensed his throat constrict around a lump of despair. Both mourned their friend who wasn't yet dead.

Raleigh arrived second in the attic, after the blond, with Sabine paces behind her. The room was bathed in summer-evening light from the small windows and shadows cast across the floor at odd angles. Dust and stillness filled the space.

"Put him on the cot." Sabine turned to her husband. "Henry, grab the chair. Raleigh, let me see your arm."

With a good tug, Raleigh tore the thin covering of fabric from her port. She twisted her arm upward, exposing the port to Sabine who immediately made the attachments. Henry put the chair behind Raleigh and she sat.

Sabine turned to the strong man. "What's your name?"

"Collin." His eyes remained focused on the friend in his arms.

"Collin, put Rho on the cot," Sabine ordered.

Slowly Collin lowered his friend down. The man rolled out of the blanket that encased him. Nearly naked, his body was a deathly gray, and his full lips were colored a corpse-like blue. A weak heart laboriously pumped blood through him, death dulling each beat a little more than the last. Around his neck hung a thin silver chain with a Greek letter, Rho, the name Sabine called him.

A nickname?

Sabine certainly didn't seem the type to indulge in nicknames, ever—and certainly not at a time like this.

Trevor, the asthmatic, finally entered the room, his eyes wide. "Why is she hooked up to that machine?"

"She makes Lucidin." Sabine worked quickly to attach tubes to Rho's port.

"Not enough. It'll kill her," whispered Trevor.

Shaking her head, Sabine gave him a look. "Do you think I would harm anyone that way?"

"We have to risk it. Anything to save Rho." Collin pointed to the on switch.

That raised Raleigh's eyebrow and caused her to do a double take. Since Collin walked in carrying his dying friend, it was easy to paint him as a hero. Now his comments were far from noble. If anything, he was a jerk.

"It isn't a risk." Sabine turned on the machine. "Raleigh easily makes more than him."

As if on cue, the machine withdrew the Lucidin from her.

"Is she his sister?" Trevor fumbled to get the inhaler from his pocket. Once in hand he took an enormous puff. Raleigh reveled in the sensation of his lungs opening. And, of course, she wasn't Rho's sister. They looked nothing alike, and she'd never met him before.

Watching Rho, Sabine shook her head. "No. Rho doesn't have any sisters. Out with you now."

"I'm not leaving him." Collin puffed up his chest and squared his shoulders in Sabine's direction.

"Give it time to take effect. You're in the way here. Downstairs. All of you." With her feet planted, Sabine pointed towards the stairwell.

Henry gave his wife a nod and ushered them out. "You stay. I'll get them calmed down and fed."

The three left, their footfalls creaking the steps in patterns. Once things quieted Sabine took out a box, brushed off the top, and fashioned it into a seat. "Raleigh, this may take a while. Tell me if you start feeling faint."

Every night she extracted before bed. This wasn't the same. She was acutely aware of the guy lying on the cot she normally occupied. He was strewn across the small bed the way his friend had left him, lying on his side with one arm extended out over the edge. Raleigh glanced at Sabine, who was spinning her rings around her nimble fingers. Then she sneaked a longer glance at the man. Ignoring the pallor of his skin, he had a handsome face, a sturdy jaw, and a thin nose. His lips were a bit larger than most, but then again it might've been his color that gave her that impression. There was something familiar about him, as if she'd seen him before, when he was younger. Raleigh knew that she would've recalled meeting him.

Her eyes went to the pictures on top of the machine. His younger self was in both.

The rain gave way to a hot muggy evening. The attic was warm, but as the extraction progressed, Raleigh's insides shuddered against the cold. Sabine sat in the corner, her brows knit in worry. Raleigh didn't want to worry her further or stop the infusion, so she remained silent. Henry came up the steps a half hour in. Raleigh couldn't sense him, but she heard the heavy steps of his dress shoes.

Henry stopped at the top of the stairs. "Maggie's finished making the dinner you started. I've managed to calm Trevor down. The other one, Collin, is insisting that he should be up here. I think once they're fed, they'll feel better." He paused and looked at the boy on the cot for a long moment. "How's he doing?"

"Fine. He's going to be fine," Sabine said.

Raleigh recognized the reassuring tone. The same one her mom faithfully used—not because the situation warranted it—but because she trusted fate and the world. Henry's shoulders relaxed at hearing Sabine's encouragement. Perhaps the words had done their job.

"Can I bring you something while you wait?"

"No. We'll be down in another half hour."

Henry stared at the boy a moment longer and left the three alone again.

They used a slower extraction rate than Raleigh's normal setting, and Rho was still frighteningly gray. This could go faster. "You can turn up the machine."

Sabine shook her head. "I'll give him a vial before bed. And, if you don't mind, tomorrow we'll do another hour-long session like this."

"But I can give more."

"It isn't necessary. He won't die tonight. Slow and steady, Raleigh. We don't want to drain you of your strength."

She didn't argue, but she didn't agree. With her Lucidin gone, she couldn't sense Rho, but he still looked bad.

"He was a student of yours?" Raleigh pointed to the picture.

Sabine shifted on the box. "Yes, he was."

"That was very fortunate... that one of your students happened to make Lucidin. Or was it not a coincidence?"

Guilt tugged on the lines of Sabine's face as a tear slipped over her cheek. She diverted her eyes from Raleigh's gaze. "It isn't. Henry and I took up positions at the orphanage, so we could keep an eye on him and his brother Kappa."

This was not the time for Sabine to keep secrets. "Someone drained his Lucidin. What are you not telling me? Up until now I thought that you didn't want to discuss Lucidin because it was a failure. If someone went through the trouble of taking it from him, that isn't the case, is it?"

After clearing the sadness from her throat Sabine spoke. "It was a failure. But people still take it. People who fall above the seventy-fifth percentile can sense. They can use it medicinally."

Raleigh's eyes widened.

"I wasn't lying when I said it harms the user. People who don't make it become dependent on it. Henry and I collected Lucidin from Rho and his brother Kappa. We had great hopes that it would change the way we approach diagnostics."

"But it didn't?"

"It had the potential to, but... I worked for a company named Grant and Able. They needed more and more Lucidin for their healers and their workers. It was impossible to keep up with the demand. Eventually they took the two boys from the orphanage. They said they were going to work with them, but they imprisoned them, instead."

"Is that who did this to him?"

"I don't know who did this. There is a black market. Usually they sell the synthetic, but they wouldn't hesitate to do this."

The cold was back in full force, and it wasn't only on account of the extraction. "And this could happen to me."

"There is a reason I told you not to tell anyone."

This was something Raleigh should have known all along. Her hands clenched and opened. "When were you going to tell me about the danger I'm in? Why convince me to leave home? I was safe there." What else had Sabine kept from her?

"Doctor Moore found me which meant it wouldn't have been long before he stumbled on Grant and Able. They would've offered to treat you, and it might've appeared like a good deal, but you wouldn't ever have been able to leave. They'd use you and your Lucidin to feed their need. This is better."

"You should have told me!"

Sabine's steely eyes bore into Raleigh. "If I had, you wouldn't have come, and you'd stayed there where they could get to you. I was involved with their research for a long time. I broke amicably with them, but I've feared them ever since."

"But their goal is to help people, as is yours."

"That isn't what they're doing. The doctors that use the Lucidin will become addicted. There are dangers in using Lucidin to which they turn a blind eye. Imprisoning Rho and Kappa was the final demonstration I needed to confirm that they are willing to do anything for the drug."

"Am I safe here? Or am I going to end up like him?"

Sabine's voice softened. "It was my intention to keep you safe when I brought you here. I expected one of them to reach out sooner or later. They're who I was going to ask for a portable machine. Then I would've sent you home with it—once I knew that you would stop using your sensing for diagnostics."

"That sensing is what will make me a great doctor one day. I have helped so many."

"It will cost you. There is much illness in the world. You can't solve it all, but they would expect you to. I'm sorry you're angry because I didn't tell you sooner. It was to save you from this harsh reality. People will use you and dispose of you as guiltlessly as they have Rho."

At the mention of his name, Raleigh had the urge to study him again. "He needs more."

Sabine placed her thin fingers on his neck. "No. He's fine. His recovery isn't going to happen overnight, though. It may take a few days. Now, you get downstairs and eat some dinner. Send Henry up with Collin. We're going to take Rho downstairs and give him a bath."

The extraction made her muscles shaky, but her frustration spurred her on. She tore the tubes from her port, disconnecting from the machine. Her legs trembled under her weight, and she edged down the steps slowly. The smell of chicken soup filled the lower level, but she had no appetite. What she really wanted to do was nap. Maybe sleep would take away the feeling of helplessness that washed over her.

"How is he?" Collin blocked her path into the kitchen.

"Sabine says he's fine."

"What does she know?"

"She is a doctor."

"You look fine. Couldn't you give him more?"

"I'm feeling weak."

"Collin, stop it." Trevor tugged on his friend's arm. It did little to move Collin. "This is more than we could've hoped for. Let Sabine call the shots."

"Just because you trust her doesn't mean I do."

Trevor leveled his eyes at Collin. "Rho does, and that should be enough."

Collin looked like an all-American boy, which was fitting with his Midwest accent, broad shoulders, close-cropped hair, and stern, yet forgettable face. He towered over scrawny, gawky Trevor. They could both only be a few years older than Raleigh, but Trevor's body had yet to fill in. His fingernails were ragged and short. They didn't seem like the type of guys who'd hang out together, yet here they were. Rho was the obvious link between them.

With little patience, Raleigh interrupted their staring match. "Sabine did say that she wanted Collin and Henry to go upstairs and carry Rho down to the bathroom. She wants him to have a bath."

"He's awake?" The news curved Collin's stiff shoulders.

Raleigh almost felt bad for getting his hopes up. "No."

Henry started towards the stairs. "He needs a sponge bath. He smells awful. Where has he been?"

"Normandy," Trevor said. "The ocean, in the mud, imprisoned, we don't really know. We found him today."

Collin put up his hand. "I think it's better for all of them if they don't know."

"It doesn't sound like you know all that much, anyway." She wanted to yell at Sabine for not telling, but she'd settle for a fight with Collin. He seemed like the type always ready to do battle.

Goosebumps sprung up on Raleigh's arm and she braced herself against the wall. Even if her mind was combative, her body had other plans. Maggie walked around the table, pressed a hand across Raleigh's forehead. "Raleigh, you're cold. I'll get you a blanket and some soup. Why don't you sit in the living room?"

"I think the extraction made me a little sick." She allowed Maggie to lead her to the sofa and fuss over her by putting a throw around her shoulders. Collin didn't care how Raleigh felt. He was already ascending the stairs, and Henry was slowly following him. Maggie went to the kitchen to get the soup while Trevor hung near the entrance of the room. He stared at Raleigh for a moment before going upstairs.

Maggie handed Raleigh a bowl of soup. "I'm going to get the rooms ready for our guests. Do you need anything?"

"No. I'll eat this and go to bed."

The world had shifted over the last hour. The time in Belgium had passed so lazily, and she hadn't any notion of the danger. This proved her mother right. Cruelty existed, the likes she'd never seen. That bitter thought dulled the taste of the soup.

CHAPTER
07

THAT NIGHT COLLIN refused to leave Rho's side. His insisting voice traveled across the house, giving little doubt he would have his way. Sabine eventually gave in since it was a good idea to have someone check on Rho and give him a vial of Lucidin, if necessary. Sabine's practice of disposing Lucidin vials every week meant they had scarcely any left. No one chided her for attempts to keep Raleigh safe. Any paranoia Sabine had about Lucidin seemed justified now given the state of Rho.

That was another thing no one was talking about—who nearly killed him. From the frantic way Collin seemed to move, Raleigh had the impression that they didn't know. The anxious tension left little doubt that the danger had only been temporarily escaped. Any time Collin passed a window he peered out, as if expecting something. Again, their hands were tied. Their most pressing issue was to get Rho better.

Concern gnawed at Raleigh, keeping her in a light sleep. Restless, she tossed and turned, the sheets bunching up under her legs. The image of Rho's frail body sat behind her eyelids. What if he didn't get better? Despite how awful she felt, Raleigh wished Sabine would've allowed her to give him a longer infusion. Normally, Raleigh would have trusted Sabine. Now Sabine's stoic disposition felt more secretive than contemplative.

She eventually fell into a listless sleep only to awake at three in the morning. At that hour her mind contentedly pretended nothing had happened, but she roused enough to remember. She wondered if Rho was doing better. After a few minutes she decided that she had to know—not simply to know— but to help if he needed it.

Slipping out of her room, she carefully listened for signs of life. No one else was up. Slowly, she headed towards the attic stairs. Carefully placing her foot on the first step, she eased her weight on it. She bit her lip as the step creaked. After pausing to make sure she hadn't woken anyone, she crept the rest of the way up as lightly as she could. When she finally made it, she opened the already ajar door. Snoring and the sound of a fan hid the noise of the hinges.

Collin slumped in the chair by the window on the far side of the room where Sabine usually sat. A fan near him oscillated cold air across the room. His scratchy snores drowned out the white noise of the fan. With his legs stretched out and his arms crossed, he didn't look comfortable. Even with his head at an odd angle, she sensed he was in the kind of deep sleep that comes after being deprived of it for too long.

It wasn't Collin she was interested in. Raleigh crept across the room and over to the bed in the far corner where Rho slept. In the last few hours her Lucidin had been partly replenished, so she could feel his heart. It was weak. Concerned, she reached over to his neck. Cold skin and a faint pulse met her fingers. It was steadier than when he'd been brought in but still not good. He wasn't out of the woods yet.

The only light in the room came through the windows. It was meager, hindering her ability to hook herself up to the machine. They'd dressed him in some of Henry's old clothes and covered him in a thick blanket. Cautiously, she untucked his arm, rolled up the sleeve, and attached the tubes to the machine the way she'd seen Sabine do it. Raleigh flipped the switch on and strained her eyes to see if the noise woke Collin. It was loud, but white noise, similar to a fan. Collin remained asleep.

Sitting down on the floor, Raleigh promised herself that she'd stop the moment she didn't feel right. With so much of her Lucidin gone from the first transfusion, she had little to give. The machine smuggled it away from her, leaving her weaker with each moment that passed. Her head lolled forward, and her eyelids weighed down. Part of her knew that she should turn off the machine, but the white noise and the dreariness of her muscles beckoned her into slumber.

Raleigh dreamt of visiting the Pacific Ocean with her older brother Ben. The sky was the same dark gray as the water and she squinted to see where the two met on the horizon. Walking down the beach, the waves playfully lapped at her feet, then her calves, and up to her waist. Floundering, she reached the surface and gasped for air when the waves were low. Cold. She was so very cold.

"Wake up," a rough voice whispered. "Please wake up."

Eyes open, her brain processed that she wasn't in the ocean, that it was a dream, and that she was still cold. It was no longer the dead of night. An early morning sunrise painted the room in tangerine and pink.

"Take it out." She clawed at the port and the clammy skin of her arm. The tubes were already out. What she'd intended to be maybe an hour-long extraction had been longer.

"Are you all right?"

Raleigh turned her attention from her port to Rho who sat on the floor less than a foot away. His color had improved.

"Are you all right?" he asked again more urgently.

"Yeah, I'm all right. Just cold."

Rho dragged the blanket from the bed and wrapped it around her shoulders. "Where are we? Who did this to you?"

"What?"

"Who hooked you up to that machine? We need to get out of here."

"I did. I set up the extraction. It made me tired, and I must've fallen asleep. We're in Belgium."

"At Sabine's?" He looked around, understanding easing the lines of his face.

"Yes. We're safe." On shaky hands she attempted to push herself up. Too weak, she lowered back down. "How are you?"

"I could've killed you." He reached out for her but stopped before his fingers touched her skin. They were close, the smell of Henry's soap clung to his hair.

Raleigh shook her head. Weary maybe, but she was nowhere near dying. Even after falling asleep attached to the machine, she was far better than him, which made her wonder how long he'd been imprisoned.

"It's fine." Raleigh diverted her eyes. His closeness made her heart race. "Like I told your friends, I make a lot of Lucidin."

Leaning forward, he rested his hands on the sides of her face, lifting it. The dim light obscured most of his own in shadow. His blue-gray eyes searched her own. "You have freckles. What's your full name?"

"Raleigh Groves." Her muscles tightened. Without the Lucidin, her other senses rushed to categorize everything about him, from the rough pads of his fingertips, to the way his lips formed his words, to the intrigued lilt of his voice.

"Do you get your brown hair from your mother or father?"

"Father. My mom's a ginger."

"How long were you hooked up?"

"I came here around three."

Rho glanced at the window. "It's at least five a.m. That's two hours. You do make a lot. It's not like mine."

"What do you mean it's not like yours?"

"In nature, Lucidin has slight variances—or at least that's what I've been told. Everyone I know has my version. Yours is wilder. Unruly."

"Rho! You're awake!" Collin staggered up from his chair, interrupting them.

Rho turned toward his friend, releasing Raleigh's face. "Collin! You brought me here, didn't you? You found me! It was such a long shot."

Going down on one knee, Collin embraced his friend. "We thought you were going to die."

"That was the last thing I remember thinking. Then I woke up here. At first, I thought I was being drained again. Then I realized that I was receiving it. Did you meet Raleigh?"

"We've met. How are you feeling?" He helped Rho back to the bed.

"Collin, she has freckles," Rho said.

Her face warmed, and she wondered if they would be visible through the blush. It was an odd thing to say. "I think he's a bit out of it, Collin."

Rho held out his hands. "I'm surprised but fine. People like you aren't supposed to exist. You're my savior, in more ways than you can know."

Pointing his finger accusingly, Collin didn't share the admiration. "Sabine said that you weren't going to do another extraction until tomorrow."

"I snuck up and did it myself."

"Make sure Sabine knows it was your idea."

Rho looked at the stairwell. "Are she and Henry both here?"

"Yes," Raleigh said. "And your friend Trevor and Henry's sister, Maggie."

"Trevor?" A smile tugged on the corners of Rho's lips lighting up his face. Gorgeous. Raleigh found herself looking away. "It was the chip he put in my shoulder that led you to me, wasn't it?"

Collin nodded.

"Never let me question him again. He's a genius, an absolute genius." Rho stood, but before he could fully rise, his legs gave out, and he flopped back down to the floor.

"Take it easy." One of Collin's hands steadied his friend while keeping him down.

Coughs barked out of Rho's throat, raw and harsh. "I'm thirsty. It feels like forever since I've had anything to drink. I can't believe I made it."

Collin handed him a nearby cup of water. "Yesterday we gave you some sips, but we couldn't get that much into you. Whoever had you, did a good job with that. Sabine said you weren't too dehydrated."

Rho took a long drink. "That, and I probably drank half the English Channel."

Collin sat on the foot of the cot. "Do you know who had you?"

"No, and I really don't want to think about it right now."

"Do you think you could eat? You've lost weight."

Rho rubbed his hand across his stomach. "Maybe something light."

With a quick flick of his head towards the door Collin said, "Raleigh, tell Sabine he's up."

Still weak, her muscles weren't much good. "I can't walk right now."

"That's my fault." Rho reached out to her again trying to stand.

"Neither of you move." Collin got up quickly. "I'll tell Sabine."

Rho's brow knit together. "What day is it?"

"July twentieth."

"They found me yesterday? It's been months."

Months? Someone had him for months? "I'm sorry."

"You, of all people, shouldn't be apologizing." Rho looked down. "Henry has really bad taste in pajamas, these look like they're from the fifties."

"I think those are small Yorkies." The tiny dogs decorating the fabric wore suits. "Rho, who took you?" If Sabine wouldn't give her answers, she would have to get them from him.

"I don't know." There was a clear shift in his voice, his happy mood at having survived evaporated. "Most of it I wasn't conscious for. I can only remember a day or two before I escaped. During that time, I figured a way out which was hard enough. Is there a reason to think we aren't safe here? Did they follow me?"

"It doesn't sound like Collin and Trevor know all that much. I don't know. Should we be calling the police? Maybe they can help you figure it out."

Rho exhaled. "You have a lot of Lucidin. Do you have a lot of receptors?"

"Tons."

"As I assumed. So, you can feel other people's sensations, right?"

Raleigh nodded. "Not right now, but usually."

"How well does it go over when you tell people you can do that?"

"They normally don't believe me, but they usually go to their doctor anyway. So maybe part of them wants to."

"The police don't know about us. The world doesn't know about us." Rho made it sound like it was better that way.

"How many of us are there? It sounds like you're speaking about a specific group."

"I'm speaking of me and my brothers. That's the extent of the "us." Or at least it was. Until you."

Raleigh was less concerned with Rho's family than hers. Dr. Moore told her about that tribe of people genetically predisposed to making Lucidin. Now she worried about her sisters and brother. "I have three siblings. Sabine never mentioned that they might make Lucidin."

"They probably don't. Mostly it's random who gets it. Can they feel other people the way you do?"

"No."

"Then they don't have to worry. Anyone who makes it has receptors. They would've been able to use the Lucidin at some point if they made it. My brothers and I are special."

"How many brothers do you have? Kappa and who else?"

"Too many." Now it was Rho's turn to look away.

"Are you all named after Greek letters?"

"We really shouldn't talk about them."

"Raleigh Groves!" Sabine shouted across the room. "I can't believe you went against my wishes and gave Rho another infusion."

"I saved him."

"You would've saved him either way! Look at you, huddled up in that blanket." Sabine examined her eyes, her forehead, and took her pulse. "You're frigid."

Raleigh pulled back, not wanting Sabine to mother her. "More crummy and tired."

"Good to see you, Sabine," Rho said meekly, transforming into the young man in the picture.

The way Sabine looked at him, it was clear she had a maternal bond. She wrapped him in her arms. It didn't matter that he was twice her size, at that moment he looked small. "You don't know how scared we were for you."

"Thanks for giving us a place to stay." He opened his mouth to say more and stopped. His face fell. "I'm sorry if we brought you trouble. I'd never want to put you or Henry in danger."

"Don't worry about that." Despite the command, Sabine's tone held a hint of concern.

"Sabine, it isn't just your safety now. It's Raleigh's, too. What if whoever did this follows me and finds her?"

"We'll address that later. I've put some water on the stove, and I'm making oatmeal. Let's get you on the mend, and then we can figure out the rest. No one is leaving today." Their conversation ended when Collin returned. "Carry him, would you?"

Collin scooped up his friend. It was a lot more awkward-looking than when Rho had been unconscious. Raleigh tried to stand, but her legs faltered beneath her.

Sabine put up her hand. "I'm sure once Collin gets Rho downstairs, he can come back up for you."

The three headed down leaving Raleigh and her thoughts. Rho didn't know if the danger had followed him. Again, Raleigh's mother was right. If Raleigh hadn't been so headstrong, she could be safely tucked away at college. But who knows how long that would've lasted?

Collin returned and lifted Raleigh up, but not in a chivalrous way. He held her slightly away from him, the way a person would carry a stinky, wet dog.

"I would've thought you'd like me after I saved your friend."

Collin walked down the first flight of stairs. "It doesn't count if you put him in more danger."

"Excuse me?"

"He's not going to want to leave without you."

"Who says that I'm going to leave with some strangers? You don't know me."

"You clearly underestimate Rho."

If anything, Raleigh was going to forget about them and go home. "Do you have a portable extraction machine?"

"Yeah, but it's ours."

"If you help me get hold of one, I can go back to Colorado."

He paused one foot on the second landing. His face loomed over hers. Then he took the next step. "Done. You'll have it in a week."

Raleigh guessed that he was making this nice gesture to be rid of her, which was fine. She was ready to go home... and away from Rho and the trouble he might attract.

CHAPTER
08

COLLIN DEPOSITED RALEIGH on the sofa beside Rho. He looked at his friend and then paced. "I can get train tickets for later today."

"No, he's not ready to travel." Sabine entered and put a tray down on the coffee table. On it sat a pair of bowls filled with oatmeal. "You need to stay at least a few more days."

After a quick glance to Raleigh, Rho gave Collin a pointed look. "Can we spare a few days?"

Collin threw up his arms. "You tell me. We found you hidden behind a rock along the coast of Normandy with nothing on. No one was around, and the only tracks we could find were the ones you probably made as you crawled there. What exactly happened?"

Rho slowly drew his breath, looking carefully at Sabine and then Raleigh.

"Raleigh, would you mind excusing us?" Collin asked.

She didn't move. There was no way she was leaving. This conversation should involve her too, especially, because she couldn't count on Sabine being up front with her. Raleigh was going to hear whatever Rho had to say so that she could make up her own mind about her situation.

Rho reached over and put a gentle hand on Raleigh's forearm. "She should stay. Raleigh has to know about this. It might be her someday."

No one spoke right away. Whatever secrets they held couldn't be good. Collin paced faster, his steps heavy on the wood floor. "Sabine, explain to him why they aren't going to hunt her. She's not the same as him. They don't even know about her."

"But I found her." Sabine sat down and looked at Raleigh.

Rho gave his friend a stony glare. "The type of girl who gives a stranger an extra Lucidin infusion, against Sabine's orders, isn't the type of girl to sit idly by. I bet she's been diagnosing diseases for a while. It's only a matter of time before someone pieces it together. Sabine, how did you discover her?"

They didn't need to talk about Raleigh as if she weren't there. "My friend, Doctor Moore, contacted her."

"Your friend, Doctor Moore? He's only your friend because you help him with his patients, right?" Rho asked. "What is he, a cardiologist?"

Sabine answered for Raleigh. "Oncologist. Which is why I brought her here. A new start."

"And since she's been here, she's kept quiet about the fact that she can sense?" Rho lifted his eyebrow.

From the way Sabine shifted in her seat it was obvious that she didn't like to be questioned by her former student. "Very. I told her to."

It was good that Raleigh had listened, not that she'd had much of a choice. "I couldn't say anything even if I wanted to. I don't speak French. But it would've been nice to know why I should keep quiet. I thought you just didn't want people to think I'm crazy. You only told me about Grant and Able yesterday." Anger built in her chest, warming her from the chill of the extraction.

Rho sat up, his face turning pallid. He looked at Raleigh and then Sabine. "You told her about Grant and Able?"

"Only that they imprisoned you... and that I worked for them. Nothing more."

The quiet exchange of glances between the two made Raleigh wonder what else there was to know about Grant and Able. She wished there was enough Lucidin back in her system to sense.

Rho turned to Raleigh. "When you helped people back home, did you send them to the doctor or did you influence?"

"Influence?" said Raleigh. "What's that?"

"A very difficult thing to do. It'll get you into a lot more trouble than sensing. Best to avoid it." Collin paused, and like a statue, towered over her. Then he started pacing again.

Rho rolled his eyes at his friend. "She needs to learn. Raleigh, it's the ability to control what happens physically in someone else's body. Think of it like a telephone. When you sense, it's like people's bodies are having a conversation with you about what's wrong. With influencing you tell the person's body how to fix whatever's wrong... or to do whatever it is you want it to do."

Raleigh raised an eyebrow. Her nose immediately started to itch. Her hand rubbed it, her eyes going to him.

"I just made your nose itch. Do you want to scratch it?"

"That's you? That's amazing."

"I can do more, when I'm not weak."

The idea made Raleigh dizzy. How did she not know about this? When she was lectured on Lucidin, that should've been one of the key points. "Sabine, did you know about this?"

"Yes."

Another bit of her trust chipped away. Sabine only gave up information when it was going to come out anyway, or when she was asked the right questions. Raleigh didn't need or want Sabine censoring things. Especially something like this. "This is a game changer. I could do so much more to help people. Can you control pain and heart problems?"

Rho moved closer to her, his eyes lighting up. "Yes. I learned about influencing unintentionally. Trevor and I were hiking, and he had an asthma attack. His inhaler was out, and help was slow in coming. I could feel his lungs getting tighter and tighter but there was nothing I could do. Finally, I willed his lungs to open up, really pictured it happening, and they did."

Wringing her hands, Sabine said, "You shouldn't be encouraging her. It will only lead to trouble."

Rho shook his head at Sabine. "She's already in trouble. At least with influencing, she can protect herself. It was nice of you to bring her here, but did you think that would save her?"

"I was trying my best. Bringing her here was a quick decision. She was sick with a growing reputation for precise diagnoses. Someone was bound to hear about her sooner or later. The only solution was to bring her here for treatment and to keep my eye on her."

Raleigh couldn't look at Sabine. She knew the woman's only motive wasn't to make her well. She wondered how long things would've dragged on if Rho hadn't shown up. Who knew if Sabine ever planned on finding Raleigh a portable extraction machine.

Rho leaned in towards Raleigh. "You're sick? What do you have?"

"I blackout from the Lucidin. It overloads my system. But the extractions have stopped the blackouts."

"That makes sense. Your Lucidin isn't as smooth as mine. Not that I'm complaining. I'm thankful you agreed to share." His eyes went to Sabine who looked off absentmindedly. Rho's eyes softened. "Sabine, you did her a favor. But one day someone else is going to find her. Now that she knows, she can be careful. I can teach her about influencing. It turned out all right in the end."

Sabine lifted her head at his words, but Raleigh seethed. Did her a favor? Who was he to forgive Sabine? He hadn't been tricked into traveling across the world without knowing the real reason.

A shadow passed by the window and Collin drew back the blind to reveal an elderly neighbor walking his dog. He let the lace curtain slide back into place. "We don't have time for you to teach her influencing. They could be tracking us down right now."

Rho ran his hands together, his thin fingers locking at the knuckle. Whoever captured him hadn't fed him well. "They think I'm dead. We have a few days."

"I want to know what happened. Otherwise I buy the tickets now," said Collin.

Reaching over to the tray, Rho grabbed a glass of water and took a large gulp. "I was at home making dinner for you, Trevor, and Brent."

"Where's home?" Sabine asked.

"My apartment in New York. I was at the stove when someone kicked in the front door and fifteen people flooded in. They shot me with some sort of tranquilizer. I stayed conscious as long as I could, trying to keep them at bay by freezing some of them with influencing. But eventually I succumbed."

"That wasn't a fair fight." Raleigh couldn't imagine fighting off one. Fifteen?

Rho gave her a dark laugh. "You'll learn quickly that this isn't a fight we'll easily win. After they took me, I don't know what happened. Around three days ago, I woke up, and they had me attached to a defibrillator and were giving me CPR. I heard them say they needed to lower the sedative and slow the extraction or I'd die. They'd been walking a fine line between keeping me alive and killing me, and they played it too loose. I was strapped to a bed, but I knew if I soiled myself, they'd have to change me. It was difficult, but I pulled out my catheter. I made my move as they were changing me."

"So that's what happened to your clothes?" Collin was back to the pacing. Raleigh wanted to shout at him to sit.

Rho ran his hands over the sleeves of Henry's pajamas. "They took off my shirt, then had started on the pants when I incapacitated them."

"Incapacitated them?" What did that mean? Rho didn't seem like the type of guy to hurt anyone. Collin, she could believe, but there was something kind about Rho. He was genuinely concerned when he found her hooked up to that machine.

Bowing his head Rho looked up through his lashes. "One of them may've died. They both went down. A lot of people revived me, but only two were there when I broke out, a young man and an old one. The old one had a fragile heart. I can't say if he made it."

Collin snorted. "You should've killed them."

At least Collin was a consistent jerk.

"They probably weren't the guys who took me," said Rho. "They were just doing their jobs."

"And their work was killing you. They sound like wonderful people." Collin put his head in his hands, shook it, and groaned.

"I stole the phone off the young one and texted Trevor. I told him I thought I was in Normandy. Thank goodness you taught me French, Sabine. The dialect made me think France instead of Africa. From the angle of the sun and the sea smell, I had a guess it was Normandy."

"That's impressive," Raleigh said.

"My life depended on it. My legs were atrophied from not

moving for months but I dragged myself over to the window which, unlike the door, didn't have locks. I hoisted myself up and jumped. I was at least four stories up, and the building was on a cliff—in case that helps us find them. Not that there's much we can do, if we do."

"One thing at a time," Collin said. "The more we all know, the better."

Raleigh hated water and didn't even swim in pools. Fainting on dry land wasn't good—in water it became lethal. The thought of jumping off a cliff into the sea was terrifying. "The fall could've killed you."

"It was better than the alternative. I'd rather drown or break my neck than be drained to death. It was clear that they were going to use me until I died."

The blood rushed from her head when Raleigh stood. "That's horrible. We need to call the police. If you remember where it is, we can have them check it out."

Collin leaned over, blocking her path. "The police would never believe it, and the people are probably long gone. These guys are part of the illegal Lucid trade. They're smart about avoiding the police."

"Lucid?"

"It's what everyone besides researchers call Lucidin." Collin stayed planted until she sat.

Rho continued. "I survived the fall, and the tide washed me ashore. I crawled as far inland as I could and attempted to hide. Then you guys found me."

Collin pointed to Rho's shoulder. "They didn't remove the tracking chip in your shoulder, so we were able to locate you. There wasn't much around besides the tracks you left on the beach from your crawl. We had to get you out of there fast and didn't think to cover them up."

"They didn't follow the plane, so we can assume we're safe for a few days." Not looking at Collin, he picked at a loose fiber on the couch. "Probably longer than that. For all they know, the fall killed me."

Collin swept his arms out. "No, not that long. We only came here hoping to find Kappa. We should find your brothers as soon as possible."

The guys both looked to Sabine. Her face fell. "He hasn't contacted me in a while. It's as it is with you, Rho. He instigates the communication."

Unsurprised, Rho turned to Collin. "You could've gone to Marcel. He keeps up with Sigma."

Finally, Collin stopped moving and flopped into the remaining chair. "Where do you think Brent is? In Paris with Marcel, which is where we should be heading. It's safer there. Grant and Able know about Sabine, and they could have their eyes on this place."

"Maybe not. Raleigh's still here."

"Because they don't know who she is, and that's why she's perfectly safe here."

"Either way, this was the right place to come. It would've been days before Marcel got hold of Sigma. I would've died."

"Yes, coming here was a good idea. But staying long isn't. We push off the moment you feel up to it." For the hundredth time, Collin's eyes went to the window.

Rho placed his head between his hands. "I'm not feeling up to it. Not yet. I need to get some sleep."

Sabine stood up. "Collin, carry him up to bed, and I'll help him get settled."

"I can walk." Rho teetered to his feet. "Or at least I can with a little help."

Rising quickly, Collin tossed Rho's arm around his shoulder, and they headed to the attic. Raleigh watched as they left. She was going to finish her oatmeal and turn in as well. There were still questions she had, but now she couldn't trust any of Sabine's answers. Before Rho left, she'd have to learn as much as she could about Lucidin and all the other things Sabine'd kept from her.

THE NEXT MORNING the rain broke, and brilliant sunshine met them, streaming through the windows. The dreariness of Rho's visit dissipated in the presence of such radiance. Danger hadn't sought them out overnight, and after a half hour extraction Rho's vitality returned. Sabine, Henry, and Maggie went to work. It was better if they didn't break their schedules because that might draw attention. Raleigh sat in the living room, observing how the three guests interacted as they ate their breakfasts one room over.

Around the table moods had improved, Collin's most of all. Collin leaned over Trevor's shoulder and spoke to Rho. "If you're feeling well enough after a half hour, we're ready for the train. Trevor, buy the tickets."

Trevor rubbed his fingers on his napkin, brushing off the toast crumbs before he put his fingers on his keyboard. The transportation website popped up, and he quickly had train tickets put into the cart. All that remained was to pay, but he didn't put in the credit card information, instead he referred to Rho.

"Not yet, Trevor." Rho bit down on a bit of toast, and then his eyes flicked up catching Raleigh's.

Collin's tension wound tighter at the prospect of staying. "There's no reason to stay. We'll get to Paris and contact your brothers through Marcel. They need to know what's happened. This is the first time in over a year that anyone has been organized enough to capture one of you. It's important that you tell them. They need to know what to watch out for."

Sighing Rho put down his toast. "What do I say? Watch out if fifteen guys kick down your door?"

"We agreed to leave the moment you felt better."

With his lips a pleasing pink, Rho couldn't claim to be sick. If he kept his promise, the tickets would be bought today. "I'm not ready to leave yet. Physically I could make the journey, but I'm hoping that the four of us can go."

Trevor spoke, a rarity. "Raleigh included?"

"Do you see how ridiculous that is?" Collin pointed at Trevor's raised eyebrows.

She had enough of people acting like she wasn't there. Raleigh stepped towards the table. "I agree with Collin."

"At least she has sense." Collin took a deep breath. The calm only filled his face and lungs, his knee shook under the table.

"You can't stay here." Rho leaned back in his chair, a storm clouding his blue-gray eyes. "I'm worried that Collin's right, and they'll follow us. In all likelihood, they'll just surveil Sabine and Henry. There's no reason to harm them. But you can't stay here as long as that's a possibility."

Luckily, she had a solution of her own. "I can go home. Collin said he could get me an extraction machine. I'll be able to defer college for a semester instead of a year. My parents have been on me to get back. This is a win for everyone."

"She'll be safer at home." Collin tapped the table.

They all waited for Rho to talk. The others might defer to Rho, but Raleigh didn't take her orders from anyone. The arguments never came, instead he lifted himself from the table, his arm muscles straining. "I need a walk. Take one with me?"

"Fine. There's a nice park around the corner. I could use getting out of here for a bit." Collin stretched his arms and walked towards his shoes piled near the door.

"I meant Raleigh."

The conversation she'd had with Collin while he'd carried her downstairs popped into her head. Rho could be persuasive, all that she'd seen so far justified that claim. She wasn't about to leave for Paris with a group of men she'd just met—a group that didn't seem very well organized, never mind that one of them almost died recently and was capable of influencing people's bodies.

"Let me put my hair up." Raleigh only agreed to go on the walk because she wanted to learn about Lucid. She jogged upstairs to get a hair tie. She heard Collin attempting to dissuade Rho from bringing her. If she did go—an idea she refused to entertain—she knew Collin would treat her horribly the whole time.

Collin intercepted her at the bottom of the stairs. "Stick to your guns. I don't care how pretty he is."

She turned her head, so he wouldn't see her cheeks flush. Rho gave her an apologetic smile, and it struck her that he could sense her. The warmth creeping up her neck was a telltale sign of an emotion she knew too well. It was disconcerting that he had the same ability she did.

"I'm more than a pretty face. Besides, Raleigh doesn't seem like that kind of girl." Rho opened the door. "If you are that kind of girl, this will go a lot smoother. I can be really charming."

Rho wasn't the same withered guy who was brought there two days ago. Dark curls hung around his gorgeous face and his natural tan had returned. He looked as though the sun had blessed him once with a kiss.

"It is a very good thing that I'm not that type of girl." Raleigh decided Rho wouldn't be interested in dating her, and he probably wasn't the type of guy that dated girls long-term. Why was she thinking like that? "Are you well enough to walk? Your legs are still a bit tired."

In answer Rho gave her a winning smile, and they headed out the door. "When I'm well enough, I'll barricade so you won't have that sort of insight. I'm not used to being the vulnerable one. Now I know how Trevor and Collin must feel. I think this walk will be good. The more I use my muscles the better."

"Barricade?" First influencing and now barricading, Sabine had failed her in so many ways.

"One of many reasons you should stay with me. You know the area better than me. Is there a park?"

"Up the street." The steep slope of the street was hard on the legs of a fit person, much less one that had been drained to an inch of their life. Raleigh sensed weakness in Rho's legs and wondered if he could handle it.

"Lead the way."

He matched her steps. They passed by the row houses without saying much. Most of Raleigh's attention was on the many familiar faces they passed, even if she didn't know their names. Would Grant and Able pursue her? What if someone else came for Rho? Collin was right, they needed to leave.

"I really am excited about getting home." Time to convince Rho to go without her and to spill everything about Lucid before he did.

"And from the conversation back there, you know that I'm set on you joining us."

"I'm touched that you want to take me with you, but have you thought this through? We're a bunch of kids."

"Trevor and I are twenty-two, and Collin is twenty-three. We're not teenagers."

"I am. I'm eighteen."

"Then you should believe me when I say that the four years I've been on this Earth longer than you have taught me a lot."

Raleigh laughed. He wasn't simply a pretty face. His lighthearted mood took the serious edge off their conversation. "My mother's plan before I met Sabine was to keep me at home until we found a cure or treatment for my blackouts. We've been looking for more than a decade. My plan was to go to college. I applied and received scholarships, got the whole thing together. Even with my illness, I wanted to move forward."

"And college is forward?"

"An education is."

"And what was your major going to be?"

"Pre-med."

"That doesn't surprise me. You'd be a good doctor."

"School isn't the only reason I want to get back."

"You have a family back home... and they mean a lot to you."

"Yes. My mom's been insanely worried since I came here. I promised to return when I got a portable machine. Collin says he'll give me one. So, I can go home now."

"Families are a sore spot. I'm an orphan, but some of my brothers aren't."

"Geez, how many do you have?"

"A lot, and some of them had adoptive families."

"So your parents kept on having kids and giving them up for adoption or to the orphanage? That's weird."

Rho's charismatic smile dropped. "My brothers and I have a very interesting story that I'm not going to share with you until you decide to come with us—and even then, only when the time is right. Suffice to say the people who were interested in Lucid were able to get to my brothers through their adopted parents."

"Grant and Able."

"Yes, Grant and Able. They might treat you better than they did me, but they'd use you all the same."

Rho looked both ways and slid his arm through Raleigh's as they crossed the street. She would've pulled away, but she knew his legs were unsteady after walking up the hill. He appeared to be making a kind gesture, but he may very well have done it just to stay on his feet. Despite feeling slightly odd walking arm in arm, she didn't step away. He was on her left, the side with the port. The hairs on her arms stood on edge, and her nerves sparked where their skin touched. Hopefully, he didn't notice.

"Raleigh, you'll go home and get your medical degree. Sometime, maybe while you're in school, or maybe after, things will catch up with you. You'll be drawn to helping people, and, as I said, all it will take is one word to the wrong person, and you'll be discovered."

"So, I should just go with you? With danger certain to find me? I can't think of a better way to attract these people than staying with you. They'll be after you and discover me in the process. It won't be a hypothetical that will happen someday. It will be a likely thing that will happen very soon."

"I can teach you how to influence and how to set up a mental barricade, so that others can't influence you. Do you know how I met Collin?"

"A dating site? Because I think he's in love with you." Raleigh instantly wished she could swallow the words. It wasn't her place to make observations about their relationship. But if it offended him, she didn't sense it.

"He was part of Grant and Able's army. The women they trained as healers, the men as soldiers. It was his job to keep me there."

Sabine had mentioned the captivity to Raleigh. Thinking of Collin in that capacity drove the point home. An army of Collins would be awful. One seemed like too much.

"Luckily, Collin flipped sides," Rho said.

"It's disturbing that they have an army. But it isn't my problem."

"It could become your problem. The army will hunt you if they have to."

"I want to go to college. We should be getting back. I'm very thankful for your concern and interested in the idea of influencing, but I can't leave with a bunch of strangers."

At the top of the hill, Liege waited below. The buildings followed the river, and the train station sat to their right. They had different paths, but for now they returned down the hill together.

Once inside Raleigh grabbed her computer from the living room. "I'm going to call my parents and let them know I'm booking a flight home."

"I think it's a mistake."

She let Rho's concern fall on the steps behind her. She'd made her decision.

CHAPTER
09

RALEIGH SAT ON her bed and checked the clock one more time. It was early Sunday morning in Colorado, but not so early that her parents would be asleep. They wouldn't mind being awakened by such good news.

After a few rings her father's large face appeared on the screen. It was nice that some things didn't change.

"Raleigh! Good to see you. Patrick's over, we're playing golf today. He'll want to say hi."

"Dad, listen, tell mom to cancel her ticket here."

Her father moved his hand across the air, as if the gesture could stop the pressure building between Raleigh and her mother. *"I know she's complained about you going, but she really does want to see where you're living. Humor her... even if she gives you grief the entire time."*

"It's not that. I'm thinking that I'll be coming home soon."

"So, your uncle told you about those people, Grant and Mable, or something like that."

Raleigh's heart plummeted into her stomach. "What?"

"I don't want you to come back until you're ready. Ignore your mother. She'd keep you here forever. Belgium is supposed to have drab winters, but it shouldn't be worse than here."

"Dad, back up. What did Patrick tell you about Grant and Able?"

"Just that they're interested in you, or more they were interested in Dr. Moore and what he knows about Lucidin. Patrick said they might call us but that we should let the doctors discuss your treatment. He seemed hesitant, said a lot of the Lucidin studies didn't work out and that we shouldn't be talking to them because they aren't very credible. Like I said, he's here now if you want to talk to him."

"I do." Queasy, she gripped the sides of her computer.

"Hey, Patrick," her father yelled off screen. *"Hey, Raleigh wants to talk to you. All you have to do is sit here and she'll be able to talk to you and see you through the camera here above the screen. Do you see her on the computer?"*

"Thanks, Theo. I've used a computer before." Patrick took a seat in front of the monitor. Unlike his brother-in-law, he sat back from the camera, so Raleigh wasn't looking up his nose.

Raleigh's dad left the room. It was for the better.

"What's up?" Patrick smiled. Clearly Grant and Able weren't weighing on him.

Raleigh's hands gripped tighter, her fingers turning white. Maybe Sabine was right about keeping secrets, maybe it was only necessary to let on some things. She tried to keep her voice light. "Patrick, what do you know about Grant and Able?"

"Your father told you. Sorry. I should've called. I didn't think it was worth mentioning. About two weeks ago, two people met Tim for lunch. They said they understood that Tim had met with Sabine who was their former colleague and that they'd heard that he had found a way to diagnose cancer earlier."

The very thing Rho warned her about wasn't years off. It had already begun.

Patrick shrugged. *"Of course, Tim was very discreet. Sabine mentioned that the Lucidin studies hadn't gone anywhere, and she told us both privately that it was best not to tell people about your treatment. Tim spun them some yarn about being active in the community and holding free screening days so people who didn't usually go to the doctor were more likely to see him when they were sick. They left when Tim started going on about public service and how all doctors should volunteer. We thought about telling you but figured that if Sabine wanted you to work with Grant and Able, you'd already be in contact with them."*

"Good. Don't tell them anything. I have to go."

"What's wrong? Should we have done more to discourage them?"

"I don't know that there's anything you can do. They aren't good people."

"They have a research center, and they're working on diagnostics. I have the link if you want to check it out. Tim said they were nice enough, and they haven't contacted him again."

"I have to go. Don't talk to them. I'll see what Sabine thinks."

"Whatever you want. Are you sure you're all right?"

"Yeah. Say hi to Mom for me."

"Take care kiddo."

"Bye." Raleigh shut her computer.

Fear tightened the muscles of her throat. They'd found her, as Rho and Sabine predicted. It wasn't hard to connect the dots. They were watching when Sabine went to the US. Raleigh had made enough of a name for herself that people were talking. It wouldn't have taken Grant and Able long to find her. She realized that they might have eyes on Sabine's house now, eyes that might've seen Rho, Trevor, and Collin. The guys needed to get on that train now.

The question was, should she go with them? If Grant and Able had no qualms about imprisoning Rho and his brothers, they'd probably do the same to her. They were still just poking around, not aggressively coming for her. But even that wasn't good.

"Rho!" Raleigh tripped down the steps, the old boards creaking as loudly as her yell. Relief, in the form of oxygen, flooded through her when she realized they were all still there hunched around the computer bickering over tickets. "They've found me!"

"Take a deep breath." Rho moved around the table in three strides and put his fingers delicately on her shoulders.

"Grant and Able met Dr. Moore two weeks ago. They said they knew he met with Sabine. They must be watching her."

Collin slammed his fist on the table. "That's why we need to leave. It isn't safe to stay here."

"Dr. Moore didn't tell them anything about me. But they know. And they'll put the pieces together, like you said."

Collin stood up and tugged Rho aside. "They might not be as dangerous to her. She's not like you. They may not try to trap her the same way."

Raleigh broke their conversation stepping between the two. Collin wasn't going to decide anything for her. "They are after Lucid. And I have it. Right? They imprison people."

Collin stepped closer to her. His breath crossed her cheek. Those fidgety muscles now strained and froze. "They imprisoned Rho and his brothers, and they didn't find anything ethically wrong with that because Rho and his brothers aren't like normal people."

Rho slowly drew Raleigh back and put a hand on Collin's chest, lightly shoving him away and becoming the focal point of his icy glare. "They're a threat to her. Who knows what they would do to keep her?"

"It might not be all bad. They will keep her away from the

black market. It might be her best option. They can give her extractions and enroll her in their healer programs."

"You aren't serious!" Rho threw up his hands. "She'll be theirs. They'll use her like they did us. Not to mention, handing her over would make them stronger. Did you forget that they're hunting me? The more Lucid they have, the better their chances against us. They might use her Lucid in one of their health programs, but they'd definitely use it with their army."

"We disabled a lot of soldiers."

"They've rebuilt, of course. It's been years and they're very driven. We aren't handing Raleigh over. The best option for her is to come with us."

"With us isn't very safe. For you or her. And she'll just be one more person to keep track of. Let her stay here. If Grant and Able are watching Sabine, they probably already know about her, and they haven't acted."

"They're biding their time. They aren't on good terms with Sabine. They're feeling Raleigh out before they make their move. Trevor, buy her a ticket."

"We should talk about it more," said Trevor.

"Trevor, she's in trouble, and she saved my life. I can't forget that. Buy. Her. The. Ticket."

Trevor's fingers flew across the keys. "It's done. She leaves with us bright and early tomorrow."

"Change the tickets," Collin said. "If they're watching, we need to leave tonight."

Rho turned towards the front door. "We should run this by Sabine. We'll tell her when she gets home."

A frantic laugh threatened to bubble up from Raleigh. Who cared what Sabine thought? Sabine was the reason Raleigh was in this position. She should've been up front with Raleigh about Grant and Able. Raleigh had to make decisions on the fly now because she didn't have the benefit of knowing sooner. Yes, they should talk to Sabine, but Raleigh wasn't staying.

RALEIGH STOOD AT the train station, the events of the past hour knotting her shoulders. Sabine and Henry had come home to find her packing her bags. Rho filled them in on the situation, and they agreed with him and encouraged her to leave. Sabine apologized multiple times in both French and English, but Raleigh mustered up little forgiveness. She'd watched Trevor and Rho say heartfelt goodbyes but couldn't produce a good farewell. After all, if Sabine had been up front, she wouldn't have needed to leave at a moment's notice.

Now at four o'clock people were taking the train home. Sunday moved at a lazier pace, the passengers unhurried. The smell of fresh baked waffles from a nearby cart sweetened the air. There would be no more days spent in the bakery. Raleigh still had her apron hanging by the oven.

"You'll be safer this way." Rho's words skipped by her ear like firework sparks.

She glanced over her shoulder, catching his small grin and Collin's stoic face beyond that. Trevor, as usual, had his eyes trained on his technology. He cupped a glossy black phone in his hands.

Their train rolled up, and the four of them boarded. Like her arrival, her bag posed a problem. The guys traveled light. Collin had a backpack with clothes and Trevor a computer bag. By comparison, she looked ridiculous. They took seats while she wrestled her bag into the corral.

Trevor and Collin sat with their back to her, but she could see

Collin's knee bouncing as she took the seat across from him beside Rho. If things weren't so tense, they could have brought down the small table and played cards. Instead Collin scrutinized every passenger that skirted the aisle and waited on the platform out the window.

The train departed smoothly, making it appear as though the terminal moved and not them. It hummed over the tracks, picking up speed quickly. They'd be in Paris in less than three hours if everything went to plan. It didn't take long for Liege to disappear from view.

Raleigh picked at the frayed edge of her jean shorts. A chill crept through the light top she wore. Both Collin and Rho wore long sleeves and jeans. The thin scarf around her port stood out. Hopefully people would consider it a poor fashion choice and not suspect anything else. Her port. She'd be leaving more than just Sabine in Belgium, she'd be leaving her treatment as well. "We'll have the extraction machine in France, right?"

"Is that why you're nervous? You're worried about treatment?" asked Rho.

He'd sensed her again. How humbling it was for the shoe to be on the other foot. "My blackouts, they're pretty bad."

"You can extract all you need." His fingers moved closer to hers on the seat.

If she stretched out her pinky, they would touch. This wasn't time to think about guys. Collin was wrong, she hadn't taken this trip because Rho was handsome. Nor would she let it cloud her judgment now. Moving her hand to her lap, she reminded herself that all three of them were strangers. Trevor seemed the most predictable—he could be counted on to say nothing. Collin considered her a risk to bring and clearly didn't want her to come along. Rho said he owed her, and that seemed to outweigh the dangers of bringing her, but she could still trip them up.

Collin wouldn't let her forget it either, he kept checking over his shoulder and fidgeting in his seat. Would he get up and pace the cabin? She'd known people who fidgeted, but never any as bad as him.

"Would you calm down?" Raleigh hated the tight feelings he radiated. It caused her own muscles to want to move.

"I'm calm."

Rho lifted the flap of their bag revealing a small pouch. "She's right. Do you want a vial? Sabine gave me the last three of Raleigh's."

Collin closed the flap and tucked the bag back under Rho's seat. "I don't need it."

Trevor snorted. "You've gotten worse. I thought finding Rho would help."

"All of you get off my back. I don't need it."

Collin placed his hands on his knees and purposely pushed his heels into the floor. The only thing twitching were his fingers. What caused him to be so unhinged? None of them were in immediate danger as far as she could tell. His eyes lingered on the bag. There might have been a very good reason Sabine thought those vials ought to go in the trash. Collin went back to checking the aisles, and Raleigh tried not to add any more worries to her collection. She had more than enough already.

Time and the train ride went faster than she'd expected. Too soon they were in Paris. Once she left this train there'd be no going back. A wild decision, even for her, she half expected her mother to jump out from behind one of the seats and scold her.

"Ever been to Paris before?" Rho steadied himself on seatbacks as they walked to the luggage area. The train slowed, and the platform came into view.

"No, but I haven't been many places." Before she could explain that the blackouts made travel difficult, her heart seized into her throat. Her bag was gone. Everything she owned was in that bag.

"I've got it." Collin said stepping to the side to reveal her suitcase. "I didn't want your dresses to slow us down."

"Thanks." Even if it was for efficiency and not to help, she was thankful.

They got off the train, and Trevor looked at his phone map and then at Raleigh. "Paris isn't that great." He looked up at the other passengers and rethought his words saying loudly, "I mean, it's not that bad... either."

"Let's go." Rho assumed the lead with Trevor as they left. They each had their role within the group. Trevor was the navigator and technology guy. Collin lifted heavy things. Rho was the leader. How Raleigh fit in, she didn't know yet.

Trevor moved them smoothly from the train station to the underground. The metro they rode had a map overhead, and she didn't recognize many of the stops. Only major ones like the Louvre. When they got off, they were greeted by loud voices ricocheting off the tiled walls of their stop. Two men barreled past. She could sense the alcohol on their tongues and a fuzziness teasing their brains. Their tipsy sensations made her feel off-kilter. Rho moved from the lead to beside her, placing himself between her and them. They weren't a real threat, but it comforted her.

Between the apprehension in the group, and the drunks, Paris was living up to Trevor's expectations. That changed as they ascended the steps to the street.

CHAPTER
10

PARIS IN JULY was beautiful. Belgium was layered in shades of gray, whereas Paris had the occasional pop of blue or white. Maybe it was that the sun shone brightly, a cheery alternative to its cozy neighbor to the north. The evening rays splashed the old architecture in a yellow hue. A fragrance of flowers, coffee, and cigarettes hung on the breeze. People who strolled by wore short outfits to accommodate the weather, and the younger ones hung on each other affectionately. Raleigh could have spent the whole day on that street corner watching them, but the others weren't impressed. Hurrying on, they treated this setting with the same attitude as the train station—another place they had to go through before their destination.

They walked for five minutes, both her and Collin searching but for different things. He searched for threats, and she scrambled to remember everything. No one told her where they were headed, and she wasn't naïve enough to ask. It was likely only Trevor knew or his phone. After turning down a short alleyway, Trevor stopped in front of a pair of large blue doors with knockers and a keypad on the side. He typed in a four-digit code. After a chirp and the sound of a lock unbolting, Trevor opened the door. Inside sat a small courtyard dotted with townhouse entrances. Trevor walked three down and knocked. After a moment the door swung open.

"Rho!" A guy with dirty-blond hair and a crooked smile rushed out. He roped Rho into the quintessential guy hug—one arm over, one arm under—and finished with a hearty pat on the back. Internally he had an even, slow heart beat and loose relaxed muscles. He turned to the others. "Collin, you're looking as grumpy as usual. Was it a good trip?"

Collin didn't seem entertained. "Hello, Brent."

"Do you have a place I can charge my phone?" Trevor asked.

Brent's crooked smile widened. "Yeah, we do."

"They don't have as many outlets here in Europe." Trevor walked in shaking his head. His pale skin was a little red from their jaunt through Paris.

"Fortunately, that's not their main selling point." Brent's eyes twinkled. Those jovial eyes swept past Collin and Trevor, past the suitcase, to Raleigh. "You brought a girl."

"Rho did," Collin said, making it clear that it wasn't his idea.

Rho took a step back and looped his arm though Raleigh's. "This is the newest addition to our group, Raleigh. Raleigh, this is our people person, Brent."

"You aren't the people person?" she asked quietly.

Rho grinned.

Brent snapped his fingers. "Rho's magnetic, but he's the product. Not safe to have him making the deals."

"We can't talk about this here. Let's get inside." Collin used Raleigh's hefty bag to prod them in. "Is this place secure?"

Brent craned his neck nodding to the high ceilings. "It belongs to a family friend. They keep it as a vacation home, and they aren't scheduled to come back for another month. It's ours as long as we need it. I've already checked for microphones and cameras."

"I'll double-check." Collin dumped the bag in the living room and headed up to the second floor. The townhouse had spacious rooms for being in the city. Like Sabine's, it had the charm of being old and lived in, but it was updated to the current style. The kitchen just off the entrance had burners so clean that they might never have been used.

"Where can I put this?" Rho held up Raleigh's bag.

"Upstairs. There are four bedrooms." Then Brent casually added, "Are you going to share with her?"

"I'll take the couch or camp out with one of you guys."

Brent bobbed his head once. "You're not sleeping together. So, why is she here?"

Raleigh didn't know if she should take offense. "Are most girls along because you're sleeping with them?"

The smile on Brent's face hinted at a laugh. "But she gets jealous. Maybe it's a work in progress."

Trevor had one eyebrow raised. "Work in progress? She makes Lucid. She saved Rho. So now we're taking care of her."

"It's supposed to be an even trade." Collin marched into the kitchen, flung open the fridge, and stole a bottle of water. "I can have this, right?"

Standing on his toes, Brent got out glasses from a high cabinet. "Would anyone else like water?"

"I could use some." Raleigh slid onto one of the stools that circled the kitchen island.

Brent opened another cabinet. "Would anyone like anything a little stronger?"

"Water," Rho said.

"Beer?" Trevor said, surprising her. His vulnerability two nights ago made her think of him as younger. Rho had said he was twenty-two, and, of course, the drinking laws were different in Europe.

Brent flipped a tumbler in the air and poured her a glass of water. He was a bit of a show-off, which reassured her. If Brent could fit in, so could she. Plus, it was clear that Collin wasn't a fan of his. That meant she shouldn't take his snub so personally.

"So Raleigh who makes Lucid, are you Designed, too?" Brent held the water marginally out of her reach and waited on the answer.

"Designed?"

"No. I guess that you won't be with those freckles."

He slid the water the rest of the way. He filled another glass and slid it to Rho, who didn't take it. Instead he glared daggers at Brent.

"Did I say something wrong? Is she insecure about them?" asked Brent. "Raleigh, you should embrace your freckles, they give you the whole innocent-girl-next-door-vibe. Although, a Designed female is something that I wouldn't mind seeing."

"What does that mean?" Too many secrets had piled up over the last day, and she was done with being out of the loop.

Brent's grin left his face, and his eyebrows rose up as he looked to Rho. "She's traveling with us, but she doesn't know who you are? How did you explain making so much Lucid?"

"Raleigh didn't question me making a lot. She makes as much as I do, and no, she's a natural, has her father's hair." Rho saw Raleigh opening her mouth. "I told you I'd tell you about my origins when it was the right time. This isn't it."

"Will it be better in the next thirty-six hours?" Brent's easygoing mood returned. "I'm not taking her to meet Marcel without her knowing."

"I'll tell her on my own terms—and she isn't meeting Marcel."

Brent sighed. "Part of the problem with you wanting to work with the nice dealers is that they aren't as seedy as their counterparts. He's not going to make her fake papers—which we'll need—without meeting her."

Dealer? That didn't sound good to her. "What does he deal?"

"Wow, you really filled her in. Raleigh, girl, why did you come along with this secretive ragtag team? Rho's pretty eyes?" Brent laughed.

She wasn't about to be the butt of the joke. "Why does everyone suggest I'd be that superficial? What do you deal?"

Rho twirled the glass in his hand. "The jokes about my appearance are directed at me, and we deal Lucid. Before you judge, hear me out. We're on the run from Grant and Able, the black market dealers, and who knows who else. It's not like I can find a nine to five job. It isn't an option. I have a commodity, and I sell it."

Brent leaned against the counter. "Don't give us that look, it's not heroin."

"But Sabine said it might be addictive." She couldn't help but notice Rho's eyes drift to Collin. Is that where his nerves came from?

"It can be if you have enough receptors and can get a hold of enough of it," Rho said. "Most people don't get addicted, and it's not like other drugs. It gives people better awareness. It makes them understand their own bodies better, improves their health. A few people can sense, but the ability to influence is so rare that we really don't worry about it."

"But you're perpetuating the same market that's hunting you."

"Yes, but I can't think of a better way to raise funds. Train tickets, plane tickets, secure apartments all cost money. Brent's parents don't have so many friends that we can live everywhere free."

"At least not enough friends that I'm on good terms with," whispered Brent. He clapped his hands together. "So, now we have more product which is good because Marcel is going to require payment, and no one likes an IOU."

"He can't have hers."

Brent asked, "Why?"

"Because it's different from mine."

"Doesn't work as well? Nature never is as good." Brent shrugged. "It would still probably be better than the synthetic."

Rho held out one of the vials Sabine gave him. "You try it."

Raleigh squirmed, was he going to inject that now? They were right, Lucid wasn't a standard street drug. It was also something that she was "on" all the time. Despite that, Brent's syringe seemed nefarious. A moment later he plunged in the Lucid, her Lucid, into a small device on his arm. It was similar to her port but smaller. It required the Lucid to go in, not out. She grasped the effect her Lucid had on Brent as it hit his system. His eyes dilated, his body tensed, and he took a long breath in.

"How many receptors does he have?" Raleigh turned to Rho, keeping her eyes off Brent and the intimate experience.

"Enough to sense for the first half hour or so after taking it."

Brent exhaled and extended his hands letting the rush slide to his fingertips. "That's pretty good. Half the population gets nada, and only a quarter can sense."

"Having any receptors means that you'll have more control over your own body. Brent will have that for a few hours." Rho noticed her confusion. "You take that for granted. The sensing you know is special because others can't do it. What you don't realize, is that you also have better control over your body, more awareness, than other people."

"How is that helpful to him?"

"If I were an athlete, I'd be able to train better," said Brent. "It could help me control any illness I had. It's insightful. Hers is better. Has more of a kick. I can tell it will wear off faster, but the sensing is easier. This would sell for more, easy. Why aren't you barricading my sensing?"

Rho bowed his head. "I'm still weak. No reason to do it while around friends."

"There's the term *barricading*. What exactly is it?" Raleigh asked.

A moment later her awareness of him slipped away. She could reach out and touch him if she wanted, but her mind had no clue what was going on inside him. Nothing. It was the same feeling she got nearing the end of an extraction. Then the connection was back.

"And you do that all the time?"

"When I haven't nearly died by being drained of Lucid, yeah."

Brent interrupted them. "Rho, it's time you figure out your terms. She needs to know a lot more than she knows now."

"I'll teach her influencing and barricading tomorrow."

Done with his scan of the house, Collin reappeared. "It takes weeks to learn both. She's not going to be up to speed for a while, until then she's a liability."

Raleigh opened her mouth ready to spit out a snarky remark, but Brent beat her to it. "You're being finicky because you don't like being shown up. From Rho and his brothers, it's understandable. From her, a natural, it's unexpected. You may be at the top of the curve, but she redefines it. Careful. Jealousy can really cloud your judgment."

"Like you should be giving anyone a lecture on judgment." Heat spread down Collin's neck.

The half hour wasn't up. Brent would still be able to sense that his words ignited the heat rising in his friend. "We have different methods of working with people, which explains why I'm the liaison between us and everyone else."

Rho stepped in. "Collin, do you want to try Raleigh's?"

"Why? We're not selling it and from what I heard you say, it doesn't work as well."

Brent tilted his head. "Works different. It might be more enticing to our customers. I could see addicts liking it more. Want to prove my theory?"

"Enough!" Rho said. "We're all stressed after this week. Let's remember this is a team. The dynamics have changed a little, but I expect that you're all smart enough to adapt."

Brent and Collin both turned down their eyes in submission, their shoulders relaxing.

"I'm going out for a late dinner with Raleigh." Rho's eyes met hers. A secret laced the iris of his eye.

Collin nodded and said, "I'll come, too."

"I don't want you there." Rho kept his back straight and spoke before Collin could protest. "I don't need your protection. I'll bring a vial, on the off chance, that I need it. But I should be able to influence."

Trevor cleared his throat and looked up from the computer. "Rho, we just got you back."

"I'll be fine. Raleigh, let's have that talk." He swigged the rest of his water and got off the stool. "You should bring a jacket. It will get colder." He hauled her bag up the stairs and poked his head into the rooms, deciding on the one with the floral motif. Then he nodded his head to her and went back down.

Her eyes admired the tasteful décor, feminine, but not too girly. She opened her case and pulled out a sweater. A few cool minutes would be welcomed after such a hot day. Wrapping the sweater around her waist, she noticed her reflection in the mirror over the dresser. She had no idea where Rho was taking her. On the street, her clothes were too casual, and, presumably, that would be the case with any place they went. She swapped her shorts for a skirt.

As she entered the kitchen, Collin stopped arguing with Brent to appraise her. "Why the skirt? It isn't a date."

Brent punched Collin lightly. "She looks like less of a tourist, and we know how important it is to blend in."

"They can find ways to bicker about anything." Rho scooped up a backpack from the counter and touched Raleigh's elbow. "Let's go."

"What's in the pack?" Raleigh asked.

"Dinner."

CHAPTER
11

RHO AND RALEIGH left the townhouse, stepping through the large navy doors onto the sidewalk. The streets thinned out as evening settled in. It was nice not having Collin scrutinizing her every move, but could they protect themselves without him? Rho's steps had grown more confident since that morning, but he wasn't fully recovered.

"So your brothers...."

Rho's steps lengthened. "Wine, food, and then the explanation."

"Or you could just tell me now."

"You'll be glad you had the wine."

Rho knew his way around Paris, winding assuredly through the streets until they reached a park. The hot July day had given way to a warm evening. Couples sat on benches and stretched out on the grass.

Unzipping his pack, Rho took out a blanket. It billowed open as he laid it down, giving them a place to sit. They could hear the

French chatter of the nearest couple, but not well, meaning their conversation could be private.

Now nothing kept her from admiring the city. The tumultuous past few days had given her little time to catch her breath. She relaxed as the city soothed her with its pleasantly warm air and ambient sounds. Rho pulled out two sandwiches and handed her one. Then he extended her a water bottle. Raleigh sat with her legs tucked neatly beneath her, regretting the skirt, as she bit into her sandwich. Its fresh taste was amazing. Pulling the bread back, she inspected it. The cheese, ham, and bread were things she'd eaten before, but, even in combination, none of the parts had tasted near this good.

Rho took out a thermos and unscrewed the lid. The smell of wine infused the air as he poured it into the cap. He handed it to her. "Here."

"Can we drink in the park?"

"As long as we don't get rowdy or drunk." He poured himself one. He took a small sip and then rested his cup on the blanket alongside the sandwich he had yet to touch. He stretched out his legs.

She didn't know if he relaxed because he could let his guard down here, or because he was too exhausted to keep it up. "How are you feeling?"

"Fine. Why don't you tell me what your family's like?"

That wasn't the purpose of their coming here, but she humored him. "I have two older siblings, Ben and Lana. Ben's out of college and working at a bank in San Diego. Lana's a sophomore in college and lives away from home. I rarely see her. Thalia, my younger sister, is going to be a junior in high school. My mom stayed home with us when we were younger and now has a flower shop. My dad's a lawyer."

"So, you're the unique one in the bunch?"

"Thalia is pretty unique. She's the rebellious one. Or maybe I get that title after coming here."

"Your mom wouldn't encourage you to join us?"

"If she knew, I'd be on the first flight home, the police would be called, and she'd seal up the house and never let me leave again."

"She's protective."

"A product of having a child with special needs. Ben says that she was much more carefree before my blackouts. I was seven and can't really remember her being any other way from how she is now. What's your family like? Pretty boring?"

"Very funny." He took another slow sip of wine. "I grew up in the boys' home."

"That's where you met Sabine and Henry." Their reminiscing the other night at dinner gave Raleigh the impression they'd had good times.

"It was great. I thrived there. At the time, I didn't know who I was. Kappa and I figured that we were probably brothers even though we don't look alike. He's blond with green eyes. We showed up at the same time, as infants with matching necklaces." He slid his fingers under the top of his T-shirt and removed the silver chain with the Greek letter.

"His picture is on top of the extraction machine at Sabine's."

"We were really similar. Both of us were in the top of our classes—Trevor and us. And when it came to sports, we were always the two captains. It wouldn't have been fair to have us both on the same team. It sounds arrogant, but it was true. Everything came easy. Really, the only thing to contend with was that we both had a liver disease which required daily filtrations."

"You don't feel like you have liver disease, not that all liver diseases feel the same. Really, it's hard to detect. Usually other stuff is off... You didn't really have liver disease."

Rho took a longer sip of wine. "It was the excuse to take our Lucid. Sabine and Henry knew we made it, but they didn't tell us. They were with Grant and Able and didn't burden us with the complexities of what we made. No one at the school knew besides them."

Sabine had a history of keeping people in the dark and hadn't reserved that behavior strictly for her. "Did they know your parents?"

Rho rolled over onto his back so he was looking up at the dusky sky. A few scattered clouds hung onto the sunset. "You don't know me well. I don't want you to hate me."

"I could never hate you for who your parents are."

"I used to think the same thing. So many kids at the orphanage had parents who had shady back stories. Trevor's mother was an awful woman. When you see how important nurture is, you can fool yourself into thinking it beats out nature."

"I don't think people are genetically predisposed to being bad."

"Neither do I. That was one of the reasons I never cared who my parents were. There was the initial interest, who gave me my eyes, did my parents like the same sorts of things I did. It didn't really matter. At most, it was curiosity. I'm sure you've read the orphan books where they find they are someone amazing due to their lineage, a hidden prince, a magical child, a man destined to fulfill an ancient prophecy. Take your pick. I knew enough orphans to know those stories were garbage."

"But you weren't a normal orphan. You could sense because of Lucid."

"So could Kappa, but we didn't ever discuss it with anyone. The few times we did they didn't understand. Sabine told us to keep quiet, and we listened. When we discovered influencing, it became a new secret to add to the other. We were the norm, Kappa and me. The rest of my brothers weren't so lucky. For all they knew, they were the only ones."

"How many brothers?"

"Twelve of us total, although two are dead. Drained."

"Twelve!" exclaimed Raleigh, glancing over at the other picnickers who thankfully didn't pay her any attention. "And no sisters?"

"Ten now, and no sisters, which was why everyone is shocked you're a girl. You probably make more Lucid than any woman in the world, maybe history."

Raleigh took another bite of her sandwich. Surely, if that many brothers made it, she wasn't that much of an anomaly. As she ate, she noticed that he'd put up his barricade. They'd ventured into the part of the conversation he didn't want to have.

"How did you meet your brothers?"

"I was fifteen. Sabine and Henry woke Kappa and me and told us that we had to go. They said our family needed us back, that there'd been some trouble, and that we needed to leave immediately. It was the middle of the night. We didn't say goodbye or pack, just left for a small airport where a private jet took us away." Rho paused and ran his fingers though his hair as he propped himself up on one arm. "We landed on an island. We were confused by why our parents would give us up if they were so rich. Frankly, by that age I was moody and didn't want to know them. That wasn't an option. Then we were escorted into the largest mansion I'd ever seen and taken to a ballroom."

"Where the rest of your brothers were?"

Rho trained his eyes on her. "It was weirder than counting up ten other guys besides the two of us. It was easy to do the math and hit twelve because there were four sets of identical triplets."

"Really? How is that possible? Isn't that super rare?"

"I guess triplets isn't technically the right word. Each one was born to a separate surrogate, but there are two guys that had the same genes as me."

"I'm not getting it? What about your parents?"

"There were none. We were made from scratch. *Designed.* The alternative would be you, a natural. It's the category the rest of the world falls into."

"Clones?"

"No, from scratch. It was a large experiment which is why we all have a Greek letter in place of a real name."

"I didn't know science could do that."

Rho sat up shaking his head. "The question is why would they do it? What would be the point? You could make a person better, but, overall, they're still only a person. I've been designed to be attractive and smart, but not so much that people should've spent years figuring out a way to make me."

Raleigh inspected him. His symmetrical face hadn't one blemish. It wasn't an exaggeration to say he was the most attractive person she'd ever seen. Up until now it had been a punch line, like Brent saying she came along because of Rho's pretty eyes. Raleigh figured that Rho had the good fortune of having looks. Now that she knew it was artificial, his attributes took on new meaning.

"You're looking at me differently." He wrapped his arms around his legs, his hands clasped together at his knees.

"But not meanly. All right, so you're created to be beautiful, smart, and witty. That's to your advantage."

Rho forced a grin. "To be fair, most of my brothers aren't witty."

A laugh escaped her. "See, they can't design everything. I'm surprised they didn't tell anyone or have it published in journals."

"It's illegal. And like I said, not worth the trouble. The real reason we were created was to make Lucidin. The rest of the stuff was secondary. They couldn't figure out how to synthesize it in a lab. They had to get it from people. Usually it happens randomly, but they had a tribe they discovered where it was passed down genetically. It's kinda like cancer in that way. Some people are pre-disposed. Others simply get it."

"I just got it."

"There you go."

"I've read about that tribe. Dr. Moore, who found Sabine, he told me about it. He said the scientists weren't generally believed. It's easy to guess why."

Rho finally took a bite of his food, the somberness shifting. Raleigh observed the other people in the park. A couple made out on a bench, and there was a trio of friends gesturing erratically and laughing. A week ago, she was sinking into the routine of Belgium. Now it was bizarre, going on the lam with an odd group of guys only to find one of them was created in a lab.

"Why make you perfect? Why not—I don't know—alter a baby to make Lucidin?"

"No one wanted to do that to a baby. To them, we aren't human, which is probably why they had no qualms about keeping us on the island. That's why Collin thinks you might be saved. But I wouldn't count on it."

"Henry and Sabine certainly don't treat you that way."

"They begged Grant and Able for us to go back home after meeting our brothers. They were denied and, shortly thereafter, Grant and Able began contacting them less."

Taking a long drink of the wine, she repositioned, the grass poking her bare legs through the thin blanket. She couldn't imagine not knowing her siblings all her life. They'd robbed Rho of his family. "Why didn't you meet your brothers sooner?"

"They tried to give us normal upbringings. They knew about sensing but not influencing, and if it were only that, it might have been possible. They used our Lucid with their healers and advanced medicine. Then we stumbled on influencing and they caught wind.

It changed everything. Chi almost killed a kid who threatened him. They called us evil and rounded us up."

"I can't see anyone thinking you're evil."

"If you met my triplet—Sigma—you'd have a hard time believing all of us aren't."

"But they've met you."

Rho poured more wine into her cup. "Even if we were good, they really didn't care. Our Lucid is all that's ever mattered."

"Will your kids make Lucid? I mean, theoretically, that's going to be a lot easier than whipping up another batch of you."

Rho laughed and stretched his legs back out. "Glad that you're okay enough with the idea of us that you're already planning more."

"I'm following their logic. If you want more people who make Lucid, then it makes sense they'd program you to pass it on. They should probably have designed a girl, so your genes aren't diluted by the general population."

"We're infertile."

Raleigh spit out some of her wine. "You've tested that? I mean, I'm sure that you wouldn't have trouble finding volunteers." She backed herself into a corner. "I mean, we've already discussed how you look."

"They told us, and, yes, some of us have taken it upon themselves to make sure and saw a fertility doctor." He paused. "I've had sex. Everything works as it should. It just affects fertility. I don't think you should feel embarrassed. I'm the one revealing all the personal stuff."

Raleigh remembered that he could sense her. It was intrusive—not that she was in a position to complain. As a rule, she responded to people's emotions but rarely brought it up.

She ignored the heat that crawled up the back of her neck. "Why did they make you infertile?"

"Like all good nerds, they read the cautionary tales. Robots and clones take over the world when given a chance, right? But we can't multiply. That was their reason for making no females. They didn't want any possibility of us reproducing."

Raleigh didn't know much about infertility. Pregnancy she could sense in other people, but infertility wasn't something she could tie down. Was Rho upset that he couldn't have kids? For her it was a "someday" sort of thing, nothing so pressing that she had to think about it anytime soon. Would she be upset if she couldn't have them?

"It's probably for the better, right? They'd be hunted, like you."

Rho nodded. "Yeah, and imagine the alternative. They expect us to have a ton of kids to get more Lucid. This is definitely better."

Raleigh's second cup of wine rested empty on the edge of the blanket, and her tongue slowed with each word. Rho'd picked at his sandwich, but she'd finished hers. He ate a few more bites.

"I told you why we wanted to leave the island. We were trapped there. When we escaped, some of my brothers killed a few people. I tried to incapacitate them. It's easy enough to make someone go unconscious. Others though, Sigma, in particular, really fought back. Many of the scientists died. I'm sure that Grant and Able will capture and use some of us. But the others, I think they'd just as soon kill."

"Oh." This was the most uncomfortable conversation she'd ever had. Not only did she have to keep a straight face, but her body couldn't betray her by showing her discomfort. Taking even breaths, she tried to steady her heart. First, the odd twist of Rho being created to make a drug, then the infertility, and now murder confessions, if it could be called murder. There was always the argument for self-defense. "What did you do after you escaped?"

"Collin stuck with me. I told him to save himself, but he kept by my side. Like most of the Receps, he's addicted to Lucid. He went off it for a year to prove he could. I think that may be why he's grumpy now. He's denying himself something that his body needs."

This news didn't endear Collin to her. *Grumpy* wasn't the word she'd use. *Asshole* was. "It was nice that he stayed with you." It was the one nice thing she could think to say.

"You're going to find out how hard it is to stay hidden. I didn't have connections back then. It was really hard going for a while. Trevor was in his freshman year of college, and he helped me find people to buy Lucid online. He also covered my tracks. Still does. A year in, I met Brent. I was at a rich kid's party, trying to sell them Lucid. I've never been great at it, and Brent said he could move it much better than me. And he did. That's when we really started making money—when athletes and other people wanted an edge. I've needed everyone on my team at one point or another."

Raleigh hadn't made up her mind about his team. Collin she could do without. Brent seemed friendly, but trusting him was entirely different than liking him. Trevor showed some real emotion when Rho was sick. A true friend. Of the three, he was the one she liked the most.

Night settled in while they spoke. The lampposts flickered on. People picked up their blankets and moved on. Other couples snuggled together, the dark romantic in a way daytime never is. The shadow of Rho's jaw made him mysterious, a beauty that had brought him such sadness for what it represented.

"You should put on your sweater," Rho told her.

"Are we leaving?"

An empty plate sat on the blanket beside her, but Rho's sandwich wasn't finished, and neither was his second glass of wine.

"The wine is making you feel warm, but you're getting cold." Her reached over and ran his fingers along the goosebumps on her arm. Warmth and electricity were left in their wake. Despite the cold, her skin flushed as she recalled what Collin said. This wasn't a date. If Paris knew that, it might not be so charming.

"I don't want to talk about my past anymore. Tell me about the blackouts."

Raleigh did, which was strange. Coming from a small community, people just knew about them. Her peers at school shared the details through gossip or concern, so she never had to. It was cathartic to tell her story to someone who would believe all of it, including the sensing. Designed or not, Rho had things in common with her that no one else did. She savored that bond as they wrapped up dinner.

CHAPTER
12

A BLARING CAR horn, followed by some yelling in French, woke Raleigh. Rubbing her eyes, she peered at the clock only to find that it was already noon. Last night she'd arrived home late with Rho, extracted, and fallen into bed around one a.m. She never slept that long. It must've been the wine and extraction. In the future, she'd stop at one drink.

The discussion last night took on a different starkness in the light of day. Grant and Able had gone to extraordinary lengths to create Lucidin, and the Designed brothers had done awful things to avoid giving it up. Solving the riddle of her illness had been freeing. Like a bird with a mended wing, she'd taken off into flight. Except now, she found the air was filled with predators. She, like the bird, couldn't go back home.

She slid out of bed and stretched. Today she was going to learn influencing, a defense, which was rapidly becoming necessary. Opening her door, she wandered down the hall to the bathroom.

Voices drifted up the stairs, Rho, Collin, and Brent in conversation. She guessed Trevor was on the computer. She was the last one up. Late or not, she was going to shower before heading down. In her slightly inebriated state, she'd neglected to brush her teeth and her hair was knotted on one side of her head. Twenty minutes later she emerged in fresh clothes with her hair clean. She padded down to the living room.

Collin stood by the table. "You slept in. We've been waiting on you."

"I'm sorry about your headache." Rho rose from the table, a smile filling his face. His beautiful face, because they'd made him that way.

Brent handed her a cup of coffee and a croissant. "Eat up. You've got a long day ahead of you."

Trevor looked up from his laptop for a moment and gave a nod. His head bobs were already becoming predictable to Raleigh.

"That's right. Influencing." She sat down at the high table with her food. Trevor adjusted his computer to avoid her crumbs.

Rho chose the seat beside her at the round table. The seed of something grew between them, something fresh, new, and weak, but undeniable. Was it more than a friendship? She didn't know, but her stomach fluttered. Maybe she should request barricading first. Rho, hearty enough now, did. "We should probably have you extract again. I'd like Collin to help us train this morning, so you'll be ready to meet Marcel."

"So I can get fake papers?" Could she really discuss violating international law so simply, let alone actually use the papers? "My stuff is fine. If you dislike him so much let's skip it."

Brent said, "We need Marcel to help us find the other Designed. None of your papers can be used."

"They're fine."

"No, they aren't." Trevor pulled his headphones down. "They can be traced. We aren't going to take any chances."

"Is it worse being caught with forged papers? Or is your idea to keep me safe by keeping me in prison?" Raleigh didn't break house rules, let alone international ones.

"Marcel is good at what he does, or, at least, the people he pays are." Brent lifted the portable machine onto the table. His warm fingers turned over Raleigh's arm, exposing her port. "Do you mind doing this while you eat?"

"It's fine." Raleigh watched him remove the small piece of cloth and hook her up. Technology was getting smaller in all areas. It wasn't only cell phones and laptops that became sleeker. This extraction machine was the size of a loaf a bread and a far cry from the person-sized one at Sabine's. After this, she wouldn't be able to train for at least half an hour.

Trevor shut his laptop. "And don't use your phone."

"My phone doesn't make international calls." She hadn't turned it on since leaving the US. Living without a phone was unimaginable the first week but a bit of a relief thereafter. "Can you help me call my parents tomorrow? I usually call them every few days."

Trevor said, "I can have it set up by then. Let's hope Marcel agrees to provide you with a driver's license and passport. Otherwise, I'm not sure how we'll travel."

Rho sat down and rolled an empty vial between his fingers. "If Marcel agrees, we'll want the papers sooner rather than later. I'd gladly pay the price in full with my Lucid, but as weak as I am, I can only extract once a day."

"If that," snorted Collin.

Since his rescue, Rho had rapidly improved. Raleigh couldn't stand the thought of him reverting, especially if it was her fault. "Maybe you should just give him mine."

Brent pointed at them. "We'll need Lucid from both of you to meet the price. This is going to cost a lot, and Rho's Lucid alone won't cut it. We'll give Marcel a vial of yours, and if he likes it— which he will—we'll ask him to keep it for his personal use."

"That way, it won't go on the black market." Rho rubbed his fingers across his port.

"Oh! Later today, I'm giving you a chip." Trevor pulled out a small tube with a fingertip-sized microchip in it.

Raleigh raised her eyebrows. "A chip?"

"A tracking chip, like the one I put in Rho. It lets us locate you within a ten-mile radius. I'll insert it under the skin on your shoulder. It doesn't hurt... and it could really help."

Raleigh let the croissant sit in her mouth.

Rho patted her shoulder. "Seems paranoid, but it saved me."

Dogs had microchips, not people. Everything was rushing toward her too quickly. Not being allowed to use her credit cards meant that she couldn't purchase a plane ticket home. She swallowed down her reservations, hiding would be hard, and they had a better idea of what that entailed. For now, she would listen.

———

FORTY MINUTES AFTER breakfast, the taste of coffee lingered in Raleigh's mouth, and fresh Lucid hummed in her veins. They held the influencing lesson in the living room next to the dining room. She and Rho were ready to start, but Collin, like most people, would have to dose first.

"You're certain you aren't ready to extract?" Collin asked Rho as he picked up a vial of Raleigh's Lucid. Tilting it in the light, he inspected it for contaminants. He fell short of implying that she might have cooties.

"No, I'm going to hold off until tonight. You don't have to teach her. I can manage that fine myself."

Collin scrunched his lips to one side of his face.

"If mine is that offensive to you, don't take it." Raleigh reached to take the vial from his hand.

Collin moved away from her quickly, took a deep breath, and injected it. Similar to Brent yesterday, Raleigh could feel his system take it up. Unlike Brent, there was a moment of jubilation followed by a wave of calm. It was akin to putting balm on a burn.

Instantly his demeanor changed, the fidgeting stopped. He sat with his feet planted in front of him on the white carpet. Rho stood, arms crossed, waiting for Collin to ready himself. Raleigh wasn't sure what she expected.

"The meditation helps him use the Lucid." Rho kept his eyes on his friend.

Collin opened his eyes. "It's wilder. I don't like it as much."

Liar. This was the most relaxed he'd been since they met. His voice was softer than normal. The change made her wonder what he was like before he took Lucid and was molded into a soldier. With his slight Midwest accent, she could picture him playing sports and being a normal guy. Lucid had negatively impacted her for years, and perhaps him as well, in a different way. Sabine did say it wasn't the miracle drug that they'd hoped it would be.

With Collin ready, Rho commenced the lesson. "Influencing uses the same pathways that your mind is already utilizing with sensing. There are two parts to it. The first is sending a signal or telling the body to create a new sensation. Me making your nose itch would be an example of that. The other is preventing something that was already happening, like freezing someone's legs when they're trying to move them by overriding the person's body with your own wants. Look at Trevor over there. Can you feel his fingers on the keys?"

Trevor sat unsuspectingly at the computer, his gigantic headphones on his ears.

"Yes." Normally she didn't pay much attention to muscle movement. It was so mundane and frequent that she rarely noticed unless someone had a bad ache or tear. Honing in, she could easily follow the finger movements.

"Try the first step. See if you can make one of his fingers press down longer than it was going too. Focus in on his fingers as if they're an extension of you. Move his finger as you would yours, will it to behave as you want."

"Shouldn't you teach her how to meditate and ground herself first?" asked Collin. "Clearing her mind will be essential if she's going to get it. She won't have the right frame of mind."

Raleigh discounted Collin. Closing her eyes, she concentrated on the muscles in Trevor's right hand, specifically, his right index finger. She made the muscles press down. If her eyes were open, she would've seen his finger holding down the H. She opened them in time to catch a scowl from him.

"Good." Rho leaned over, his mouth hovering closer to her ear. "Now override the control he has over his movement."

Trevor tried to stand, and she stopped him by interrupting the message to his legs. It wasn't the stiffening trick that she'd used with his fingers. Instead, she simply made it as though his brain never sent the message.

She hadn't frozen his mouth. "Find someone else! Isn't this what you have Collin for?"

Raleigh let his finger go slack and allowed him to stand up. He did, only to give them a deep sigh and sit down.

"I did it! That was so easy!"

Brent came in. "She already did it?"

Collin's calm dissolved. "You've done this before."

Raleigh spun around and looked at Collin. "No, I haven't. I never thought to try before, which is a shame. How many people could I have helped?"

"Be careful, you can really overdo some things. You can try to slow down a racing heart and accidentally make it stop. There's a lot of fine tuning you'll have to do before you can really use it." Rho smiled as he issued the warning.

Brent patted Collin on the shoulder. "How long did influencing take you? A few weeks? Months? I guess we were right in thinking that she would far surpass you."

Collin narrowed his eyes. "Now let's see how well she does with barricading."

Rho rubbed his hands together. "All right, Raleigh, you're going to want to...."

Sharp pain. So sharp she reached up and clasped her head, holding it together even though it only seemed like it was ripped apart. She screamed, clawing to make it stop. Falling to the ground she rolled, trying to do something to alleviate it.

It stopped, and her yells were replaced by Collin's deep howls. His hands balled into fists at his sides. Rho positioned himself over Raleigh squaring off against his friend.

The yelling stopped, and Collin stepped forward, unclenching his fists and shoving Rho. "Why did you do that?" Collin shouted.

Rho stepped over Raleigh instead of falling on her. "You were hurting her!"

"That's how we teach it. Pain is something people instinctually push out."

Rho shook his head. "That's not how I learned."

"Well, you're different!"

"So's she!"

"She's not like you and your brothers. You're going to figure that out when you introduce them to her. You're different. She's the same as everyone else."

"You just hate being upstaged." Rho knelt down and helped Raleigh up. His hand cupped the side of her face, her pain gone but not her memory of it.

"Whatever! I guess you don't need me now!" Collin charged past them, flipping a chair over before yanking open the door and storming out.

All eyes rested on the overturned chair. Brent said, "He's right. With her here to watch your back, you don't need him."

Trevor gnawed the edge of his nail. "She can't pilot a plane."

"How often does that really come up?" asked Brent.

"That turned violent quickly. Who knew he'd be so irrational about Raleigh?" Rho stared at the door.

Brent answered the rhetorical question. "Who couldn't? He's an addict. You can't keep acting like being around us is good for him. Now that she's here, we can let him go."

Rho pointed at Brent. "Keep talking like that, and he'll leave. We don't drop people when someone better comes along."

"You admit she's better."

"Of course she is."

"Please, by all means, if you find someone better at selling, go with them. Don't keep me on because you feel like you owe me."

Trevor opened his mouth, thought for a moment, and said, "I don't think you'll find anyone as good at computers. Still, there is something to be said for loyalty. Collin has always had that. I don't think you can turn someone out who's stood by you."

Brent's eyes rolled up and then focused on Rho. "It's better for him to not be around Lucid, to forget it exists."

Raleigh didn't take sides. It wasn't her place. If Collin was addicted, it wasn't his fault. She could understand the feeling of coming in a distant second. On the other hand, she wouldn't be sad to see Collin go.

Rho inhaled, his shoulders moving up and down with the breath. He walked over, opened the door, and waited in the doorframe. "I'm going after him. Raleigh, we'll have to work on barricading another time."

The door snapped shut behind him leaving them in an awkward silence. Raleigh pursed her lips. That barricading lesson was an important one. Collin's temper tantrum might end up costing her.

Brent said, "We should get you ready for tonight. It will take you longer to get ready than us."

"Sure."

She and Brent went upstairs, her mind going over the inventory of her suitcase. The skirt last night was one of the dressier things she had, and she doubted it would work for the meeting. "Do you think I could borrow something out of one of the closets?"

"Sure—if you want to dress like a fifty-year-old. I bought you something, though."

"When?"

"Not all of us slept in until noon. Don't get testy. I got Rho stuff, too. I guessed that skirt was the nicest thing you had, and it's not going to cut it tonight."

"Where are we meeting Marcel?"

"At his nightclub, where he conducts all his business."

Brent led her to his room and pulled an outfit from the closet. "I'll step out while you put it on. Then I can help with your makeup."

After Brent left, Raleigh removed the outfit from the bag, wondering how good his makeup skills could be. The shimmery red top hung low in the front and laced up the back. The black leather skirt would help tone down the glitz. Thalia would have loved it, but could Raleigh pull it off? With the blackouts, she'd always attempted to draw attention away from herself. This outfit would do the opposite. Putting it on, she walked to the attached bathroom so she could admire the outfit from all angles. It showed more skin than she would've liked, but Brent had done a good job.

"Am I awesome or what?" Brent said from the doorway.

"It might get cold."

"With all the hoops Rho's going through to bring you along, it's safe to say he'd give you the shirt off his back. I'm sure he'll lend you his jacket."

"What about shoes?"

Brent held up boots. "Heels would go better, but we want you to be in something you can run in. Let's do your makeup, and then you can extract before we leave."

"Will Rho be back in time?"

"He better be. There's no point in going without him. Sit down, and let me do your eyes."

They went to the adjoined bathroom. He closed the toilet lid, and Raleigh sat on the edge of the tub. She shut her eyes trying not to flinch at the pressure of the eye lining pencil. This was going to be different from wearing makeup to prom and other dances.

"Do you put makeup on girls often?" Raleigh asked.

"I'm no orphan like Rho and Trevor. I come from a blended family. Lots of full, half, and step siblings. Each of my parents has been married two or three times. I've had my share of sisters. Nothing wins the heart of a five-year-old like putting on her makeup."

Raleigh smiled as he worked on her lashes. "Does it help you pick up girls?"

"That and a lot of other charms. It's easy to pick them up when Collin is around, harder when Rho is."

"Is Collin in love with Rho? Because the way he looks at him and feels inside, it's more than protective. There's a sense of ownership."

"That's the addiction." Brent's hand paused right by her eyebrow, and he stared into her eyes. "Please don't tell me you're the type of girl that goes for jerks like Collin. You don't seem like the type. I've seen the looks you give Rho."

"What looks?"

"The ones everyone gives him. I've never been attracted to him, and I've caught myself staring. People aren't supposed to look like that. Stay away from Collin."

"You won't have a hard time convincing me of that."

Brent finished her eyes. Wanting to say something else, his mouth opened twice before he reconsidered and shut it.

It was odd to see Brent not talking, holding back. It made her curious as to what he wanted to say. "Brent, what are you thinking?"

"That you need to put on some of this lipstick." Brent held up a tube of blood-red lipstick.

It was darker than she liked, but it went well with the shirt. Raleigh took it but didn't apply it, waiting for Brent to answer her.

"I was wondering if Rho got around to telling you about the rules of dating," Brent said.

"No. But I'd assume that sort of thing is on the back burner, with us being chased and all."

"It's a bit more complicated than that. But I'm going to let him give you the talk about the birds and bees."

Raleigh ran the lipstick across her bottom lip and then slid it around the top. "I've had that talk."

"Not this particular one. Now tonight, you should know that Marcel is really forward. He's not a bad guy, but he can be intimidating. You hold your ground. Answer his questions honestly. This is going to be one of the only times you'll do that. Rho and his brothers use him to sell, and he's honest. Just because we all dislike him doesn't mean we don't all trust him."

"Is he unpleasant like Collin?"

"No one is as unpleasant as Collin." His laugh grazed her cheek. "He's not mean, but he's a ruthless type of person which happens to benefit us more often than not. A moral person wouldn't be able to get hold of fake papers. You look perfect. I'm going to change. I'll meet you in the living room."

Raleigh looked in the mirror. Thalia would approve. The thought of home tightened her chest. For a few moments, she sat in the silence, bolstering her confidence. Then she went into the living room where Brent and Rho waited. "How's Collin?"

Rho motioned towards the door. "Staying with us. It's time to meet Marcel."

CHAPTER
13

THE ENTRANCE TO Marcel's club sat on a side street and, despite her expectations, was more sleek than sleazy. The last rays of summer sun left the sky a muted mustard, but here shadows engulfed them. She moved her toes around in her boots. Not only were they going to ask Marcel to do something illegal on their behalf, they were going to pay him with the Lucid from her body.

She'd become a commodity, like oil or gold.

Rho flattened the collar of his shirt. "Let's go."

They walked up to a door with *Orange* written across it playfully. Peering through the large windows, Raleigh thought that a better name would be White. Once they entered that was all she saw, white tables, chairs, tiles, and walls. The orange popped out in surprising places—the occasional chair, lamp, and napkin. LED strip lights from under the bar illuminated the room in the perky color.

"This is a mistake," Trevor whispered.

Rho led them in. "You don't have to go up. Collin and you are staying down here."

"Why isn't Collin coming with us?" Raleigh surprised herself. It wasn't like she wanted him along.

Brent surveyed the room. "Marcel considers Collin a bodyguard, and he doesn't do business with bodyguards."

"There aren't many people," she said. Beyond a few waiters and a couple in the corner booth, they were the only ones.

Brent headed in the direction of the steps, donning a wide smile. "They just opened. Give it an hour, and we won't be able to walk across the floor without bumping into people."

Rho squeezed Raleigh's shoulder as they approached a bouncer guarding the stairwell. Underneath the bouncer's fat, she sensed tight muscles, and the skin along his knuckles ached. This guy enjoyed fighting.

"Brent." The bouncer's thick French twisted the name. After scanning Rho and Raleigh, he moved to the side, letting them pass. Rho's hand went to the small of her back as they climbed the steps. Before stepping foot on the landing, she knew there were two people up there, one near the landing, the other further in.

A bar greeted them at the top of the stairs. The color scheme was similar to downstairs with whimsical touches of orange, but everything else was black instead of white. Tables scattered across the second floor in a random pattern with deep leather sofas and chairs in conference around them. One of the men she'd sensed was a bartender running a cloth through a damp glass. The other sat farther in at a table.

The man at the table rose from his leather chair and walked in Rho's direction. "Good to see you again, Rho."

Rho replied with a curt nod. "Marcel."

There must've been an unspoken dress code. Rho, Brent, and

Marcel wore the same metallic-collared shirts. Marcel and Rho donned dark colors, but Brent wore bright purple, the color striking against the dark hues. His time to shine was now.

"Thanks for meeting with us." Brent's smooth smile quirked up a corner of his lips. He shook Marcel's hand. She would never have guessed that the two were anything but friends.

Marcel turned and clasped Rho's hand between his. "I'm sorry that I was unable to give in to Brent's request of your brother's location the other day. As you know, I'm under strict rules to only provide it to one of you."

"Yes, and we thank you for your discretion."

"I see that you made it. Nasty people, those in the synthetic trade. One day, we will have to work on pushing them out of the market permanently." He studied Rho's face. "Maybe that is a better proposition for Sigma. That man was made without a heart."

Rho had mentioned Sigma being evil. If Marcel, with his reputation, felt that way, she could imagine how bad he must be.

"It's your choice to do business with him." The charm that normally graced Rho was nowhere to be found. With his rigid posture and direct gaze, he exuded strength.

"True enough but beneficial for you. A lot has happened in your absence."

Rho wisely barricaded around Marcel. Raleigh could only tell he was concerned by the falter of his face. "What news do you have?"

Marcel tapped his nose. "You bring a lover?"

Heat blossomed across her cheeks, and her mouth went dry.

Brent introduced her. "This is Raleigh, and she's a friend."

Marcel leaned forward, kissing the air alongside her cheeks. He smelled of spice and cigarettes. "Lovely to meet you, Raleigh. You've made an interesting choice in friends. Please sit." He held his hand open, ushering them to a low table surrounded by four chairs.

Raleigh sank into one of four deep chairs positioned around the table, grabbing the hem of her skirt as it inched indecently up her leg. Adjusting herself delicately, she balanced on the edge of the chair, she crossed her legs attempting to be modest. The men, by contrast, plopped into their chairs, leaning back, like kings lounging on thrones. Rho sat to one side and Marcel to the other. She and Brent were bystanders to the deal.

"You sound surprised to learn that things have happened to your brothers. Is there another reason you came here?" Marcel asked.

"Yes. But first, what's happened to them?"

"Sigma has gathered most of you. I have a phone number that you are to call. Just you. Not your team. I know you have your rules." He gave Raleigh a curious glance. "I'm to assume you wish for her to be part of the discussion?"

"Raleigh is one of us."

"Let's hope for her sake, that's not true." Marcel studied her a moment longer. His light-brown hair was brushed back from his very stern, thin, and angular face. He was sharp like his words. "Mu and Tau have been captured by Grant and Able."

Rho gripped the arms of his chair. "How long?"

"Shortly after you went missing. There were rumors that you'd been killed. That was why I could not, in good faith, give the phone number to Brent." Taking out a pen, he scribbled a number on a scrap of paper and handed it to Rho. "How is it that you're alive? Brent told me that you were drained within inches of death."

"That's why we're here."

"Revenge. I knew it." Marcel rubbed his hands together, Raleigh sensed elation boiling in his chest.

"Not revenge." Rho turned to Raleigh, an apology in his eyes. "I need papers. A passport, American driver's license, and anything else you think might be useful for Raleigh."

Marcel shook his finger. "I don't do that often. Forgery has a hefty sentence."

Brent stepped in. "We'll pay you well." He removed four vials from his pocket. "Take these. We'll have more in a week."

"A week sounds fair, if I decide to do it. My dealers can move much more than that. Can I buy more?"

Rho shook his head. "It's not mine. You have to promise to keep this for personal use."

"Not yours?" Marcel chuckled. "Don't tell me you have found a way to make a synthetic? We'll all be rich."

"It's Raleigh's. That's how I survived... with hers."

Marcel's smiled faded as he leaned towards Raleigh. "There is no way you are going to convince me she's Designed."

"She's not. She's a natural. Remember, people can make it."

"They never make much. I remember the biology lesson about receptors. You can spare me."

"Because she's a natural, hers is different."

Brent added, "Better."

Marcel raised his hand and snapped his fingers. Instantly, the bartender was on his feet and a moment later Marcel had a syringe. Raleigh didn't watch as he injected it. Like Brent, he had the endorphins of euphoria warm his nerves. Raleigh caught Rho's eye. What was Marcel capable of? Rho motioned toward Brent. Sensing, earlier he'd said almost no one could influence.

"It's savage." Marcel's thin lips parting into a wicked smile. "I could sell this for more. Really, where did you get it?"

"We told you. Raleigh," Brent said.

Marcel rolled down his shirt sleeve shaking his head. "You expect me to believe that doe-eyed girl makes this!"

"I do," she said.

Marcel sat back, drumming his hand on the arm of the chair.

"This is your story? You want papers for a girl who makes Lucid? I'm not buying it. See those scars on her arms and legs. Old. This girl has seen pain. What are you getting her out of? If you're trying to traffic her, it's a serious offense, even if you are trying to save her."

Raleigh had to give Marcel credit. He noticed things and didn't seem willing to give papers over unless it was for good cause. A creepy guy, but one with morals—or at least lines he was unwilling to cross.

"Have I ever lied to you, Marcel?" Rho asked.

Marcel rubbed his chin, inspecting Raleigh. "I can think of a way to prove it."

Brent shook his head. "I didn't bring the extraction machine. We try our best to not draw attention to that."

Marcel turned to Brent. "Sigma likes to take the company of some of the women I know. For a small fee, I give him their names. They line up. Do you know why?"

"He looks like Rho?" She bit her lip.

Marcel laughed in a hearty way that filled his lungs. "Yes, that would probably be enough to form a line out the door. No, in this case they are women with some receptors, and they get a small hit from engaging with him. A kiss is worth a fraction of a vial, but they can tell. The first time one asked I had to assure her that he had dosed up before he took her to bed. I didn't want your secret getting out, Rho. Most people dose before sex. Sensing during that is phenomenal. But then, I don't need to tell you that."

Rho perched on the edge of his seat, no longer stoic. Raleigh didn't like the direction this was going.

Brent mirrored the casualness of their host but wasn't smiling. "Raleigh isn't going to have sex with you."

"Usually the girl is the one who answers that question." Marcel grinned. "And sex isn't needed. Merely a kiss."

Rho jumped out of his seat. "This is ridiculous. If you can't take me at my word...."

Marcel flipped a his hand in the air indicating Rho's chair. "Sit down. You prudish Americans get squeamish about the silliest things."

The skin on her arms stood on edge, she wanted to be one floor down or, better yet, gone. Even with the barricade, she knew Rho itched to fight. It was just a kiss. "I'll do it."

"Raleigh, you don't have to." Rho spoke to her, but his eyes were on Marcel.

"It's fine." She'd kissed two boys before. The first was awkward and something told her this was going to be worse. She tried to appear indifferent.

Marcel shifted to the front of his seat, and she did the same. His fingers drifted along her jawline.

"My, your heart is beating fast." He drew her gently to him and slowly opened her mouth with his. It was a deep kiss, his fingers holding her face in place. After swirling his tongue against hers, they separated. She expected him to sit back, but he whispered in her ear, "Give me one night, and I'll let you keep your week's worth of vials."

She sensed a force moving him back in his chair against his will, Rho and the bartender now on their feet. Marcel's pupils dilated despite the room being relatively dark. Even a man like him feared things.

Marcel smiled. "Message received. I'm surprised she makes it, but I can see you're telling the truth."

Rho released him and reached down to take Raleigh's hand.

Brent removed an envelope from his pocket. "You have your proof. I'll be back in a week. Here are her real documents."

Marcel stood and took the envelope, checking inside. "Done. I hope that I will see you all again. You should be going now. Collin is no doubt downstairs pacing a hole in my floor."

Rho and Brent shook Marcel's hand, and Raleigh made a point of sticking hers out before he could say farewell the same way he'd greeted her.

Marcel shook it but didn't let go right away. "I can offer you more safety than they can. Rho is the kindest of the brothers I've met. I know I make you nervous, but I am the safer alternative. Take my card."

"She won't need it." Rho wrapped his arm around her shoulder, folding her into him.

"Your brothers believe that naturals are lesser. Don't fool yourself into thinking Lucid is what matters. To Sigma, Lucid is a tool to control and buy people. He will not like that he can do neither with her. She will not be seen as an equal. You may not like it, but I have the resources and the reputation to keep her safe."

Brent stepped between the two. "Thanks. It's something to consider. But you can understand why we're keeping her with us."

"Yes." Marcel gave them a long, considering look. "See you in a week."

The three left their host and returned downstairs, Rho's arm tightly knit around her waist as they passed the bouncer.

Tossing up his arms, Brent grabbed Rho before they found Collin. "Did you have to influence him? You do know that you could've been shot!"

"I had my attention on the bartender's trigger finger, too. Raleigh, don't you ever agree to something like that again."

Brent shook his head and pointed to Rho's chest. "It was one kiss, you overreacted. He'd want to get his hooks into her either way. Part of it, I'm sure, was to see how you'd react. And yes, you behaved as he thought you would."

Collin made his way through the crowd and over to them. Trevor followed steps behind, his shoulders pulled in as to not touch the other patrons.

Collin studied Rho's face. "What's wrong?"

None of them answered, and Rho draped his arm over Raleigh as they navigated the crowd. As predicted, things picked up, but the crowd separated as Rho marched through to the exit. She enjoyed the warmth of his arm around her but could feel the muscles strained underneath his skin. The touch's main purpose was protection, not flirtation.

Outside a breeze lifted the skirts of a few girls smoking near the door. Rho withdrew his arm from Raleigh and shrugged out of his jacket. Then he wrapped it over her shoulders and led his team and her a few yards from the club.

Trevor grabbed Rho's arm. "Are you mad because the deal's off?"

Rho didn't answer, instead putting more distance between them and Marcel's. Soon they arrived at a busier intersection, the car lights illuminating their path.

Brent shook his head. "The deal's on, and we have the phone number. Mu and Tau have been captured by Grant and Able."

"That's bad." Trevor's lungs tightened due to the clipped pace, and Rho slowed.

Collin held out his hands. "Calm down, Rho. We can work on getting them out. I'm sure that's what Sigma and the others are planning."

"I'm sure we will," Rho said. "If G and A wanted them dead, they would be. It may not be pleasant, but they're probably not in danger of dying anytime soon."

"Then you can calm down."

Brent whistled through his teeth. "That's not what's bugging him." He tilted his head in Raleigh's direction.

Collin squinted his eyes, and Rho held up his hand. "It's not Raleigh's fault. It's Marcel's—but I should've expected that."

The wind tugged her hair, and she reached her hand out from the tent of jacket to put it back. "Really, it wasn't that bad. Marcel isn't a bad kisser, and it was over pretty quickly."

"I am so glad to hear that," Rho said sarcastically, tossing up his hands.

"He's kind of good-looking, in a slightly scary way," Brent added. "Besides, influencing him was way out of line. You acted as if you don't know who he is."

"You influenced Marcel?" Collin moved closer to Rho.

Brent flanked Rho on the other side. "You need to tell Raleigh about Mu. You're naive if you think Marcel's the only one who will make her that kind of offer."

Rho stopped walking and held up his hand. A taxi skidded to the curb and he opened the door. "Guys, go home. Raleigh, you and I are taking a walk."

Brent shoved Collin in before he complained, and Trevor slid in next. The car drove off, and Raleigh and Rho stood together alone on the sidewalk. Rho liked to discuss difficult topics during walks. Before meeting him, walks to her had always been such quiet, peaceful things.

Rho's sour mood evaporated. He fell into an easy pace beside her. "You have to be careful about who you become romantically involved with."

"Yeah, I got that. I'm not getting romantically involved with Marcel. I just kissed him, so he'd agree to get the papers."

Rho sighed, and his gait elongated. "I'm going to tell you about what happened to Mu."

"*One* of your brothers?"

"Yes, one of the nicer ones. Some of us had girlfriends before we went to the island at fifteen, but most of us hadn't. After we got out, dating wasn't really an option. Relationships are hard to have when you might leave at any moment, and danger tends to follow us. Mu hid out in the city and eventually met a girl. They were friends at first, and then the lines blurred, and she became his girlfriend."

"Did she know he was Designed?"

"No. Everything went well the first month. But as time passed Mu started to think that maybe she wasn't the girl for him. When he tried to break things off, she got violent with him. She stalked him for months until he left. It was uncharacteristic of her, and it didn't take much for Mu to figure out it was his Lucid she missed. Each time they kissed, like you did back there with Marcel, she got a small hit. Addiction appears to be related to receptor volume and exposure, and she was being exposed."

"I have a lot. Does that mean I'm addicted?" Raleigh stopped, her feet tired. The empty buildings on the side of the street had their metal gates down for the night. Only the occasional person could be heard in the distance.

"You're like me. You can't live without it, but you don't have to take it. So, no, I don't put us in that category."

"Could I get addicted to yours since it's different?"

Rho shook his head. "It's not that different. It's smoother. I guess you can try it if you want."

Raleigh gazed at his lips. "Maybe another day."

"Geez, Raleigh. Lighten up. I meant a vial." But he didn't move away from her.

She turned away. "So... no dating. How lonely."

"You can date. It just has to be a guy who doesn't have receptors, which limits you to half the population. I would hate to think of you being in the position Mu was in. It was scary enough, and she was a sweet girl to start."

"Should we be worried about Collin?"

"He's not going to force himself on you like Mu's girlfriend tried with him." He paused.

"What?"

"It was one of the reasons we left the island. Some of the Receps in the private army were disobedient when they were taken off Lucid. It was a bad situation for the guys with a lot of receptors who were used to a daily dose. Gamma was assaulted."

"That's horrible." The wind blew harder, bringing with it a chill. She pictured someone as strong and heartless as Collin forcing himself on her and shuttered.

"They were stopped pretty early. But yeah, it was obvious by then what Lucid was doing to the Receps. People act out of character when they need something like that."

"But you're not worried about Collin?"

"He went a year without it."

"He certainly wants you, but Brent says it isn't sexual."

"It isn't. I could cut Collin loose, but I'm worried about him. This has become his life. I'm not sure what he would do back in the Midwest. College? After this life? Some of the Receps resorted to taking the synthetic. I don't want that to be him."

"He needs help."

"He's a mess right now. Even though it wasn't his fault that I was taken, he believes it is. Then, when they found me, he couldn't save me. Then you do the impossible. Now he feels his role in the group is under threat."

"You think I could be your bodyguard?" Raleigh punched his shoulder playfully.

"It would have to be a mutual watch each other's back thing. But yes. Given the ease with which you picked up influencing, I'd say that one day you're going to be incredibly strong. Stronger than Collin could ever hope to be." Rho backed up to the main street and hailed a cab. "I know he's being a jerk, but can you cut him some slack?"

Raleigh nodded her head. She wanted to be strong. She wanted to have an idea about where she belonged. But most of all, she didn't want to feel like she was just along for the ride. She wanted to be the driver.

CHAPTER
14

A WEEK PASSED in a haze of influencing and barricading lessons. Brent went alone to see Marcel the second time and returned with Raleigh's real and fake passports. As promised, the counterfeits were indistinguishable from the real. Raleigh spoke to her parents twice, and they hadn't noticed the bags under their daughter's eyes or listened well enough to hear the household of males she now stayed with. Thalia was due to start her junior year, and that distracted them well enough. Life in Colorado moved on without Raleigh, and no one questioned if she was still in Belgium. Unfortunately, the good times in Paris had an expiration date.

With the freshly-minted passport just hours in her hand, Raleigh and Rho headed for the airport, States bound. Their destination a secret to the group, Raleigh's only clue was that their final stop was San Francisco. When the Designed met, they didn't bring their entourages. Collin had pressed Rho, but the others seemed happier not to know.

The plane's flaps caught the foggy air, and it bounced the passengers on landing. Raleigh's stomach, already knotted, dropped. "My brother lives in California," she told Rho as they disembarked. "San Diego. We flew out two years ago. It's one of the few places that I've visited."

"San Francisco is different." Cloudy skies proved his point, and the weather reminded her of autumn rather than summer. Rho hailed a cab. "We probably won't be here long."

"Why is that?" She stepped back as the cab parked on the curb.

"It puts a large target on us. Easier for people who are looking for us to find us if we're all in the same place. Slip-ups happen, and we're more likely to have them if we're all holed up together."

With both hands, Rho heaved the bag into the trunk and handed the cabbie a small piece of paper with the address. The bag was impractical for these short trips. She vowed to travel light from now on, but there was little she could do now.

The inside of the cab smelled of body odor. She cracked the window, noticing that Rho did the same, his eyes lingering on the airport as they drove off. He'd been pleasant, but more contemplative, since the meeting with Marcel.

"Do you regret bringing me?" Marcel's warning about the Designed not accepting her curled her toes.

"Why would you think that?"

"You're sad."

Rho flicked his eyes to the rearview mirror, the driver's techno music loud enough to muffle his words. "I can't stop thinking about Mu. He's a great guy, creative, hilarious. He's from Austin. His parents are a couple of hippies. Every year he dyes his hair a new wild color."

"That can't be good for blending in."

"Neither is playing in a band, but that hasn't stopped him. The guy is crazy-talented on guitar, and now he's in trouble."

"They'll get him back, right?"

"There are only so many near misses before one of us gets hit." He rested his hand absentmindedly on his port as they drove.

"Did you tell them you were bringing me?" Raleigh asked.

"I didn't speak to any of them. I talked to one of the guys on Sigma's team. All he gave me was an address."

"What if they don't want me along?"

"If they don't want us, we'll leave."

"Where will we go?"

"We'll figure that out if we have to."

None of these answers satisfied her. She pulled on a loose fiber of her jacket. If she needed, she could go home. California was closer to Colorado than Belgium, a two-day drive or a few hours on a plane.

The breeze fluttering through the top of the window smelled sweeter as they entered wine country, the rolling hills and open spaces a welcomed reprieve from the past weeks of city living. The sun splayed out from puffy white clouds bathing her face in warmth. Uncongested, houses here sat far apart and isolated. The driver rolled up to a winery, parked, and retrieved Raleigh's bag while Rho paid.

Raleigh slid out of the car, her eyes on the vineyards and the tourists that were buzzed on alcohol. Their minds were fuzzy, but she doubted so unobservant that they wouldn't notice four sets of triplets. Surely they weren't stopping here.

Rho extended the telescoping handle of her bag with a click and pointed at a path. "We have a walk. I didn't want the driver to know our location."

They trekked through the green hills, their shoes and the wheels of her bag were caked with mud by the time they reached a lone house. She wiped the back of her neck with her hand and turned towards Rho. Unlike her, he didn't have bags under his eyes from the turbulent flight or splotches from the sunshine-filled hike. He stood facing the house, perfect as always. Their differences shone through in the little things, and she wondered if Lucid would be enough of a common bond for his brothers to accept her.

"This place is huge. Quite the place to hide out," she said. If it had been Raleigh's choice, she would've chosen a small space in a busy area—one that had people coming and going, not one where everyone knew each other well enough to recognize a stranger.

"Sigma owns it but rents it out for most of the year. We can't go just anywhere. With the number of us that look alike, we stand out."

"So, two of them look like you?"

"Two did. Just one now. Sigma. My other triplet, Pi, was drained to death a year ago."

Raleigh's heart twisted. She'd seen Rho when death was upon him, and she could imagine what Pi had endured.

As they climbed the front steps, she scrambled to tame the hairs that had escaped her ponytail. Straightening her shirt, she sniffed to make sure she didn't smell too ripe from the trip. Rho pressed the doorbell, and a small chime announced them.

The door cracked open. Raleigh had expected Sigma, but the guy who stood on the other side had blond hair and eyes as green as the surrounding hills. "Rho!" He rushed out and wrapped Rho up in a tight embrace, his smile hidden in his brother's shirt.

"Good to see you, Kappa."

Kappa moved back, his hands on his brother's arms, his eyes inspecting him. "We thought you were dead! You've been out of contact so long. When I called weeks ago, Collin said you'd been taken."

"The synthetic dealers caught me."

Kappa's smile faded, and he caught sight of Raleigh. First his eyebrows rose and then dipped. "You know the rule. No team."

"She's not on my team."

"You have a girlfriend? How did you find the time for that, being locked up? Aren't you the one who's always preaching to me that it isn't something we have time for?"

"I'm not his girlfriend."

Rho sheltered his eyes with his hand. "It's a long story. We should go inside. I may as well explain it to everyone at the same time."

A voice startled her from the doorway. "Yes, please do come in. Please explain why you've compromised our hideout by bringing an outsider. I'm happy to see you, brother, but we have rules." A man, who could only be Sigma, stepped slowly backward, his eyes feral as they entered.

Rho was wrong, he didn't look like Sigma. The two had the same body and hair, but Sigma held his head back with contempt, the slight sneer on his lips far uglier than Rho's enchanting smiles.

"This is Sigma." Rho made the unnecessary introduction to Raleigh before turning his attention to him. "Can we talk about why I've brought Raleigh here?

Sigma sauntered over and ran a finger down his chin considering her. "Kinda plain, isn't she? I know you can do better, and she's a bit young."

"I'm eighteen." She didn't back down and kept her eyes level at him. From her mountain training, she knew that sometimes you played dead when confronted by an animal, other times you showed them how big you were. This time warranted the latter.

"You look younger." Sigma shrugged. "Naive and young. Not surprising that Rho goes for that. He has a thing about playing the hero. Although, you should know that by being with you he's putting you in danger."

"I'm not his girlfriend or his type." She needed them to know she was there on her own merit, not because of some guy.

Sigma snapped his fingers. "Kappa, gather the others. There better be an extraordinary reason for her being here."

Rho dashed over and took Kappa's arm before he could leave. "Can you also grab an extraction machine?"

"You want to extract now?" asked Kappa.

"You'll see."

Five minutes later Raleigh found herself at a long table. Everyone but her barricaded, she'd yet to master it for long periods. The division was clear—the only people on her side of the table were Kappa and Rho. Across the way, staring them down, was the opposition. Sigma sat in the middle of the five chairs, to his left Kappa's shorter-haired triplet, Psi. The Gamma, Upsilon, and Xi triplets occupied the remaining seats. They all had dark-brown skin and eyes so brown they verged on black. Like the others, they were beautiful. But she couldn't tell them apart.

Rho slid his fingers onto the wooden table and turned his palms upward. "As you know, I was captured by one of the synthetic dealers. They held me for three months before I managed to escape."

Sigma sighed and leaned back, arms crossed. "We know this. Kappa tried to contact you when Mu and Tau were taken. You do know that Mu and Tau are captured? Marcel must've told you when he gave you this number."

Rho nodded his head. "That's all I know. I need to be filled in."

"First, explain her." Sigma nodded his head at Raleigh, his eyes sharp and unflinching.

"Collin, Brent, and Trevor found me barely alive in Normandy. It was after I was washed ashore and had dragged myself into hiding. I was dying and don't remember what happened, only what Collin told me."

Sigma focused his scowl on Rho. "Yet another discussion. Tell us about the girl."

"They took me to Dr. Sabine Orman's house. Brent went to Marcel to try to get in touch with all of you, but Marcel wouldn't give him the phone number."

Kappa rose his hand to attract their attention. "I think that we should have some kind of system in place to address that problem. Our teams are people we trust. Surely, we can share our information with them."

Sigma shook his head once. "Collin, like most of the people I hire, is an addict. He's loyal as long as he has Lucid. It's a great way to control people, but it doesn't make them honest. We seem to be straying from the point."

Rho continued. "Raleigh was at Sabine's. She was receiving treatment for her overproduction of Lucid. A continuous infusion of Lucid from her saved my life."

Sigma's ugly sneer dipped deeper into a scowl. "What? Is she some afterthought Grant and Able had?"

"Nope. She's a natural." Rho took the extraction machine from Kappa, attached Raleigh, and turned it on. The light hum of the machine reverberated in the now silent room.

"A natural," whispered Gamma.

Psi lips thinned, and he pounded his fist on the table. "It explains how they did it."

"How they did what?" Rho asked.

Sigma leveled his gaze at Rho. "Grant and Able have had Lucid for a while, enough that they could take down both Mu and Tau. They've been training a whole new batch of Receps to come after us. If they had a new synthetic, there'd be no reason to capture Mu and Tau. They would've killed them. So, they must've had some Lucid to start. The question has been, where did they get it? It wouldn't be one of us. So, it had to be a natural."

The pride in Rho's face was replaced by concern. "It wasn't

Raleigh." He paused, as if chewing on the possibility. His face resolved. "It wasn't her."

Sigma clucked his tongue. "We thought maybe they'd concocted the inducer, the original drink that tribe used so long ago. But if they did, why would they need us? They must've obtained a small amount from somewhere. Now we know."

"When I found her in Belgium, she was completely unaware of what Lucid does."

"Please. Sabine used to work with G and A," Sigma said. "It was only a matter of time before you or Kappa reconnected, however briefly, with her. Both of you have done it over the years. No reason to suspect you wouldn't again at some point."

Everything he said rang true. Sabine had anticipated that very thing. Kappa and Rho were the contacts she was going to get the portable machine from.

The mood of the room changed, and with the extraction still in progress she couldn't barricade. "I've never met Grant and Able. They're after me, too."

Rho said, "They are. Her uncle said they were poking around. That's why we took her from Sabine. She's one of us, and she needs our help."

Sitting back in his seat, Sigma slowly shook his head. "Brother, you're a fool. Grant and Able have been using her Lucid to help train their soldiers. Then they see their opportunity and place her with your old mentor—knowing that one day you or Kappa would stumble on her. She pretends to be in trouble and you, hero that you are, not only whisk her away from Sabine's, but bring her here."

"It isn't true!" Raleigh stood, jostling the extraction machine and wrapping up the tubes. There was no evidence though, no proof that Sigma was wrong. All she had was her word.

Xi turned to Sigma. "What do we do?"

Sigma narrowed his eyes. "I think that we all know what happens to people who cross us."

The thud of Kappa's fist against the table broke the tension. "We aren't doing anything! This is a far-fetched theory. It could've been another natural they got the Lucid from."

"I doubt it," Sigma said. "If she makes as much Lucid as us, she's an anomaly. The whole reason they created us was because people like her don't exist. To have two suddenly appear is too much of a coincidence."

Rho put his hand on Raleigh's arm lightly tugging her to her sit. "We came here to ask for your help, because she's one of us."

Leaning on the table, Sigma clasped his hands pointing his to index fingers in Raleigh's direction. "She makes Lucid, but is she as smart as we are? No. Otherwise she wouldn't have entered here so naively. What defines us isn't that we make Lucid. That's what Grant and Able intended, but we're more than that."

Kappa gave Rho a worried look. "Then I guess Raleigh will have to go."

"She's seen where I live. Is she done extracting? Let me have the vial." Sigma's outstretched hand wrapped around the vial in the machine. Easily he administered it to his port. His nose crinkled. "It's different."

"It's Lucid," Rho said. "She will certainly be hunted, as we are. Grant and Able have already expressed interest. Without your help, we may be the next two they get."

Raleigh could tell that Kappa was on their side, but the others were suspicious. This was how it was always going to be. Collin and these guys had forged bonds through impossibly hard times. Now she asked for their help and offered nothing. Rho couldn't split from his brothers. That network was important, even if Sigma was an asshole. If they left, they'd surely be caught. Grant and

Able were going to get her. It felt inevitable. A crazy idea popped into her head.

"What if I get Tau and Mu out?" Raleigh asked.

"What?" Sigma and Rho said at the same time, their voices sounding almost identical except that one was curious and the other shocked.

"Grant and Able already are interested in me. I could have Sabine set up an introduction. They'll trust me for all the reasons you don't. They want a natural who makes Lucid and doesn't know about their shady past, right? That's what I'll be. Then I'll figure out where Mu and Tau are and rescue them."

"No way." Rho scooted his chair away from the table. "That's never going to work. We're leaving."

Sigma grinned at Raleigh, not looking anything like his brother. "Sit, Rho. Let's think this out. They won't treat her like they treated us. To them, we aren't human. But look at her. I've never seen anyone less threatening." He caught Raleigh's glare. "Oh, I'm sure you'll master influencing, and I bet he taught you how to barricade, too. But that isn't how you look, and all of us can tell you that appearance plays a large role in how you're treated."

"None of us know how they'll treat her. For all we know she'll end up in the same pen as Mu and Tau." Rho tried to get Raleigh's attention, but she kept her eyes on Sigma.

"They won't jump to that. They'll want to seem civilized and have her appear free, as they did with us originally," Sigma said. "If she's able to successfully bring back Mu and Tau, then it will prove she isn't with them."

"She isn't with them! Her telling us is all the proof we need." Rho put his hand on Raleigh's shoulder. "It's all I need."

Psi leaned forward his expression excited. "This is good. We thought of using one of our guys as a mole. But Sigma's right.

They're loyal to the Lucid, not us. We risk losing any Recep if Grant and Able offers them enough Lucid. We don't have that problem with her."

"Collin is loyal to me, and he's a Recep," Rho said.

Sigma shook his head. "But we can't send him in. They know him, and I don't trust any of my team."

Rho snorted. "I can't imagine that any of them would want to betray you. There must be team members we can trust. I refuse to believe that none of you have someone like Collin."

"Only Sigma and I keep addicts on our crews," Psi said. "And they're unruly. Collin's a wreck. They all are. It has to be Raleigh."

Rho looked to Kappa. "Come on. This is a horrible idea."

Nodding Kappa said, "It is. Rho's right. This is far too dangerous for Raleigh. She just met us. We can't expect her to go."

"This is how she becomes one of us." Sigma stood up and put his hand on the back of his chair pushing it in. "Raleigh, you can stay the night. Thank you for offering to rescue our brothers. Rho, thank you for bringing such a tidy solution to our problem. Get some sleep. You're jet lagged, and Raleigh has quite the task ahead of her."

Rho stalked out the room, pounding the side of the doorframe as he went. Sigma's eyes were on Raleigh, a sinister smile hitching up the corner of his lips. Rho was mad, and Sigma was pleased, but she knew this was the best option. She lifted her chin and marched out of the room to find Rho. He was in the adjoining room, his fingers gripping the side of the sofa like he was about to rip it apart. She closed the door, letting her hand rest on the knob as she processed her arguments.

Quietly Rho said, "Why did you do that? If you cross Grant and Able, they won't make the mistake they did with us. They'll kill you."

"Don't you want Mu and Tau back?" Raleigh moved closer to him, thinking of his face when he discussed Mu. He had to know this was the best shot at saving him.

Rho's fist tightened then relaxed. "Not at the cost of losing you." He turned to her. "You'll tell my brothers you've had a change of heart. None of them will blame you."

"Then they won't trust me, and you'll lose them."

"Not Kappa. We'll run and bring him with us."

"But Grant and Able will catch us someday. They're already looking into me. If it's not them, it'll be the synthetic dealers."

"We can hide. I was caught once, but if Kappa comes, too, that'll help."

"It also puts a target on our backs."

He angled towards her, letting his fingers trace down the inside of her arm near her port. "Then it'll be the two of us. We don't need my brothers. I can keep you safe."

The nerves on her arm stood at attention, trying to predict where his fingers would touch next. Rho was charming. There'd been jokes about her following him because he was. What would waking up to Rho every day be like? The thought of his intense eyes took her breath away.

"You're beautiful." She figured she might as well say it, the sentiment was probably written across her face.

"So are you, and yours isn't artificial." Slowly, he slid his fingers up her neck until they were tangled in her hair. "You saved me, Raleigh. Let me repay the favor."

Raleigh focused on his lips. If she kissed him, she'd get to experience his Lucid. He said she had to date people with no receptors. That wasn't true. The alternative was dating someone who made enough Lucid that they didn't care about hers.

"Will you stay with me?" he asked softly.

Would he date her if she stayed? Did she care? Would it be enough to convince her? Rho described his Lucid as smooth, much like him. She was more like her Lucid—a bit wild. Would a reasonable girl have gone to Belgium? Maybe. Would she have followed Rho? Probably not.

A heavy knock on the door interrupted them. Not waiting for an answer, Kappa stuck his head in. "Rho, if we don't want Raleigh to go to Grant and Able, we should leave now."

"We aren't leaving now." Raleigh took a step back away from Rho. "I'm going to go to Grant and Able to get Mu and Tau."

The image of Rho near death made her sympathize with Tau and Mu. The fear that she'd taken on too much dogged her, but no one deserved that fate. Someone had to go in, and she was in the unique position of being that person. When she returned, the others would have to accept her. She knew that Grant and Able would chase her and Rho. All she wanted was to go to college and become a doctor. Neither of those things could happen if she was in hiding. Grant and Able had to be faced.

CHAPTER
15

RALEIGH DIDN'T SPEAK with Rho again, but she caught a glimpse of him as she left for the airport. She hadn't told her parents that she was coming home. There was a chance that her mother would want to talk to Sabine, and Raleigh didn't want to explain that she was in California. She simply booked a flight and landed in Denver.

In the departures line of the airport, she hailed a cab. She inhaled two large breaths of the thin dry air, both the altitude and the climate welcoming her home. Getting into the car, her legs twitched, she was so close. They drove by buildings that she'd seen at a distance most her life, and then by familiar complexes, and then into her development. She kept scooting to the edge of her seat, but the seatbelt tugged her back.

The hot sun of late afternoon pooled into the car as she stepped out. A distant lawn mower could be heard, infusing the air with the smell of fresh cut grass. Her two-story blue house brought on a pang of nostalgia. The basketball hoop over the garage begged a game, reminding her of the scrimmages against Ben and Lana. Everything had changed, yet this remained preserved. At the front door her fingers instinctually went to the bell before she thought better of it and opened the door. This place would be home no matter how far she'd come.

"Hello?" Her father's voice sounded warmer without the computer speakers to distort it. His footfalls echoed through the foyer as he left his office. His face turned from worry to jubilation, his heart picking up to match her joy. "Raleigh! You're back."

Raleigh tucked herself into the folds of his arms. The surge of emotion made her want to spill everything and to talk to him like she used to when no secrets existed between them. For years he'd helped her pick apart her problems, but this one was too heavy for her to hand off to him.

"You're back?" Her mother would not wait her turn an embraced both Raleigh and Theo. Lilacs from the flower shop incensed her hair. In that embrace the anger and conflict from the last few months was nowhere to be found.

How easy it would have been to pretend that nothing had changed and that she was safe just because she was home. That wasn't the case and she stepped back. "I need to get the number for Grant and Able from Uncle Patrick."

THE DECEPTION WAS surprisingly easy. Dr. Moore contacted Grant and Able, and Rho pleaded with Sabine to corroborate her story. He must have been convincing, because whatever Sabine said to Grant and Able made them very interested in Raleigh.

Grant and Able requested Raleigh's blood work and scans and Dr. Moore sent them. They were ecstatic, to say the least. They did a background check on Raleigh and nothing suspicious turned up. With her perfect record, Raleigh was an ideal candidate. Soon enough, she found herself sitting in her living room waiting on an interview with the head of the company, Agatha Grant.

"Do you think she'll want lemonade or tea?" Beth rearranged the serving tray in the living room for the sixth time that morning. The tables were polished, and the cabinets had been dusted. As far as she was concerned, this was a job interview, and she was desperate for her ill daughter to get the position. The blackouts had already resumed, and she didn't want her daughter to return to Liege.

Raleigh reached out to grab a cracker and cheese but caught her mother's glance and refrained. They were for presentation not eating. A bunch of work for nothing, Raleigh was a shoo-in. Grant and Able needed her far more than she needed them. Never the less, she let her mother fret and fuss, it added authenticity.

Beth pressed her hand to her curled hair. "Thalia's at the pool, and I've told her that if she comes back while Agatha is here, she should say as little as possible. Remember to sit up straight and don't fidget."

"Raleigh will be fine." Theo put a hand on his wife's shoulder. They'd both taken the day off work.

The doorbell sounded, and Beth jumped into hostess mode. Gliding to the door, she opened it. "Hello. I'm Beth Groves. Such a pleasure to meet you."

Raleigh perceived two people at the door. Agatha's strong heart and toned body made her physically seem younger than forty, which Raleigh guessed had to be her age from the way she held herself and the way her white hairs mingled with the blonde. The young man accompanying her was in his early twenties. His muscles ached from a recent workout, and there was a yearning in him similar to Collin's. This could easily be one of the men in the Recep army Rho warned her about.

Theo sat next to his daughter and unwound her clasped hands. "You're going to do fine. They don't send the CEO out to interview people they aren't really interested in."

Raleigh managed a half-smile and smoothed her dress as the two guests entered.

"Please, have a seat." Beth motioned to the coffee table and food before seating herself next to Raleigh on the couch.

Agatha reached her hand across the coffee table and offered Raleigh a firm handshake. Her short blonde hair and navy dress gave her an air of sophistication. However, her smile was the kind that belonged on a hiking trail or sitting around a board game. It was genuine.

"I'm Agatha Grant, head of Grant and Able."

"My name is Raleigh."

"Yes, we've heard a bit about you. Sabine and I spoke."

Raleigh bobbed her head. "Sabine felt you'd be a better fit. Not that Belgium wasn't great."

"And the treatment works," interjected Beth.

Agatha sat back in her seat. "I'm happy to hear that. Sabine said as much. We should be able to continue the same extraction schedule at our facility in Arizona. This is Gabe," she said, introducing the young man. "He's been with our company for several years."

If he'd been there for years, he would have met Collin and the Designed. Had he been there for the escape? Surely Agatha would have been with the company at that time.

Agatha rested her thin attache case on her lap, unzipped it, and removed a brochure. "Grant and Able is committed to improving health and outcomes in a variety of patients. Lucidin helps us do this."

"But that's what's making our daughter sick." Beth took the pamphlet and unfolded it.

Agatha delicately put her hands in her lap. "That's usually not the case. Most people can use it to help with diagnosing and treating illnesses. Patrick and Sabine told us that Raleigh had already been using her talents to do just that, well before the Lucidin was discovered."

Beth flicked away the idea. "It's something that she pretends. The therapist theorized that it's probably her mechanism for coping with her illness, thinking everyone else is sick."

Agatha leaned forward and knitted her eyebrows. "Mrs. Groves, what your daughter can do is not fabricated. We have quite a few people who can do it."

Raleigh flinched, knowing the direction this conversation was headed. Agatha would provide evidence and her mother would reject it. It was amazing how unwilling her mother was to consider the possibility.

"What happens with the Lucidin is of secondary importance," Theo said. "The key is that Raleigh gets treatment."

"And she will." Agatha tapped the brochure over a picture of the buildings with cacti in the foreground. "Our complex in Phoenix is a research facility. We have a state-of-the-art extraction room. Many of our scientists live in the city, but we have some on-site housing. It was a retreat before we acquired it, and we've kept some of the rooms. That's where Raleigh will stay."

"I want to go to college," said Raleigh. Phoenix must have at least one college. She might as well get something out of the deal, she didn't just have to rescue Mu and Tau.

"Wonderful. We're close enough to the city that you could take classes at Arizona State," Agatha said. "I don't see any reason why you shouldn't get in. You'll just have to apply."

"How much is this going to cost?" Theo studied the clean white campus that looked not only modern but pricey.

Agatha paused. "It's free."

"Really?" Raleigh pretended to act surprised, but she knew that her Lucid would go for a lot on the black market. If anything, they should be paying her.

Agatha's reassuring smile returned. "Yes. You can work in the labs and with Gabe. He specializes in training people to use Lucidin."

"I think you'll do well." Gabe's voice was low and stern.

"The labs would be good for your résumé if you go on to become a doctor," Theo told Raleigh.

Beth handed back the brochure. "When can you take her?"

"She could accompany us back tomorrow. Am I correct in thinking that it's been a few days since you last extracted?"

"Yeah." Raleigh thought of the blackout she had yesterday at breakfast, uneasy about how quickly they'd returned.

"She's already having blackouts." Beth's eye went to the bruise her daughter had sustained during the most recent fall. "The sooner she goes the better."

"What do you think, Raleigh? Does it sound good?" Theo asked.

Raleigh plastered a big smile on her face. "It sounds wonderful."

A DAY LATER Raleigh sat on a sleek private jet, her hands twisting in her hair as the bags were stowed. Over the past few weeks, she'd overcome many of her fears of commercial flying, but that confidence didn't extend to the tiny jet. The news often featured stories on how small planes went down, and she could imagine the local newscasters describing her fate in the same sorrowful tone as the others.

She sat facing a pair of chairs, a glossy table between them. The buttery soft seat she perched on now was far more comfortable than the rough fabrics of the larger planes.

"Don't fly often?" Gabe sank into one of the identical seats across from her. He was more social now that they weren't with her parents.

"Just to Belgium and back, and a few years ago I went to California to visit my brother. But I've never been on a small jet like this."

"You'll get used to it."

"So, you're going to teach me how to use Lucidin?" She mindfully called it by its proper name. "I've been detecting illnesses for a long time. Sabine said I did it better than anyone she knew."

The engines revved, and the force of take-off pressed her into her seat. Gabe lounged in his, although his fingers tapped absently on the armrest. He displayed the same tics as Collin—the craving for Lucid affected them similarly. Agatha sat across the aisle, smiling politely whenever their glances crossed.

In the air, the plane rocked a few times, the water inside the plastic bottles on the edge of the table slid up the sides. She tried not to think about the distance accumulating between her and the ground.

Gabe pressed his lips together. "You've sensed, but have you ever influenced?"

This was going to be the tricky part of being a spy. Her backstory was mostly true, minus the time in France. Anything she learned from Rho, she'd have to feign ignorance to. "Influencing?" She opened her eyes in the same ditzy way Thalia did when tricking their parents.

Gabe clearly had no mischievous younger sisters, as he seemed eager to explain. "Yes. Lucidin not only allows you to feel what other people feel, you can also control how their bodies work. It's called influencing."

"I've been diagnosing for a while, but I've never done that."

Gabe leaned on his knees. "You have to will it to be. If you don't have resolve behind it, then it won't work. Likely you never had the right mindset. We'll teach you. Very few people can do it. But I'm certain, after looking at the information Sabine forwarded, you will."

"Is it just going to be you and me?" Raleigh hoped that Sigma was wrong, that the private army had been disbanded.

"No." Gabe sat back, his eyes slipping to the side, resting for a second on Agatha. "Anyone in the ninety-sixth percentile for Lucidin receptors should be able to influence. Anyone over the seventy-sixth should be able to sense. We search the country for people in the former category."

"Four percent of the population?"

"Not everyone with that level of receptors will be able to influence well. Some people will require more Lucidin to do so." From the way he spoke, it was clear that he was adept at it. He just fell short of puffing up his chest like a proud bird.

"And you train them to be doctors?"

"The women, yes. They aren't in Arizona. They have clinics in New York and Chicago. The women you'll meet in Arizona are our scientists."

Her heart sank. "What about the men?"

"We'll be training with them in Arizona."

"Shouldn't I be going to Chicago or New York?"

Agatha interrupted. "No. It wouldn't be as safe."

"Safe?" Raleigh pretended to not know about the synthetic trade—an easy feat. She honestly couldn't think of what could be more dangerous than an army of Collins and Gabes. "I know big cities can be intimidating...."

Gabe shook his head. "You'll learn all about the relevant safety issues tonight."

"Is this something I should be worried about? Sabine never mentioned anything. She said that I might not want to announce what I can do, but I was under the impression that was more to keep people from thinking I was crazy."

Gabe crossed his arms. "The situation is complex. But you needn't worry. I'm here to keep you safe."

Raleigh wasn't sure if he expected a thank you for that. "All right. I won't worry."

After that brief exchange on influencing, the conversation turned to mundane things like the weather and Raleigh's family. Agatha closed her laptop and joined in. Besides Gabe's militant posture, there was nothing off-putting about them. She tried to view the conversation as if she'd never met Rho. The scary thing was that without her preconceived notions she found herself liking Agatha. Grant and Able, on a whole, seemed friendly and organized, two things the Designed lacked. Soon enough they were on the ground and headed towards the facility.

In the limo, air-conditioning blasted across Raleigh's arm, making the hairs stand on edge. Outside heat made its presence known in the scorched earth. Buildings here were a different style, and she couldn't be sure if it was to accommodate the climate or cultural influence. Once they left the city the desert stretched out, an open scar on the landscape. After a while, the white stucco buildings from the brochure came into view like a mirage.

"This is home." Gabe held open the car door for her and Agatha.

Raleigh stepped out of the car, shielding her eyes with her hand as the hot sun overhead beat down on her. "You live here, too?"

"Yes, in the dorms." He motioned to a building to the left of the main one. "I live with the people I'm training."

"But I won't live there?"

Agatha signaled to the driver to bring in their bags and then led the procession into the building. "No. We have something special for you. This used to be a retreat." The automatic doors parted for her and cold air rushed out as they went in. "It was for artists."

With the technological advances taking place, Raleigh assumed the decor would be modern and sterile. Instead, a bison head hung over the entrance, rugs covered the walls, and potted cacti peeked out behind doorframes.

Agatha's heels clacked on the tiles as she gave the tour. Gabe stayed back a few paces, but still within earshot. "This is the central building. The others you saw are the dorm, gym, and laboratory. This main building is where you'll eat and spend your free time."

As if on cue, the cafeteria came into view. With its round tables and a buffet skirting one wall, it wasn't as homey as the entrance. What it left wanting for charm, it made up for in functionality, it was large enough to accommodate a crowd. Mexican spices filled the air, trays clattered, and open tables were few.

The two types of diners separated themselves accordingly. The first wore shirts with collars, slacks, and were generally older. They reminded Raleigh of the doctors in the hospital cafeteria, and she assumed they were the researchers. The second set was younger, male, and dressed in black. They sported the same haircut as Gabe. She didn't need to be told that they were the Receps. They joshed around and spoke in the same boisterous way boys at her school had. It would be easy to mistake them for jocks, but that would be underestimating them. Influencing made them powerful, and the Lucid addiction made them unpredictable.

While Raleigh sized up the Receps, Agatha prattled on about the nutritional content of the food. Apparently, Grant and Able wasn't only vested in the health of their patients but also their employees. "We have vegetarian and vegan options." Agatha didn't miss a beat. It was a well-rehearsed spiel.

A twosome in the corner caught Raleigh's attention. They couldn't have been any older than her, and they lacked the professionalism of the researchers and the uniformity of the Receps. Ironically, their normalness made them stand out. "Who are those two boys?"

"Dale and Quinn. They undergo extractions, like you." Agatha kept walking, her steps leading away from the cafeteria to the next segment of the tour.

Raleigh stopped dead in her tracks. Her eyes scanned their faces, Dale's plump and Quinn's spotted with acne along the chin. Not Designed, they must be naturals—a phenomena that she was supposed to have the monopoly on. "Like me? Sabine thought that I was one of a kind. I guess she was wrong. How many people are like me?"

"You are unique. Sabine was correct. There's a special reason Dale and Quinn are able to produce enough Lucidin to need extraction. We'll discuss it tonight. You'll have plenty of time to meet them. They live next door to you. Let's go there now."

Raleigh remained staring at them. This is why Grant and Able had enough Lucid to hunt down Mu and Tau. Sigma had been right, they'd gotten it from somewhere. Agatha checked her watch and Raleigh turned, a mystery for another time.

Going unnoticed by the diners they headed out of the cafeteria and down a hall to the back doors. Outside tiny cottages dotted the pebble path. Flowers that weren't deterred by the aridness released soothing fragrances.

"You have a pool." Raleigh walked up to the edge of the kidney shaped pool, her reflection bouncing back to her.

Agatha stood alongside her. "The water helps thwart the heat. Do you swim?"

"No. It was always a bad idea with the blackouts. If I faint on dry land, I just have to worry about how I fall. In the water, I might drown. I haven't done it in years."

"You're past the blackouts. We're going to help you the way Sabine did. I'll make sure that we find you a suit."

Raleigh stepped back from the poolside. Even without the blackouts, she had a distrust of water, one that wouldn't be overcome in the presence of a suit. Agatha followed her lead, leaving the pool and continuing on.

"There are eight of these small homes." Agatha handed her a key card with a large number 4 on it. "You're in this one."

Raleigh held the thin white card to the rectangle lock. After a faint chime, it opened. The inside contained a main room, kitchenette, bathroom, and bedroom. Pretty standard, but even so it had personality. A cacti painting hung over the bed, its paint rising off the canvas in tiny peaks and a quilt covered the bed. Raleigh brushed her hand along the soft fabric, the uneven stitching and colors too imperfect to be commercial. The bedroom window overlooked the Arizona desert where barren hills layered the distance. No wonder artists were inspired here.

Agatha remained outside. "Gabe and I will let you get settled. I'd like you to join us for a formal sit-down dinner at the restaurant on the second floor at six. Unless that's too early? Mister Able is a little older and would have us all eating at five if he could."

"It sounds fine." The small apartment instilled an illusion of freedom. In reality, she'd traded in her mother's rules for Agatha and Gabe's schedule.

With the door shut, Raleigh found herself alone. Wandering over to the window, she chewed on the corner of her fingernail. The campus had a few buildings, none of them an obvious place to capture Mu and Tau. It would be a difficult arrangement. Like Rho's captors, they'd have to devise a way to keep the boys sedated enough not to influence. Tomorrow she'd start searching. She couldn't risk it now, not if she wanted them to think she was there solely for treatment.

For the second time, Raleigh closed her eyes and tried to envision what this would be like if she hadn't visited Belgium, met Rho, or learned all of G and A's secrets. No doubt she would've been excited. This was a big change from home, and they were committed to helping patients. A passion she shared, and one that she couldn't pursue if she was on the run with Rho.

If she didn't know what they'd done to the Designed, she would've bought into all of this. Had they seemed benign to Rho and his brothers when they first arrived on the island? Rho didn't discuss it much. To Raleigh, Agatha appeared welcoming and Gabe protective. She hoped that they intended to leave her in the small cottage and not a cell.

CHAPTER
16

THE CLOCK OVER the second story dining hall door read 6 pm sharp when Raleigh arrived. Pausing, she poked her head in, not sure it was open. The twenty large wooden tables sat vacant, the sturdy chairs empty, and the thick cloth napkins untouched. A low rumble of an air conditioner drifted through the open space. Stepping inside she found an older man standing by the far window, his eyes directed to Phoenix in the distance, but it seemed his mind was elsewhere.

"Excuse me?" Raleigh wasn't sure if she was in the right place.

The man turned, his suit uncomfortably bunching up on his large stomach. "You must be Raleigh." His contemplative scowl transformed into a wide smile. "I'm Oliver Able."

"Nice to meet you." She reached out to take his extended hand.

The thin dry skin over his meaty hand pulled taunt as he shook hers. A pain shocked his knee as he leaned toward her—distracting her from the heart disease and diabetes that plagued him. Unlike his business partner, Agatha, he wasn't healthy.

He slapped his knee with a metal cane. "You can feel my arthritis, can't you? I know it's a sin to be so unhealthy around people who can sense it. But I'm old and haven't aged well."

Raleigh didn't know how to respond. "I'm sorry it hurts."

"Have a seat." He lumbered into one of the chairs at the far table and motioned for her to take the one across from him.

Glancing towards the door she wondered if it would just be the two of them. "Thanks for inviting me."

"The pleasure is mine. I've spent a long time studying Lucidin, and I've never met a person like you. The lab results Sabine provided us are nothing short of extraordinary."

"Thanks."

"How is Sabine doing these days?"

"Good. She seemed good."

"It feels like ages since I've spoken with her."

Raleigh observed that his unhealthy heart kept an even rhythm. Being the head of Grant and Able, he surely would've known how Sabine was... if they were keeping tabs her. Maybe they weren't watching as close as Rho feared. There was something familiar about Oliver's face. "You were in the article." The picture she'd seen of him was from thirty years ago when he was considerably thinner, but this was the same man. "You're the scientist who discovered the tribe."

"That's me. Back then, there was no Grant and Able. It was only me slogging through accounts of people like you. There are many stories of healers, and it took a lot of time to tease out the ones who used Lucidin. After I found the tribe, I managed to set up a small team, and years later we have this." He waved his arm expansively.

"The article didn't say where the tribe was from."

Oliver tapped his nose. "Few people know that. I promised to keep it a secret."

"They drank something to help them use the Lucidin, right?"

"Yes, an inducer. It causes a person to make more Lucidin for a short time. I never did get them to tell me the ingredients. To this day, we have people tinkering in the lab trying to recreate it."

"I'm late, and you're starting without me." Agatha hurried across the floor to their table taking a seat between them.

Oliver leaned back in his chair, adjusting so he could turn to Agatha. "We're discussing the tribe. All you've missed is a history lesson. It's time to eat."

A waiter appeared with salads and tiny boats of dressing. He positioned them in front of the three, the thick ranch dressing jiggling as he set them down.

Raleigh did her best to remember all the etiquette pointers her mother had chided her for over the years. Politely, she opened the crimson napkin and placed it neatly across her lap. She poured some dressing on her salad. Agatha put so little on hers that it probably wasn't worth doing and Oliver acted as though he was trying to drown his.

"Is the inducer one of the things I'll be working on in the lab?" Raleigh asked.

Agatha speared a few leaves. "Yes, but we hope to have you not only in the lab but training with Gabe and the other Receps."

"We call them that because they have a lot of Receptors," Oliver explained.

After chewing her delicate bite Agatha turned to Oliver. "Gabe explained who they were. Raleigh seems to have an elementary understanding of Lucidin, and her personal experience gives her insight into it."

Raleigh didn't want to train with the Recep army. Her heart tugged her towards medicine and helping people, not being a cog in their weaponry. However, if she was going to find Mu and Tau, training with the Receps would give her the best chance.

"If Receps aren't being trained as doctors, what's their purpose?" Raleigh asked. This had been glossed over, she wanted answers and to see how truthful they would be.

The lines of Agatha's face fell into a flat seriousness, and Oliver let out a laugh. "She's a smart girl. Don't look so upset, Aggs. The purpose of this dinner was to bring that up, and it was your idea."

Agatha put down her fork. "Normally, Raleigh, the Receps have a month at home before they're brought here. During that month, the trainer Recep in charge teaches them meditation and determines if they'd be a good fit for our program. When they come here, they're eased into training and learn what's expected of them."

Oliver said, "We can't train people at home. The logistics of it don't work."

"Yes, that's why we bring them here." Agatha rested her hands on the edge of the table, not gripping, but stabilizing herself. "But we didn't have a month with you at home. That puts you in the awkward position of being thrust into training."

Raleigh sensed the jumble of emotions competing in Agatha, a heart aching sadness, a long dormant anger strung in her muscles, and a worry pinching right between her eyes. Raleigh kept her own face neutral. "I'm a fast study. I've been sensing for years, and Gabe seems to think that influencing won't be too hard for me."

A ragged sigh escaped Agatha. "It isn't the actual training I'm concerned about... it's what you're being trained for. We've done a lot of good here at Grant and Able. Our doctors in Chicago and New York are making a lot of progress. However, there have been a few missteps and mistakes made along the way."

Oliver stopped eating and opened his hands. "The problem with Lucidin is that there isn't enough of it. I discovered a miracle drug but never found a good way to make it. Most people who create it do so randomly, like you. But some people inherit the trait from a parent or parents. The tribe is a good example. Marriages were established to help give the babies the best chance of creating Lucidin. I contacted a geneticist, John Grant, Agatha's father, to help figure out what was going on in these people. Around the same time, I had organic chemists working to synthesize the drug in a lab."

"My father was eccentric, but one of the best minds in his field." Agatha picked her fork back up but didn't eat.

Oliver gave Agatha a fatherly smile. "The synthetic we made was a poor substitute for the real thing."

"We still use it though," Agatha quickly said. "We mix it with real Lucidin so that it stretches. It's sort of like stretching lemonade with water—did your mother ever do that?—but instead of diluting it, the real Lucidin makes the synthetic stronger."

Everyone quieted as the waiter arrived at the table. Enchiladas, keeping with the Southwest theme, were the main course. Cilantro leaves on top gave them a clean aroma, and they were fancier than the ones she ate with her family at the local Tex-Mex restaurant back home.

Oliver hovered his fork over his food as he dutifully continued. "Ideally, we would've had an animal produce Lucidin. We looked into cows and monkeys, but it didn't work."

Raleigh winced, not liking the idea of using animals that way.

Agatha flicked her hand in the air. "It's not unusual. Hormones like Lucidin can often be produced in other animals and used in humans. Pigs are used to make thyroid, cows made insulin, and horses are still used to make estrogen."

Oliver cut into his food. "Lucidin is uniquely human and that caused some problems. We couldn't get the secret of the inducer from the tribe, and, even if we had, it may not have been enough. We were desperate and had one of the best geneticists at our disposal."

A chill ran down her spine, and she fought the urge to shiver from it. Good thing only she could sense. For a moment, she wondered how different things would be if they'd succeeded with an animal. Lucidin would be readily available. There would be no Designed. No Rho.

"Ethically, it was a gray area," Agatha said. "I was young then, in my early twenties, and my dad was confounded by how to use what he'd learned to enable people to make more. Ultimately, we decided that it wasn't ethical to alter embryos. Who do you choose? Your own children? Other people's? Who do you set up to have this sort of power?"

"Does a person have to have a lot of receptors to make Lucidin?" asked Raleigh. "Sabine said that they're found together. But if you have the choice of having one and not the other...."

"I'm going to be happy to have you in our labs. You're a clever one." Oliver pointed the tongs of his fork approvingly in her direction. "Yes, you can have one without the other. But we didn't want that. We wanted them to have receptors so that they would be able to heal and use the drug. For all I'd learned about Lucidin, I had no inkling that people could influence. We didn't know the power that we'd be bestowing."

The heartache in Agatha won out over the other emotions. "And we bestowed it. My father made twelve babies from scratch. He joked that he felt a bit like Frankenstein. But his creations weren't ugly. They were beautiful, intelligent babies. We adopted them out to families to give them a normal upbringing. Sabine and Henry raised two of them in their orphanage."

"They didn't mention that." Raleigh tested the waters of lying. It didn't come naturally to her, and she was careful not to overdo it. "She said that she'd never known anyone who makes Lucidin like I do."

"No one natural. You're the only one who does that hasn't been designed to. That's what we called the twelve, the Designed. Sabine wouldn't have brought that up," Agatha said. "It's a dark part of our history, and we all wish it to remain that way."

"Are they here, the people who make it?" Raleigh prayed that her youthful face made her appear innocent.

Oliver adjusted in his chair. "They're evil. Slowly they stumbled on influencing. We hoped to bring them here when they were older, to train them as doctors. Then one of them nearly killed another boy by stopping his heart."

"With influencing?" Raleigh tried to act surprised.

Oliver nodded. "He claimed it was a mistake, but there were warning signs along the way. They are charismatic, but something was always off. You can't design a soul, and I believe they don't have them."

Agatha's fork scraped the top of her food, the conversation dulling her appetite. "They were rounded up and brought to an island where some of our Receps conducted research. We hoped to inspire them with the good work we were doing with Lucidin. Some of them showed genuine interest in what we did, or at least they had us believe that they were on the same side as us. That wasn't the case."

Oliver picked up the story. "They betrayed us a few years ago. Agatha and I were in Chicago to establish our clinic. While we were gone, they massacred everyone... scientists, Receps, even some of the janitorial staff."

"My father and husband were killed." Agatha gulped down the sadness that filled her throat. The memories evoked a physical pain in her. Raleigh was taken aback by such a raw display of emotion. She wanted to comfort Agatha but didn't know how.

"Why wasn't this in the news? Why haven't I heard about

this? Did you go to the police?" Raleigh was still shocked that the technology and the Designed were never brought to the attention of the authorities or the public.

Oliver twisted in his seat. "We couldn't. Ethically, creating people is a gray area. We could never convince people that it was worth pushing the ethical limits. For them to understand the importance of our work they'd have to see the value of Lucidin. People don't want to believe Lucidin can do all that it does. Even with our progress and our outcomes, people would rather pin its success on things like God, luck, and fate. It wasn't possible to convince them that Lucidin is important enough for us to create people who make it."

With glossy eyes, Agatha gripped the table. "Most of the dead were suffocated. The Designed influenced them simply... well, not to breathe."

"Agatha, she doesn't need the details," Oliver said.

Not following Oliver's directions, Agatha continued. "We told the families of the Receps, boys younger than the ones we train now, that there'd been a carbon monoxide leak. A few ran into the sea to escape... and drowned."

Oliver patted Agatha's hand. "Enough. Don't put yourself through that again."

"Where are the Designed now?" Raleigh pictured them sitting around that large table in California.

"Two are dead." Agatha straightened her back and wiped a tear from her eye. "The synthetic was leaked before the Designed escaped. An illegal trade has been set up around it. Gabe will talk to you about that in depth sometime soon. It's why Sabine wanted you here. All you need to know is that the two who died were drained to death by people in the illegal trade. We've captured another two of them. Their Lucidin fuels our Receps. The other eight are at large."

Agatha touched Raleigh's hand. "That's why we had to bring you here, to keep you safe. Gabe will see to that. He was my bodyguard on the trip to Chicago. I remember telling him that I didn't need one. How naive we all were."

"You think they'd do me harm?"

Oliver didn't hesitate with his answer. "They would. The fact that you're as powerful as they are is reason enough. They're a crime against nature. You're what nature created to combat them."

Grant and Able wasn't only interested in her Lucid. They would have her be a soldier in their war. Not a soldier, their champion. High expectations, but everyone at the table knew she was capable of living up to them. Part of her wanted to tell them that the Designed weren't as evil as they thought, that they hadn't hurt her, or at least Rho hadn't.

Agatha turned so she looked at Raleigh directly. "We need you to help us defeat them."

The whole meal soured for Raleigh. Rho'd said a few people died during their escape. He didn't say that they'd killed innocent people like the custodians. Sigma's arrogance chilled her, he wasn't bluffing when he said he would've killed her. Taking a sip of water, she fought the sinking feeling that she might be on the wrong side. Mu and Tau were more like Rho, weren't they? For now, she had to focus on rescuing them. That thought caused a wave of apprehension to flow across her shoulders.

Everyone quieted. Agatha and Oliver let Raleigh process what she'd been told.

"Yes. I will help you," Raleigh said. If nothing else, she respected their candor. Sabine hadn't been honest. Raleigh thought Rho had been, but now she wondered how much he glossed over. If nothing else, Agatha and Oliver wore their emotions, exposing their vulnerability in a forthright fashion. Out of the three people at the table, Raleigh was the one keeping secrets. Lying and spying was only altruistic if she was on the right side of things.

Small talk proved impossible after discussing the massacre. They ate the remainder in silence. Raleigh tried to picture how she would act learning of the Designed in this context. Would she eagerly take up their cause? Hearing Rho's side first had drawn her to it. After hearing what Grant and Able said, she was on the fence. One thing wasn't changing. She was going to stay here, either to help Grant and Able or Rho, and that meant training as Agatha proposed.

After dinner Agatha walked Raleigh down the steps to the main lobby. At night, with no one around, it looked larger.

"We'll extract twice a day, opposed to once," said Agatha. "Before, you were doing it simply to ward off the blackouts. Our goal now is to get more Lucidin to train our Receps and aid our doctors."

"Twice should be fine." In Paris she'd undergone twice daily extractions with no consequence.

"It's right through here." Agatha escorted her past a recreation hall with a pool table and pinball games. "Receps and lab workers go there to blow off steam. Feel free to hang out there if you're bored. This is our extraction room. You access it with your thumbprint. I'll put mine down first, and then you will register yours by placing it down next."

Agatha pressed her thumb over the tiny light and then motioned for Raleigh to do the same. A high pitch beep sounded, and the thick door slid open. Raleigh followed Agatha into a narrow room. To her surprise, the two normal-appearing boys from the cafeteria were inside. Exposed ports on their arms connected to an extraction machine.

"Who's she?" one asked. He had shaggy blond hair, ripped jeans, and a T-shirt for a band she'd never heard of. A skater kid, he was younger than her. So was the other one. The second one didn't attempt to look cool. His khaki pants and polo shirt were better suited for someone twice his age. He was heavyset and had difficulty keeping eye contact. Raleigh knew the type.

Agatha made the introductions. "This is Raleigh. She's a natural who makes Lucidin. Raleigh, this is Quinn and Dale."

Quinn whistled. "A girl. Finally."

Agatha raised her palm clearly indicating he should stop. "There's no fraternizing. One of the benefits of having our girls in Chicago and New York is that we don't have to worry about people being distracted."

"Because that would give us something to fill the time," Dale said under his breath.

Raleigh scrunched up her nose. Agatha had explained Raleigh to them, but she was yet to explain them to Raleigh. "How is it that they create Lucidin?"

"We forgot to tell you!" Agatha touched her head. "We got so caught up in discussing the Designed that I neglected to mention the Modified."

Dale sighed loudly. "That's us. We were modified as fertilized eggs to make Lucidin."

"I thought you didn't feel that was ethically right." Raleigh instantly regretted saying those words in front of Quinn and Dale.

Agatha quickly explained. "It was a backup plan... after we realized there might be a problem. The Modified are about five years younger than the Designed. They have no receptors. As you suggested, they only make Lucidin. We modified babies from fertility clinics. The Lucidin has absolutely no effect on them at all because they don't have receptors. They're normal in every other way. No sensing. No influencing."

Quinn leaned back shrugging. "It isn't bad. We're normal. I wouldn't even know what Lucidin was if they hadn't told me. Grant and Able called our parents and said we had a 'blood' disorder and now pay us for our Lucidin."

"We weren't moved here until recently," Dale said. "A few months ago."

Agatha led Raleigh to a chair. "Safety concerns arose. Once we captured the two Designed, we worried the other eight would retaliate. We needed to keep Dale and Quinn safe. Having them here makes that possible."

Raleigh wanted to ask if they were infertile, too, like the Designed. That wasn't an appropriate question, plus, she wasn't supposed to know that about the Designed. Dale and Quinn did appear normal. With Dale's chubby face and Quinn's uneven teeth, it was clear that just the Lucidin had been messed with.

"Let's get you started." Agatha attached the equipment.

"Are there more Modified?" asked Raleigh.

Stepping back Agatha turned on the machine. "Yes. So far Dale and Quinn are the only two we've needed to contact. Their Lucidin has given us a one-up on capturing the Designed."

Of course, it had. Sigma had accused Raleigh of giving them hers. Raleigh assumed that the Designed didn't know about the Modified, or they would've mentioned something.

"So here's a TV and a remote." Agatha used it to turn on the television. "Just relax, and I'll be back in twenty minutes or so."

"Where are you from?" Quinn asked.

"Colorado."

"You're lucky you're here. This is the coolest job ever. All we have to do is give extractions twice a day and we're set. Nothing else is expected. You can spend the day by the pool or improving your gaming."

Neither gaming or the pool appealed to her. "That sounds nice."

Dale stared at the ceiling. "It's damn boring. All this free time gets old fast. I'm hoping that they capture all the Designed so that we can get out of here and on with our lives."

"We're an important part of that," Quinn said. "They couldn't have caught Mu and Tau without us. Those are their names, because, you know, they're monster lab freaks."

Dale and Quinn obviously viewed their situation differently.

"Agatha didn't describe them quite like that." She glanced at the free chairs. "Do they extract here too, the captured Designed?"

With wide eyes, Dale shook his head. "No! That would be too dangerous. They're locked up somewhere, but nowhere near us. That's the one good thing. We get to sit back and let the Receps do the work. I wouldn't want to go up against them."

"I don't think I'm going to have that luck. I'm training with Gabe and the others tomorrow."

Dale said, "Of course, you have receptors."

Quinn lifted his free hand motioning excitedly. "They're so cool. You've gotta tell us what they're like."

"I'll keep you posted." She wished she could muster up that sort of excitement. The Receps topped the list of things she dreaded about Grant and Able.

CHAPTER
17

THE ANTICIPATION OF meeting the Receps woke Raleigh early. She slipped into the extraction room before breakfast. The bakery hours gave her an appreciation for getting things done early, and the desert morning was serene and beautiful. No doubt the sun would work tirelessly to scorch the Earth, but in the early hours it was no more than a threat.

She'd just finished the extraction when the door clicked open. Her eyes jumped to the entrance, surprised that one of the Modified would be up this early. Gabe strolled in stopping a few paces from her, his legs a shoulder width apart. "Are you ready for today?"

"Yes." She got up from the chair, and the two of them exited the extraction room and then the building as a whole. The early Arizona desert smelled of dust, flowers, and sunscreen. Out of her pocket she withdrew a white cotton sweatband that she adjusted into place over the port. "Where are we going?"

"I've pointed out the dorms, where the Receps and I live. That two-story building with windows is the lab. We're going to the gym over there."

The different buildings stood out from one another. The dorms were similar to the ones at the university she'd applied to. The gym had a large dome. She pictured basketball courts and a track underneath it. As they walked past the buildings, she almost missed a small cement bunker off to the side.

Gabe didn't say anything about the simple structure with high windows and metal doors that gave the impression of an enlarged maintenance shed. Even after her extraction, she could surmise that there were people inside. Creating a visor with her hands, she squinted. The building had a small keypad to the right of the door. Raleigh didn't ask Gabe about it. If he wanted her to know, he would've told her. Maybe Mu and Tau were closer than Dale said. They'd have to be someplace secure. Why not there? Later she would check it out. For now, she stayed on course to the gym.

The wide clear doors to the gym slid open. The dust from outside collected on the mat inside the door, otherwise it was spotless. Chlorine and cleaning solvent competed in the air. They faced a glassed-in room, where the waters of an Olympic-sized pool rested pristine and unbroken. Signs for weight rooms and yoga centers pointed the way further down the hall.

"All this for the Receps?" With training an army, she'd expected something more functional, like a shooting range.

"And you and the researchers. That's why we have a women's locker room." The tour ended in front of a large door with a little metallic symbol of a lady. "Agatha left clothes for you in locker ten."

"Why do I need special clothes for mostly mind work?"

"Lucidin gives us a better understanding of our bodies, and usually, a person has to be mentally and physically fit before they can move onto sensing and influencing. Only a small portion of our time is spent on working with Lucidin. The rest is focused on fitness and team building. When you go into the field, the guys you train with here will be your team."

"I'll get ready then."

The panel of white lockers sat untouched. The only noise passing through the narrow cavern of a room was the low rumble of an air conditioner. Raleigh found locker ten and opened it. Folded in neat squares was a set of workout clothes. Black, like the ones she'd seen the Receps in the cafeteria wear. She slid out of her clothes and pulled the new cotton shirt over her head. It hung loosely on her, not snug. The shorts too were unflattering and shapeless. It didn't matter, she had no one to impress. Lacing up her shoes, she wondered who made the foolish choice of black clothes in a place as sunny as Arizona.

Leaving the locker room, she discovered Gabe waiting for her. His eyes raked over her, from her head down to her feet. "Good. You're going to fit in."

"Yeah, hopefully. Is this what it was like when you started?"

"I started before the massacre, so, no. Things were more light-hearted then, a lot of fooling around and pranks."

"Things are less fun now?"

"Things are more serious. But don't worry, it's still a lot of fun."

The quiet building wasn't unoccupied. Raleigh sensed the room full of men before they entered the meditations room. Inside around twenty guys loafed around, some sitting cross-legged on the floor, others yawning. A few spoke in hushed voices.

"The newest arrival is always overseen by the second newest." Gabe put a hand on her shoulder, halting her near a young man. He was about her age, with cropped brown hair and wide brown eyes. "Adam, you're in charge of bringing Raleigh up to speed." Gabe went to the front of the room to talk to a few of the Receps.

"I'm Adam." The guy said as he rocked on the balls of his feet, his raised eyebrows made him less severe than some of the others.

"Raleigh."

"You're a girl." Not a question, more an observation said aloud. "All right, Raleigh, first things first, we all dose up before class. Just go over to that machine and scan your thumb."

In the corner sat a large vending machine with a short line of Receps waiting to use it. The nearest one put his finger on the scanner and a door opened, revealing a vial. He injected its contents, disposed of the needle, and covered his port with a sweatband. Their ports, like Brent's, were smaller. Raleigh sensed that Adam had already dosed, the Lucid clawing through him and the other guys. It was different than hers and Rho's. It erratically hit their receptors and nerves. She recalled Agatha saying they used the synthetic to stretch the real Lucid.

Adam gave her a sympathetic grimace. "It's a bit weird to see people taking it. Needles suck, but at least you have your port. Go over and dose up."

"I'm good for now."

"Gabe already showed you the machine? He personally recruited you, too, didn't he? That's where he and Agatha have been. They rarely take such an interest. Most of us are thrown in, helps with the camaraderie. What percentile are you in?"

"Excuse me?"

"I'm in the ninety-seventh percentile. Anyone over the ninety-sixth should be able to influence, but it's tough. Those guys standing around Gabe are both ninety-nine."

"What's Gabe?"

"One hundredth. He should've told you what you were."

"He didn't mention it." Percentiles didn't matter. Like Brent had said to Collin, she redefined their curves.

"You should find out. It determines the hierarchy around here. You shouldn't feel bad about being in the ninety-sixth, if that's where you are. It's not as though you won't be capable of influencing. You'll just have to work harder. That redhead over there, Carter, he's a ninety-sixth, and he's doing fine."

"All right, everyone!" Gabe hollered, and silence replaced the chatter. "We have a new Recep. Her name is Raleigh."

Raleigh waved. None of them waved back. In a roomful of girls, there would've probably been some kind smiles. As it was, they showed no emotion about her.

Gabe pointed to one of the ninety-ninth percentile guys. "Dustin, do you want to lead meditation?"

Dustin jumped up—like the prized student who clamors for the teacher's attention. But it wasn't grade school, and Gabe wasn't a traditional teacher.

"Let's start with some yoga," Dustin said.

Years ago, Raleigh had taken a yoga class at the Y. She recalled some poses, but it didn't give her much of an edge. The Receps were surprisingly limber. Adam kept whispering points about technique, but Raleigh wasn't flexible enough. By the end, her muscles were shaky and aching. At least it was followed by twenty minutes of quiet meditation.

Gabe wove through the Receps that sat cross-legged in neat rows. "Now that you're all feeling centered, find a partner, and we'll work on our Lucidin exercises."

Adam gave Raleigh a worried look. He clearly expected her Lucidin skills to be on par with her yoga ones. "Did you do any sensing during your home training?"

"You could say that."

Gabe interrupted before Adam could ask what that meant. "Adam, you're with Wyatt. I'll be working with Raleigh."

"Not with Dustin?"

"Dustin will be fine. Get to it before the drug wears off."

Adam gave Raleigh a meek smile and then dashed off.

Gabe watched him leave and turned to Raleigh. "I'm going to tell you how influencing works, and then you can try. Do you have enough Lucidin in your system?"

"Yeah."

Gabe gave her the rundown on how to influence. It was word for word the way Rho'd put it. There must be some influencing handbook they quoted from, or some teacher they both had who first described it the way they did now. Her back bristled under the scrutiny of so many pairs of eyes sizing her up. Recep culture was competitive. Gabe finished up the explanations, his facial expression not unlike Collin's when talking to Rho. She wondered if they'd known each other.

"Earth to Raleigh." Gabe snapped his fingers. "Am I making this too complicated for you?"

"No. I was just thinking of all the ways I could use influencing."

"Influencing has many uses, but you have to master the basics first. Will me to feel pain in my finger."

"You really want me to make your finger hurt?"

"You probably won't be able to do it... right away."

That certainly wasn't going to be the case. Lying was one thing, but scaling down her skills was something she didn't know how to do. The last thing she needed was for him to figure out that she was holding back. She focused on his finger causing the nerves to shock, as if being pricked by a pin.

Instinctually, he shook his hand. "Great! I knew you were going to be great at this."

A nearby pair took notice of them.

She glared at Gabe. "Shh. I'm not ready for them to know yet."

"Why not?"

These guys made her skin crawl, the last thing she needed was for them to know her secret. Collin had been jealous of her. The fact that she produced the Lucid they needed to inject created an uncomfortable dynamic. It would establish her as their superior, and she knew it was easier to bond with equals.

"Are you going to answer me?" asked Gabe.

Raleigh attempted to explain herself. "How am I going to fit in with them if they think I'm better? Do you really like that kid who shows you up?"

Gabe rubbed his chin, his eyes taking in his students. "They'll be envious."

"I'd rather have them as friends than admirers."

"Then tell them on your terms. But be aware, there are plenty of ways they surpass you, and they don't hold back."

"Noted."

They had a chance to prove Gabe right. The next activity on the schedule was basketball. One by one they marched down the hall to a large gym. It smelled of rubber and sweat. She'd watched Lana and Ben compete in sports, but with her blackouts it hadn't been realistic for her. The Recep voices filled up the large space altering the mood from a quiet to loud one. Gabe gave a speech about how this would strengthen their bodies and teamwork. Then he assigned captains, and they selected teams. The captains picked Raleigh last, but at least she was with Adam.

Gabe blew his whistle, and the guys jumped into action. Raleigh's team had the first chance with the ball, and they raced towards the basket. She reached the other side after the others but had a clean shot. Waving her arms in the air, she signaled she wanted the ball. Her teammate turned to her, scrunched his nose, and passed it to another Recep who missed.

Now, the opposition had their turn. They stampeded down the court.

"Hey, Ninety-Seven, throw it to me!" Dustin shouted to his teammate with the ball, who obeyed.

Raleigh reached half court as he sunk a basket. Her teammates joined in a chorus of groans and then went back to the game. Now her team had the ball a second time, and again the other team found no point in guarding her. This time she positioned herself right under the hoop, it would be an easy shot, she'd played enough times with Ben in driveway back home to make it.

"Here!" She yelled.

The boy reluctantly threw it to her. With the textured ball in her hand, she rocked on her feet the way her father had taught her. Extending her arms, her hands propelled it towards the basket. She could picture the part of the backboard it would hit. She was going to get a basket. Then Dustin's hand flew up, knocking the ball off course.

"Should have stayed home, Ninety-Six." He laughed, barreling past her and knocking her arm.

"Maybe you'd be better as a healer," one of them suggested after the botched basket. "That's where all the other girls go. Why aren't you there?"

"Because I'm here to train."

She gave it her all, with each step she stretched her legs to keep up with theirs. Her lungs wheezed from the dry air that she roughly inhaled. Even with her efforts, she failed to keep up. They sneered at her, her team's loss falling on her shoulders.

By the time Gabe's whistle pierced the air, she was more than ready for practice to end. The day proved that these guys wouldn't be won over easily. Their camaraderie had to be earned. Being a girl, and a novice to Grant and Able, were two obstacles. It didn't help that Gabe favored her. The Receps were condescending to her, making her rethink hiding her percentile. If they knew, there was still no guarantee that they'd treat her better. It certainly hadn't endeared her to Collin. He hated her more for it. No. She would keep her head down.

Everyone headed toward the locker room. They prodded and teased one another, their jabs echoing down the hall. She turned the opposite direction towards her locker room, the sound of the air conditioning blasting the silence.

Gabe jogged over to her before she could duck inside to the privacy of the white room. "Don't worry, things will get easier. You'll be sore tomorrow. It would be a good idea to skip training. Agatha wants to give you a tour of the lab. You'll be back here the day after tomorrow. Clean up and then get some lunch."

"Sure." Raleigh pushed through the door, wishing that she'd had a month to prepare for this.

She tore off her smelly clothes and went straight to the showers. The steamy water opened her pores and rinsed the sweat from her skin. Scrubbing her arms red, she tried unsuccessfully to wash off the failure. Tomorrow would be a better day. It was always hard being the new kid. She bolstered her hope in a way that would make her mother proud. As the conditioner slithered from her hair down her back, she vowed that she would fit in.

The chatter of female voices echoed through the shower stall after she turned off the stream. Researchers. Maybe she could make a few friends. Many of her friends back home had been untraditional. Dr. Moore and Uncle Patrick weren't the kind of friends who could braid her hair, but they had something in common. The labs could be her solution to fitting in. The researchers were older, but who cared? Straightening her shoulders, she figured she should introduce herself.

She dressed, preparing a proper introduction in her head, then she stopped. She wasn't here to make friends. No. She was here to gain information about Mu and Tau. Researchers would not be involved with their imprisonment. The Receps, who were charged with capturing them, would know a lot more. She yanked the laces of her shoes tight. Adam was the nicest. He'd have to let her in. It was time for lunch.

CHAPTER
18

RALEIGH'S HIGH SCHOOL had loosely-formed cliques. Lunch tables were organized more or less by interest and friend groups. Everyone had their place, but it wasn't so unwelcoming that you couldn't sit at a different table for a day and feel uncomfortable. That wasn't the case in Grant and Able's cafeteria.

Yesterday she'd noticed the obvious differences between Receps and scientists. Today she saw that the Receps further divided themselves, based on receptor volume. Adam, at ninety-seven, ranked low. The people at his table struggled during practice with Lucidin. People in the top ninety-ninth percentile and above filled up Gabe's table. It seemed like an arbitrary way to choose dining companions.

Gabe caught her eye, his head motioning to the chair on his left. To his right sat Dustin. It was Dustin who had berated her for not running fast enough, and he called guys like Adam by their percentile rather than name. Now he stared daggers at her, the message clear, they didn't want her. It was imperative that she fit it, but she couldn't bring herself to sit there. They would never befriend her if they considered her Gabe's pet.

Adam sat at the next table, and it had an empty seat. He waved to her. These guys on the lower rungs would be more inclusive, having worked hard to get by themselves. If she wanted to make friends, it would be easier with them.

Straightening her spine, she went over to the vacant seat. Her tray clanged against the tabletop gaining the attention of the others. She didn't sit, waiting to make sure none of them protested. No one spoke, and she plopped into the plastic chair. Reluctantly they continued their conversation.

"Did you know that's not real chocolate mousse?" one of the guys asked, pointing to her tray. "It's made from avocados. It doesn't have any milk in it, just added chocolate."

Adam licked the edge of his spoon shrugging. "It tastes the same. You'd never know."

"That's what's so creepy about it!" the guy said.

Raleigh grinned, remembering Thalia's vegan stage. "My sister used to eat cheese made from nuts instead of dairy."

"Did it taste like cheese?" the guy asked.

"No."

"Exactly my point! Watch out. Agatha is like my mom, always hiding vegetables in things. I'm Brandon, by the way."

Raleigh reached out and shook his hand, the greeting strangely formal. A few of the guys fist bumped during the game, something too awkward for her to do, at least yet.

"Who cares if it tastes good?" asked Adam.

Raleigh tried a bite. "It does taste good."

With her blackouts, she never tried out for a team sport. But her sister Lana had been tight with her girls' volleyball team. She envied that bond and now had a small thrill go up her spine imagining that she too would be part of a team—even if it was a team of Lucid-driven Receps.

Predictably, the conversation during lunch revolved around receptor volume, training, and what the field would be like. Mu and Tau weren't discussed. As the guys stood up with their trays, she wondered how much Receps this low down knew. She didn't dare ask about them the first day.

After stowing their dirtied trays, they spilled into the foyer of the building. Adam hung back for her, his hand rubbing the sweat from the back of his neck. "Technically we're done with training for the day, but in an hour a lot of us are going to meet up in the weight room to lift."

Raleigh hadn't really ever lifted weights. She'd have to ignore her reservations, lifting was the best way to get stronger. "Sure, maybe."

"Cool, see you in a bit." Adam gave her a nod before heading off with the others to the dorms.

She watched as they all disappeared. Raleigh's homey cottage now revealed its downside. By living separately, she missed out on some of the bonding.

Shielding her eyes, she stepped out into the sweltering afternoon sun. Nobody else lingered outside. The unbearable climate made it so people rushed from one air-conditioned building to another. Beads of sweat formed along her hairline and dripped down her back. Mu and Tau had to be here somewhere, and her money was on the squat, unwelcoming building Gabe failed to mention on the tour.

She circled the gymnasium and the squat bunker from earlier came into view. A short path led to its metal door, making it a destination rather than a place to pass. Rolling her shoulders back, she kept her steps measured and calm as she approached it.

This was the type of place that would make a good prison. The narrow windows were too high to see through and only served to allow light in.

Carefully, Raleigh went to the side of the building where she couldn't be seen from the gym or path. She surveyed the area. Even the desert critters hid from the heat. Reaching out her mind, she attempted to sense Mu and Tau. They could be barricading even if they were asleep, but not if they were drugged. Grant and Able's best chance of holding them was to keep them doped up—the same way Rho'd been when he was in captivity.

She sought two male bodies in a drug-induced haze. Many people worked inside, none fitting that description. The inside of the building was cool, as evidenced by the goosebumps on the arms of the people she sensed. Most of them sat hunched over, their back muscles aching and their eyes strained. She guessed they were working at computers. She leaned closer, her hands pressing against the rough white adobe wall. There were maybe thirty people inside, but she didn't sense any bodies that seemed like they could be Mu and Tau. What was this place?

"Raleigh?" said Gabe.

His voice skipped up her spine, causing her to jump. Whipping around, her hand fell on her chest. "Gabe. You scared me."

"What are you doing out here?"

She didn't have an answer because she didn't think anyone was going to sneak up on her. She wasn't used to people barricading. Now she stood a foot from the building, looking suspicious. Would he guess that she was trying to sense the people inside? If he did, would he jump to the idea that she was a spy?

"When did you learn to barricade?" Gabe studied her face.

"I was scared." She hadn't meant to barricade. Dropping it she let him sense her racing heart. "I closed off. Instinct."

Gabe seemed to approve. "It figures that barricading comes naturally to you. What scared you?"

Snakes. Thalia once saw a snake when they were little, and ever since she'd always been vigilant when hiking. Raleigh used to tease her about it. "I saw a snake. Adam said there was weight training in the gym, and I was headed there when something slithered over here. I thought I'd check it out."

"There are diamondbacks around here. They're poisonous."

Raleigh rubbed her arms. "We have garter snakes back home. Anyhow, I came over here but couldn't find it. What is this place?"

"Our intelligence building." Gabe wasn't interested in the building, he stood lightly on his toes. "Let's get out of here. I don't want to get bit."

"Yeah." Raleigh followed him away.

Gabe smiled. "You were getting along with Adam at lunch."

"Yeah. I think it's working out not to tell them about the extractions." She snapped the elastic of the sweatband on her arm. "They seem friendly enough."

"How many times have you lifted?"

"A few times in high school. Enough to know I need a spotter."

"I can do that."

Raleigh was relieved that Gabe bought her story. In the future, she'd have to be more careful when she poked around.

THE DUAL TRAINING sessions made for a long day. On aching legs, she ambled to the extraction room. The lactic acid irritated her muscles as she waited for her thumbprint to be scanned. Once inside she discovered both Dale and Quinn, she gave a small wave and sunk into the extraction chair.

"How'd it go with the Receps?" Dale asked.

"I bet it was awesome!" Quinn said. "We've reached level twenty-five of...."

"Don't, Quinn. She doesn't care." Dale exhaled loudly and then turned to Raleigh. "I overhead them at the table saying that you sucked at basketball."

Even if Dale and Quinn weren't social with the others, they kept in the loop.

"I'm really out of shape." The last thing she needed was for them to judge her, too.

Dale snorted. "Compared to them, who wouldn't be? They work out nonstop."

"They're dedicated. I wish I had receptors." Quinn made a muscle with his arm and frowned at it. The moment of regret passed quickly. His machine stopped, and he disconnected the tubes from his arm. "I'm done. Back to the game."

Dale watched him leave, then leaned his head back with a soft thud. "I'm getting sick of gaming. So, what are you doing tomorrow?"

"I'm going with Agatha to the labs. I'm hoping to work there. She says that I can apply to college, so I can become a doctor."

"I bet they'd love to have you as a healer. That's the whole point of this place, to understand Lucidin well enough that we can save lives. Why aren't you in Chicago or New York?"

"Agatha said it's safer here."

"Yea, the Designed think they're better than everyone because of their Lucidin. Agatha worries that they'll target us because they don't like that anyone else has that power. I've never been to the labs. I've always wondered what they did in there."

"Haven't you been here for a couple of months?"

"They treat us well, but they really aren't all that interested in us beyond the Lucidin."

The gears turned hungrily in the extraction machine. It was the same thing Rho had complained about. Quinn clearly enjoyed the free time and the praise. Dale wasn't the type of person who'd be satisfied with this kind of life. Raleigh wasn't either.

"Do you want to come to the labs tomorrow?" she asked.

"I don't know if they'll let me."

"It's your Lucidin. Shouldn't you get to see where it goes?" Dale had to prove to these people that he was more than a source of Lucid. Agatha and the others needed to involve the Modified, and she would insist that he come.

Dale bit his bottom lip. "I've been interested."

"Then you'll come with me tomorrow when I go. We'll do it after extraction. Do you think Quinn will want to come too?"

"He's in an online tournament tomorrow. Be careful not to bring it up, or that's all you'll hear about."

"I'll be careful then." Raleigh laughed, and her side, still sore from the workout, protested. She was going to need that downtime from training tomorrow.

CHAPTER 19

THE NEXT DAY they stared at brains that bobbed lightly in their cylindrical jars. Raleigh leaned in closer while Dale paled. She sensed the blood drain from his face and settle in his legs. The repulsion crept up his spine, and his eyes widened. It surprised her that he didn't run out of the room. Of all the things Raleigh expected to see in the labs, human brains weren't one of them.

In the hospital, the laboratory was the place where blood work was done. It smelled on account of the stool and urine samples. The grossest thing was bacterial plating of the medical swabs. There were no brains swimming in briny-smelling broth.

"What are they?" Dale asked.

Agatha remained unfazed. "We're attempting to grow brains that produce Lucidin."

Dale cleared his throat fighting his nausea. "Don't they—um, you know—need a *body?*"

"To make Lucid, you don't need a body. The hormone is made

in the brain and then, theoretically, leaches into the surrounding solution." Dr. Gustav, Raleigh's new boss, tapped the glass. "We haven't succeeded yet. In a few days we'll slice up this one open and see if it produced any receptors."

"Can they think?" Dale asked.

"No." Raleigh couldn't sense them and assumed they were sending no messages. Even tiny embryos had the spark of life. "These are more like cells arranged in a brain fashion."

Dr. Gustav shook his index finger. "We never claimed to be close. You two will be responsible for keeping the broth between certain temperatures. And later, you'll stain and mount the brain sections after they've been sliced."

Dale gave Raleigh a look. "The other lab had nice clean beakers."

It was true. The first lab they visited was working to construct a better synthetic. In the second one they toured, the scientists tried to recreate the illusive inducer used by the tribe all those years ago. Both would be heavy in organic and biochemistry. This was more hands-on.

Dr. Gustav snapped on a pair of gloves and turned to Dale. "You can feed the lab rats. The rats smell worse, and they bite, but if you want to help out in the synthetics lab they'd appreciate it."

"I thought only people could use Lucidin," Raleigh said. "Rats wouldn't be able to test if any of their samples worked."

Agatha pulled her attention from the brains. "You listen well. It's for toxicity. We would never inject something into a human until we tried it on other animals first."

So, the Designed weren't the only guinea pigs, but there was nothing to say that some synthetics wouldn't be exclusively toxic to humans. Raleigh dropped it. Her eyes went to the brains. They were the same translucent pink as the hamster babies in her fourth-grade classroom. Dr. Gustav put on gloves and reached in and delicately grabbed one, it squished between his fingers. Dale's stomach clenched.

"I'll show you how we rinse them." Dr. Gustav rested the brain on a metal tray and motioned to Dale to follow.

Agatha's gloves snapped as she tugged them off. "That's fine. Show Dale, and I'll take Raleigh to the video conference I've arranged."

Dr. Gustav rested the brain on the tray on the counter and wrapped his hand around it, his meaty fingers turning it over to reveal the tail-like brainstem. "Right, thanks for your visit Agatha. Raleigh, it's going to be a pleasure working with you. Dale, put on a pair of gloves, I'll teach you the cleaning process."

Dale furrowed his brow and grabbed two of the gloves from a box. Raleigh gave him a smile and followed Agatha through the doors into the hall. The icy temperature in the labs made her shiver in her summer clothes.

She waited for the door to shut behind them before saying, "Dale's anxious."

"The brains are a bit off-putting at first. Once he figures out that none of them are going to talk to him, he'll be fine."

Raleigh wondered what a brain would say. I'm here to take your Lucidin job, Dale. Grant and Able weren't fools. They made the Designed too strong and the Modified free, but the brains would have none of that. If they worked, it would be a victimless method.

The first floor of the building was undeniably devoted to the labs—with their high ceilings, black counters, and deep sinks that gave them an industrial look. Agatha led Raleigh toward the elevators, passing whiteboards and large equipment that hummed and beeped. When the elevator doors opened onto the second floor, Raleigh felt like she was in a standard office building. Offices lined the walls, and a kitchenette with a coffee maker percolated in the corner.

"We'll take this meeting in my office." Agatha moved down the hall stopping at a door with her name written in precise script. She opened it and welcomed Raleigh in.

The earth tones and clean lines that Agatha seemed to prefer made the office bland. Agatha motioned Raleigh to sit in a back straightening ergonomic chair. Raleigh delicately sat, her back held straight, and her muscles, sore from the workout yesterday, ached.

Agatha sat in an identical chair at her desk. She swiveled the computer monitor so that both she and Raleigh could see the screen. Then she typed a password, and a call went through.

"Hello, Agatha." A middle-aged woman appeared on the other end. A pair of thick black lenses hid her dark brown eyes, and her ebony skin contrasted nicely with the white lab coat. She sat in an office, a patchwork of anatomy posters peeking out from behind her. To the side of them was a window, and skyscrapers dotted the view.

Agatha nodded at the screen. "Dr. Arthur, this is Raleigh."

"Hi, Raleigh." Dr. Arthur beamed, her eyes almost disappearing from the smile. *"I'm Gabe's equivalent in the healer world, which is to say that I train the doctors in our program how to use Lucidin in diagnostics and healing in the New York clinic."*

Raleigh leaned forward trying better to see the skyline in the distance. She hoped to be sitting in that seat one day. Her mind pushed out the thoughts about the Designed and trying to find Mu and Tau. The jitters of being a spy were replaced with a curiosity that tugged on her heart. She had so many questions for Dr. Arthur, but they all became tangled on her tongue. Should she ask what they'd been able to cure? If people believed her? And the most pressing, when could she start?

Agatha said, "We're going to be enrolling Raleigh in college in the spring."

Dr. Arthur nodded to Agatha, and then spoke to Raleigh. *"We want to have you here as soon as possible. Gabe says that you're working on finding the Designed. Round them up, so it's safe for you to come."*

Eight years of school and eight Designed on the lam, one of which would be Rho. Raleigh swallowed that thought. "What do you treat?"

Dr. Arthur held out her hands. *"Everything. We get neuropathic pain cases, and we help the brain rewire how it processes that pain. We diagnose heart disease, hormone imbalance, and clotting disorders. Our most promising work is with cancer. We all hesitate to use the word cure, but, in most patients, we can work with the body so that it targets and eliminates those cells, including metastasis."*

"An end to cancer." The giddiness rose up in Raleigh. She couldn't wait to tell Dr. Moore. His patients put on brave faces, but there was fear and pain in them that had left Raleigh scarred. "What do the patients think?"

"We see the most desperate ones. We're who people go to when they have no other options. Most of them think it's New Age voodoo. Others think we're miracle workers sent by God. Most of them are happy to be better. Speaking of which, I have to be going. Do the best you can in the field and come be one of my doctors as quickly as possible." Dr. Arthur winked.

That was it. The crux of the whole thing. Grant and Able offered her everything she could ever want. Raleigh would no longer helplessly sense diseases in others. She would cure them. It was more than she dreamt it would be. All she had to do was forget about Rho. His beautiful face lingered in her memory. No. Forgetting him wasn't an option. All she had to do was never see him again.

"I know you have patients, so we'll let you go. Thanks for your time." Agatha's hand reached to end the call.

Dr. Arthur interjected before she could. *"Let me know which doctors you want me to bring to the benefactors' dinner next month."*

Agatha checked her phone. "Is it really next month? All right, I'll let you know. That's when the two of you can meet in person." Agatha finished the call and clicked out of the app.

Raleigh stood up and said, "This changes everything." This trumped what the Designed had against Grant and Able. Had they been horrible and created people to make their drug? Yes. There was no denying that they'd made mistakes along the way. The outcome though, the end, was justified by the means. Or for the moment it seemed that way, the thought of Tau's and Mu's fate gnawed at her.

"It is a game changer," Agatha agreed.

She had no idea of the full effect it had on Raleigh. Not only did it make her call into question her faithfulness to the Designed, it brought about a personal aspiration she had ever since she started sensing disease.

"Come, I want to show you something." Agatha stood and went over to a thin sliding door in the corner. She took a breath and steadied herself before opening it and stepping inside.

"What is this?" Raleigh glanced around.

"This is where I come whenever I'm feeling frustrated or in the mood to feel nostalgic."

Thus far, the decor of all the buildings seemed to reflect Agatha's style—minimalist with a focus on function. There were the occasional nods to the Southwest that were more of a tribute to their location than a design choice. This room didn't have the standard scenery picture every few feet. Instead, it was hard to see the paint with all the photos crammed on the wall.

"Those are the original Receps," Agatha said.

Young, vibrant faces squeezed into the frame of the nearest picture. They weren't posing. It was as if they'd been rounded up for the camera at a moment's notice. Watching Agatha cry over their loss two nights ago had been heartbreaking. This was chilling. Caked in mud and unapologetic about their ruffled hair, they seemed like an adventurous bunch.

Agatha didn't say much. She allowed Raleigh to look at their faces and imagine what it might've been like to know them. Raleigh recognized Gabe and Collin even though they were younger with longer hair and wider smiles. They stood with their arms looped over each other's shoulders, a football under Gabe's arm.

"That's Gabe." Raleigh turned to Agatha.

"And his friend Collin. We believe he died. They never found his body, but a few of the Receps ran into the water and drowned when the Designed influenced their muscles to stop. Most of the bodies washed up, but his never did. Gabe spent months searching and never found him. They were close."

How would Gabe react to finding out that Collin was alive and fighting against his cause?

Agatha directed her attention to the next wall. "And these are the scientists."

With their white lab coats and concentrated expressions, similarities could be drawn to the current scientists. She could easily see these scientists working here. But the Receps seemed different. The current Receps were a more resolved, somber group.

"I brought you here, so you could see the people that we're doing this for. We told you a couple of nights ago, but I wanted you to see them. That's my dad there."

The photo was of a blond man who resembled Agatha standing over a bassinet gazing down. At first, she wondered if the baby was Agatha and his face was that of a proud father, but a younger version of Agatha stood in the corner. Raleigh realized that one of the Designed was in the crib.

"He was so enamored of his creations." Agatha sighed deeply.

"I still can't believe he was able to make them."

"He treated them like his own. Every parent wants the best for their child. They want them to be strong, smart, and beautiful. Those wishes turned into gifts that he gave them, gifts that they would use to murder him. It's a sweet picture when you don't know what happened. I'm sure he looked at me with much of the same adoration. They were family to us."

Guilt and loss weren't the only things plaguing Agatha. There was also the betrayal. Agatha had wanted the best for the Designed, too, and they'd destroyed her life.

"That one's my husband." Agatha pointed to a picture further down the wall. It was of a nerdy man with large eyes and a crooked smile. His hand was in mid-wave. Raleigh wouldn't have been surprised if it was Agatha who'd been on the other side of the lens, snapping the photo.

Agatha ran her thin, manicured fingers over the glass with the tenderness one uses to touch a cheek. "I saw his face so often that I never saw a need for pictures. Why look at something like this when you have the original? This is one of the very few that I took."

"I've never lost anyone. It must be very painful." In the hospital she'd seen family after family lose their loved ones, and they all had knots in their chests.

"It's hard. But we're committed to this never happening again. I wish we would've found someone like you first. If there were more people like you, we wouldn't have made them. We have you now." She rested her hand on Raleigh's shoulder. "I know that you want to become a doctor, and you will be good at it, potentially the best we'll ever have. However, I also need you to help right the wrong that was committed against these men. Will you help these souls find justice?"

In that moment, Raleigh understood the depth of the loss residing in Agatha. "I will try."

After leaving Agatha with her pictures, Raleigh wasn't sure she could be around the Receps. Guilt curdled in her stomach like milk in lemon tea. She'd gotten better at keeping the emotions from her face, but the Receps would sense her unease. She went back to her cottage and called her parents. Now that she was back in the states, she could use her cell phone without the camera, which was good because her mother had a way of seeing right through her. Luckily, Agatha didn't know her so well.

Her mother picked up on the first ring. *"Hello, Raleigh. How was the move in?"*

"Good. It's a great place, exactly like the brochure."

"I've been keeping track of your weather, and I hope you're wearing your sunscreen."

"I am. Usually I'm inside most of the day."

"Is there something wrong?" Even without seeing her daughter she could read volumes in the tone of her voice.

Raleigh was sick of lies, but she couldn't stop telling them. The truth, once lost, sunk deeper. "No. Grant and Able are great. I'm worried that I'm not going to live up to their expectations."

"What sort of expectations do they have?"

"College, becoming a doctor." That wasn't a lie, but it wasn't the thing that sat heavy on her.

"You're a very resilient young lady. I was very surprised when you said you were going to college, but I shouldn't have been. The ways you overcame your disease over the years is nothing short of remarkable. Each time you blacked out on your bike, I thought it would be the last time you rode it. All you did was put on more padding. That's the type of person you are Raleigh, the kind who perseveres. Those are the kind of people who make it in the world. Am I saying you're going to

be a doctor? I don't know, it's too soon to tell. A lot of Patrick's friends began on that path with him and quit. What I do know is that you will make something of your life. I have no doubt about that."

"How do I know I'm doing the right thing?" Raleigh wanted to tell her about Rho, the Designed, Agatha's dead family, and what she was being trained for. If her mother knew a word of it she'd be down in Arizona, instantly... right after she called the police.

"You've never been the type of person that struggles with these sorts of questions."

"I guess I am now."

"Well, don't be. You have a good gut. Use it. Now, your sister Thalia, she tends to have horrible instincts, and your brother Ben is too much of a risk taker. But you, you're cautious and considerate. You've got a great head on your shoulders."

"Thanks, Mom."

"Anytime, sweetie. Call back sometime when your sister is around. I don't think she's adjusting well to being the last kid left at home."

"I'll call."

"Take care. Don't forget to wear sunglasses. You don't want to end up with cataracts."

"Okay."

"Love you."

"Love you, too, bye." Raleigh hung up.

When she shut her eyes, she could see the pictures of the Receps that hung on Agatha's wall—boys who were innocent and now dead. She could imagine Rho near death just as easily. Grant and Able were wrong about him being a monster. It all would've been so much easier if Grant and Able had been as malevolent as she assumed they were. She closed herself in for the day, she couldn't risk any more emotional surprises.

CHAPTER
20

RALEIGH SAT BOLT upright in bed, the hairs on her arms bristling as her mind jolted her out of sleep. Someone rapped on her window. Was something wrong? She sensed a young, fit man. From the underlying tension in his muscles, her bet was on him being a Recep.

She slid out of bed and opened the curtains. "Adam?"

"Do you want to go for a run?"

She was shocked to see him. Could he honestly want to run when they had a day of training ahead of them? She checked the clock. It was six a.m. Was this some kind of hazing ritual?

"Do you want to go for a run?" Adam asked again.

"A run?"

"Yes. It's just like walking, except faster."

Adam really wanted to go running, with her. "All right. I'll meet you in front." Raleigh threw on the gym clothes she wore yesterday. They stunk of sweat, but they were what she had. She yawned as she tied up her hair, slipped on her shoes, and went out the front door.

"All right, let's go." He pointed to a side road that wound behind the labs and out into the desert landscape.

Between breaths, she managed to speak. "Aren't there snakes out here?" Gabe believed her when she told him she'd seen a snake, so it was a valid concern.

Adam's eyes widened. "I've never thought about it. But I've been out here before and never had a problem. A lot of guys run this trail, and no one's ever said they saw a snake. We'll keep our eyes open."

That was good enough for Raleigh. Adam had a strong heart and toned thighs. He could run much faster than her, but he held back. Raleigh's face flushed, her legs protested, and her heartbeat echoed in her ears. They'd been running for ten minutes. She knew because she'd checked her watch eight times.

"You'll get used to it." When he spoke, his breath didn't come out scratchy with exhaustion.

"Why are we doing this?"

"Because you're the weakest. There's no shame being in the ninety-sixth percentile."

"But there is." Raleigh slowed, unable to talk and run at that pace. "You have to sit at a separate table and people like Dustin call you ninety-sixth instead of your name. But you're right. There shouldn't be any shame in it, but why do you think I'm in the ninety-sixth?"

"That's just what we figured. Otherwise you would've told us."

"Okay, so you guys just made an assumption. Is that why they hate me?"

Adam shook out his shoulders delaying answering her right away. "There isn't much Lucidin to go around. There's talk that we might have to scale back soon."

"But you have two captured Designed, right? That's what Agatha said."

"Their Lucidin goes mostly to the medicine side of things. The guys don't want you here because another Recep means another person to dose. When I came, it was because the last guy broke his leg, so I got what he used to. There was a time when Receps dosed daily. It hasn't been that way for a while. In the field you get more, but you have to make it that far first. So, we wondered why you're here."

"Can we stop for a moment?"

Adam slowed to a walk. It was hard for Raleigh to come up with lies on the spot, and even harder when it was super-early, and she'd been running.

"The sky is gorgeous." She'd meant it as a distraction, but it was true. A pink and orange sunrise playfully picked apart the blue horizon.

"Do you know why you're along?"

"Same reason as you. I'm here to train."

"You're a girl."

"I have been for a while."

"You don't think that's weird?"

"Did you bring me on this run to interrogate me?" Exhausted, she didn't hide her agitation well.

"No. I brought you because you're going to have to train harder than the rest of us if you want to keep up. You're not starting with a strong foundation."

"Why do you care?"

"Second-newest guy looks out for the newest. I know how it is to fall in the ninety-seventh. It isn't much better than being in the ninety-sixth."

There it was.

Those at the top were arrogant assholes like Dustin, and the less able stuck together. Raleigh didn't know if the olive branch would extend beyond this, but it felt good to have a friend.

They ran for another half hour. Adam insisted that it would get easier. As they reached the complex, the sun happily started its trek across the sky, and the Arizona landscape prepared for its scorching embrace.

They made their way straight to the gym. There was no point in showering to get the ruddy dirt off their calves when they were just going to get dirtier. It was true that she would have to do additional work to keep up, but that didn't mean her muscles would comply. She ignored her discomfort as they joined the guys in the training room.

Testosterone and competitiveness thumped through the Receps, but only Raleigh could hear that anthem. They looked militant, like Gabe, but she felt the tumultuous need to win tugging at their veins. Today's training excited them.

"What are we doing?" Raleigh asked Adam.

"One-on-one challenges."

Gabe clapped his hands. "As you know, we're sending a team out in a month. Some of you will be ready, others won't. This is one of the many ways you can stand out." Gabe motioned to a large circle in the middle of the floor. "Your goal is to incapacitate your opponent. Dustin, Carlos, you're up first."

Raleigh raised her hand. "With influencing?"

Gabe shook his head. "Without it. It's safe to say the Designed will be able to break your barricade. Thus, it will be a game of brute strength."

Raleigh scrunched her nose. "But they'll win, won't they? I mean, they're big right?"

Dustin flexed his muscles. "We're big, too."

Raleigh rolled her eyes. Maybe *big* wasn't the right word. Strong was. Despite being drained nearly to death, Rho's muscles still had a strength none of these guys possessed. They wouldn't have been able to beat him even if it was four against one. "There will never be a fistfight because if it's hand-to-hand they'll influence and win," Raleigh whispered under her breath.

"We have an inhibitor," Adam told her quietly. "It keeps them from sensing and influencing. Didn't you learn about it in the labs?"

An inhibitor would rob the Designed of their advantage. The skin along her back prickled. "That's how you're holding the two imprisoned ones?"

"Yeah. How did you think?"

Raleigh didn't want to say anything that would reveal what she knew about Rho—or his imprisonment. She tried to undo the knot that was forming in her stomach. "Does the inhibitor stop their barricade?"

"No. That's why we'll have to fight them hand-to-hand."

Gabe's whistle sliced through their conversation. Adam turned his attention to Dustin and Carlos. They circled each other, waiting for the moment to strike. Carlos managed a few good hits, but Dustin took him down with a well-placed swipe to the legs. Gloating, Dustin stood over his opponent chest puffed up like a bird.

Gabe turned to Raleigh. "You ready to go?"

"Against who?" She'd lose to every one of these guys if she couldn't influence.

"Ninety-seventh here will take her," one of the guys whooped as he hit Adam on the back. "Or I can take her, but not in the ring."

Gabe shot the guy a look that was so severe it shut everyone up. Then he turned to Raleigh. "I'll go up against you, and we can do it over here, so we don't get comments like that." They moved into a corner. "Show me your stance."

Raleigh positioned her body the way she'd seen the guys in the circle do it. Gabe repositioned her arms.

"Hit me," he said.

Raleigh's fist flew past his jaw without making contact.

"How many fights have you been in?"

"None. Are we in some bad fifties' sitcom? People don't get in playground fights in real life."

"We don't send teams to playgrounds." He motioned for her to come at him again.

"Maybe if you didn't favor me, they wouldn't dislike me."

"Or you could tell them the truth about why you're here."

"If I tell them the only thing they'll care about is my Lucidin. I'm more than that. I don't want to end up sitting by the pool like Dale."

Gabe repositioned her arms again. Then he showed her how to adjust her weight as she threw a punch. "They'll respect you. That's why you're training. When we're out in the field, I'll pair you with some of the bigger guys. That way, if influencing is out, you'll have them."

Raleigh turned her attention to the guys in the circle. One of them gave her a wink. "They're assholes."

"There aren't many girls around. They've lost their manners. I'll talk to them again about not fraternizing."

"They just joke about being interested. Their bodies are more concerned with Lucidin than sex. Not having girls here because it would be a distraction doesn't hold water as an excuse."

"We don't usually train girls as Receps because we don't want them to get the shit kicked out of them by the Designed." Gabe made his point by taking her down with one fluid move.

Her back hit the mat hard, jarring the wind from her lungs. She coughed once and pushed herself back up.

"Did that make you angry? Come on, Raleigh. Show me what you got."

She went for him and he easily dodged her. "If I could influence, you'd be screwed."

"All right. Let's see it." Gabe secured his mental barricade and assumed his sparring position.

"You're barricading."

"Yeah. Can you break it?"

Raleigh pushed out her mind, trying to tease out any holes in his mental defenses. His barricade reminded her of a sheet of cardboard. Some of the other barricades were as flimsy as paper. She'd sensed those two days ago. Her own barricade was more like a brick wall. She sent the strongest signal to Gabe she could. Using the phone analogy to explain it, she'd say the ringer was set to deafening. In her head she screamed at him to listen and the barricade fell, giving way to her power.

Gabe's eyes grew wide, and the playful smile disappeared from his lips. She could feel a slight bounce in his feet as he bobbed away from her. He paused, and she threw a punch, cutting him across the cheek. It wasn't hard enough to repay him for flooring her.

Emotion flickered in his eye. Was it anger? She pushed up her barricade to be on the safe side. This wasn't like with Collin. She didn't need Rho to save her now, but instead of attacking her, Gabe grinned.

He walked over and placed a hand on each of her shoulders. "Good. Very good. You're amazing. After practice I'm going to take you to meet the intelligence crew. I want you to get involved with their work."

They returned to the group. The sparring increased their competitiveness. Fires simmered in their chests—from the fighting, the Lucidin, or both.

Dustin's eyes traversed between her and Gabe. His eyes darkened, and his mouth pressed into an angry line. She was going to have to keep her eye on him. Luckily, with his large size and thundering steps, he wouldn't be able to sneak up on her even if he barricaded.

Dustin squared off against Adam. With no influencing it was a relatively fair fight. A lot of the lower percentiles compensated with extra strength training, and Adam's morning runs made him quick. Dustin landed a blunt hit on Adam's shoulder, harder than necessary. Dustin's eyes darted to Raleigh. If he was going to target her friends, then she might have to put him in his place, but not today. Adam could hold his own for now.

The session wrapped up, and Raleigh left the gym. Despite the ache in her calves, her feet moved quickly in the direction of the locker room. The intelligence team sounded like a promising lead. It should help her find Mu and Tau. Stripping down quickly, she turned on the shower and scrubbed the smell of sweat and mud from her skin. There was no languishing under the water today.

As she put on the fresh black clothes, she considered Mu and Tau. If she did find them, would she be able to get them out? Would they be in the same weakened state as Rho? Or physically abused? Or on the inducer? The task felt insurmountable. Could she leave without them? Rho was angry that she'd defied him. If she returned empty-handed, he may withdraw the offer of running away. Even if they did run, it would probably be futile. With the inhibitor and the tenacity of Grant and Able, it seemed inevitable that the Designed would be caught. She didn't want to leave here just to be captured in a raid on the Designed. There was also the heavy thought that abandoning Grant and Able robbed her of the chance to become a doctor. There was no doubt in her mind that Mu and Tau deserved to be free, but so much good came out of the

Lucidin they provided the doctors. How many lives would be saved by forfeiting theirs?

Raleigh jogged out of the locker room.

"Hey Ninety-six!" a Recep named Felix said.

Whirling around, Raleigh found him close to her. Too close. She shoved his chest. Some of his testosterone must have rubbed off. "Do you know how dehumanizing that is?"

"Call me Ninety-Nine anytime you want."

"I'll keep that in mind, *Felix*. I've got to be going."

"Where are you running off to?"

Raleigh flipped her damp hair over her shoulder. "That isn't your business."

"It's to hang out with Gabe, isn't it? Are you sleeping with him? Is that why he's giving you preferential treatment?"

"No" Raleigh used her shoulder to push past him.

He turned and darted in front of her, preventing her from getting outside. "Because fraternization is against the rules. You know that, right? Even if Gabe might give you extra doses."

"I know." Raleigh took a step to the side. "I'm not with Gabe."

He still didn't move, but his sneer dissolved. "I wanted you to know that I've never been one for rules, and, well, I wouldn't mind breaking that one."

Raleigh stopped trying to skip around him and focused on his eyes, which were wide and questioning. It was clear that she'd misjudged. Felix clearly maintained his sex drive with or without the yearning for Lucidin.

"No."

"Think about it. A ninety-sixth could do much worse. That, and I could make sure some of the guys go easier on you."

"I won't need that."

"You know, a good Recep uses all the tools at their disposal.

Since you're lacking strength, you might think about what that means for you."

"Raleigh!" Gabe approached them his hands open. "I thought we were meeting out front."

Felix didn't scurry away, but he gave her a sly wink that Gabe didn't see before he turned and walked toward the main door.

"It's nice to see that not only the lower percentiles are talking to you now. Felix is one of the higher ones."

"I don't consider it talking when he's making a pass at me."

Gabe's face hardened. "He shouldn't have. I'll talk to him."

"Don't bother. I'm sure it's just another way for him to 'bolster the competition.'"

"You can't date any of them." Gabe furrowed his brow.

She wondered if he'd tell her about Gamma being assaulted on the island for his Lucidin. Raleigh couldn't say for sure that Gabe wasn't one of the attackers, but on second thought, she couldn't see it. Gabe was the type of guy who clung to morals and the notions of right and wrong.

"Promise me you won't date any of them."

"I won't." She didn't want to date any of the Receps. Thoughts of Collin filled her head. She pictured the way he looked at Rho, and they weren't sleeping together. No way. And none of them came close to Rho. The thought of never seeing him again produced an aching in her chest. "Felix accused me of getting extra doses from you."

Gabe rubbed his chin and looked at the gymnasium. "I've told the guys that we're going to need to start rationing. None of us like it, but the stockpiles are running out, and those in the field and the doctors need it more."

"But Dale, Quinn, and I have been giving."

"That and we have the two captured Designed, and Dale and Quinn are extracting three times a day. Still, it's going to be a much larger problem if we don't head it off now with rationing. It won't affect you."

"I could give three times."

"Honestly, the most helpful thing you could do would be to get the Designed. And to do that, you need to familiarize yourself with them. Let's go to Intelligence."

CHAPTER
21

GABE SWIPED HIS keycard to open the door of the squat cement Intelligence building. A burst of cold air drifted out of the antechamber. Additional security features in the form of an eye scanner and keypad awaited them. Whatever they kept in here, they didn't want very many people seeing. Gabe leveled his face with the narrow box in the corner of the antechamber. A flash lit up his eyes, and a beep changed the light over the door from red to green. Gabe turned to her. "Put your eye to that green screen. I'm going to register you with the system."

Obeying, she stepped forward, her eyes staring into the box. Her eyelid itched to close, fearful that it would be like the alarming puff of a glaucoma test. Thankfully, it was only a flash of dull light. Gabe typed in a series of commands on the nearby box.

"Put your index finger on the red dot," he said, pointing to a quarter-sized spot.

Raleigh pressed her finger against the light. She waited until it turned green, and the heavy door slid open. They stepped in, the dark interior a stark contrast to the Arizona sunshine outside. The door slid shut behind them, and the ominous lock clicked into place.

"What's all this security for? You aren't keeping the two captured Designed here, are you?" Surely, anyone would be curious about their whereabouts, not just a spy.

"No. They're on a boat in the ocean that docks occasionally for supplies and to drop off the Lucidin. They're on the inhibitor, so they aren't a danger to the crew. We assume that eventually the others will come to break them out. They're fiercely loyal to one another. This adds an extra level of difficulty for them."

Unfortunately, it added an extra level of difficulty for her, too—perhaps insurmountable. Her chest tightened. There was a good chance that she would never get the opportunity. If so, her mission here was an utter failure. She inhaled, willing away the frustration, she had to mask her emotions around Gabe. "That's very clever."

"The security here is to protect our information. We keep track of the synthetic trade and the Designed. We can't risk having just anyone see it. I know it's a lot of cloaks and daggers, but most of the people in here are geeks."

It was true. The fluorescent and natural light revealed computers lining the walls. Intelligent-seeming men and women hunched over the keyboards. Trevor would've been at home here. The stale air slipped into her lungs leaving a metallic taste in her mouth, the static kind that reminded her of the computer banks back at school. Back pains ailed the programmers who had sat too long. These were the folks she'd sensed when she was snooping. None of them looked up, or seemed to care, that she and Gabe were there.

A gigantic four-by-three electronic grid caught her attention. Each column had a Designed triplet set with green, blue, or red backlighting. The first of the four columns was Sigma's. Sigma, distinguished by his lack of smile and small symbol, sat above Rho's grinning picture. Both were backlit in red. Underneath Rho was their third triplet, Pi. His square was dimmed. The next column was the Psi, Kappa, Mu triplet. Psi in red, Kappa backlit in green, and Mu in blue. The remaining triplet trios occupied the last two columns.

Gabe pointed to the board. "Red means that we kill them on sight, green means we capture them, and blue means they're already taken. The images that aren't lit are dead. When we started, all of them were lit up. The synthetic dealers are doing some of the work for us."

The red border around Rho made her squirm. Kappa, at least, was in green. Psi, Sigma's right-hand man, was red like Rho. Personality-wise Psi and Kappa were different, but physically they were replicas. "How can you tell Kappa apart from Psi?"

"They each wear a necklace with their symbol. If you aren't sure, then err on the side of caution."

"You mean kill them?"

"You're making the mistake of thinking they're human. They look it, but they aren't." Gabe went to a nearby computer, typed in his password, and pulled up a video.

The grainy quality of the video made it hard to discern details. Raleigh moved closer to the monitor to see better. On the screen, scientists, very similar to the ones she'd met in the lab yesterday, were at their stations. They clawed at their necks and clutched their chests. Their faces contorted in pain, their mouths open. She didn't need the sound to know the depths of their agony. One by one they crumpled to the ground. The twelve Designed passed through the lab leaving a trail of death in their wake. Sigma led the grim march—the way he mercilessly walked past the bodies, it had to be him. These weren't peaceful deaths. They were vicious and not necessary.

"Why kill the scientists?" She wanted to look away but her eyes fixed in place. The Receps, who held them prisoner, she could understand fighting in self-defense, but this was the murder of defenseless workers.

"They didn't want them to continue their work on Lucidin. They set fire to the building. Those that were injured burned to death. The ones that died before the fire were lucky."

"And Agatha's husband?"

"Is one of them."

"And it was all the Designed?"

"Count them up if you want. There are twelve."

Raleigh tried to tell their faces apart. Xi, Gamma, and Upsilon, with their black skin, stood out from the other nine. One with dark hair, she guessed was Rho, checked bodies before he ran over and grabbed Sigma. Arms flew in a heated exchange, but the killings didn't stop. This couldn't have been a plan Rho agreed to. But how could he not have known Sigma would do it? Once it started, he could've fought his brothers, he could've stopped the killings. The weight of those deaths hung on all twelve of them. And it wasn't in self-defense—as she'd been led to believe.

Raleigh's stomach flipped, and her mouth dried. She was on the wrong side of things. Gabe was right about them being monsters.

"I don't need to see anymore." She turned her face from the screen unable to stomach it.

Respecting her wishes, he turned it off. "Let's talk about something else."

They hadn't really talked about the Designed. They didn't need to. The video spoke volumes. A jolt of regret shot down her spine. It had been wrong to trust them. She'd known Rho for what, a week or two? The joke was that he was charismatic, but his looks alone would've been enough to sway her. Raleigh wasn't the type of girl who fell prey to that, at least she thought she wasn't. But now, as she examined her feelings closely, how many times had she thought about him since coming here? The answer was a lot. She was smitten, and that clouded her judgment.

A fire rose in her belly as she clenched her jaw. She could tell Gabe about the home in California, and he and the Receps could be there with the inhibitor in hours. No, she couldn't do that. Rho and Kappa didn't deserve to be killed and captured. Sigma had led the massacre, they'd just failed to stop it. She couldn't see any way to give Sigma to Gabe without all the others. So, it had to be none.

Yesterday she'd come to the realization that staying with Grant and Able would help her become a doctor. Not only a doctor, a savior to all the sick who'd lost hope—like her before treatment. Today she saw the error of the Designed. Even if some of them weren't bad, a few were wicked.

"It's really upsetting," Gabe hovered over her shoulder, but didn't touch her. "Do you want to talk about it? Are you ready to see some of our intelligence?"

"Show me." If she was going to be a Recep, she might as well know everything.

He led her to a table with a large monitor displaying a map of the world. "This is a map of the Lucidin trade, or as much as we know about it anyway. It's called Lucid on the streets." Gabe twisted his finger over Europe, causing that portion of the map to expand across the whole screen. Bright dots, with small pictures next to them, covered the map. He slid his finger over a dot and pulled up the information about that particular dealer. Raleigh's eyes quickly scanned for Brent's name. He wasn't there, but Marcel was.

"There are two or three synthetics out there. Most of them are worse quality than the one we make. The market is odd. Since Lucidin isn't a street drug, it doesn't have the same laws associated with it. That's to their advantage. Their main problem is that so few people use it. Anyone can get high off heroin, but only a handful of people can sense on Lucidin. Because of that, the cliental is different for Lucidin than other drugs. The goal with most drugs is to get high, but with Lucidin, it's to have more power. They make some back-alley deals, but most of it's done in broad daylight with people who can afford to take it regularly. Once they get a client, they have them for a while."

"Do the clients become addicted?"

"With the synthetic there is more of a pull, but I still wouldn't use that word. Sometimes, after long use, there can be a minor withdrawal. I'd classify it as minor addiction."

Raleigh bottled up her outrage. If Gabe didn't consider his own addiction anything other than a preference for the drug, he was in no position to be calling what these people had minor. Dressed in his militant gear, it was tempting to label him as a collected, orderly man. But she knew otherwise. He might not pace holes in the floorboards like Collin, but inside he was as much of a powder keg.

"Will I be learning about the Lucidin market?"

"No, not yet. You'll have to familiarize yourself with it because the Designed sell their stuff on the market. Their trade is represented by the turquoise lines."

Raleigh traced the paths of the turquoise and yellow lines. Some dealers had duel lines coming from them but not Marcel. The yellow wove across the board in thick lines while the turquoise ones were thin.

Gabe turned toward a computer. "Before we can have you jumping in, you need to read about the Designed. I'm sorry, it's troubling reading, especially when you put it in context. Many of the adoptive parents loved their Designed sons. Some of the things they reported were red flags for the type of evil they would become, but they were largely overlooked. Grant and Able have to shoulder the blame on that as well. Everyone wanted to assume they were good. It's a human thing to do, assume people are good at heart. They simply forgot that these boys don't have hearts."

"Men, they're men now." The video changed her perception of them. The men that had sat around that table in California weren't boys. "Using the term boy makes them seem innocent in a way they can't be. Not after what they did."

"They were boys at the time of the accounts." Gabe grabbed a chair and set her up on the computer. "You don't have a password yet, but you don't need it to read up on them. You will need one to have access to the intelligence, but we'll get to that in time."

Raleigh scrolled to the twelve files. Their history. Gabe opened Sigma's file, as if to drive home his point about the Designed. Then he stepped back, letting her read.

The first few documents read like a lab book. There were observations, comparisons between normal development, and findings. It was clear that while Agatha and the others were changing diapers, they were also collecting a lot of data and testing the infants every day for things like motor development, eye tracking, and, eventually, speech. Some notes compared the brothers. Developmentally, they were all well ahead of the normal population.

By the time Sigma went to live with his adoptive family in Nebraska, he was already recognized as a prodigy. His adoptive mother took up recording his progress, and her notes weren't as thorough as the scientists'. They contained a lot of emotion, claiming he was "adorable" and a "special little guy." Sometimes she slipped and wrote his nickname—Siggy. Funny, when Rho said he didn't have parents, Raleigh'd had a hard time wrapping her mind around it. Now, even with proof that Sigma had been adopted, she couldn't believe it.

Red flags began to pop up by the time Sigma was in grade school. His mother wrote that she felt bad for her son because he was clearly superior to the other children. This remained the case even after he was sent to the best school. There were accounts of how he tormented the other children, because he was frustrated that "his intelligence didn't have an outlet." Everyone justified his actions. The only time his mother didn't give Sigma the benefit of the doubt was when he picked on his younger sister, who was his parents' biological child. The mother lamented that it was unfair to his sister to be in his shadow. By the time he was a teenager and shipped off to the island, it was clear that he was the Sigma that Raleigh had met.

Raleigh became so engrossed in the reading that Gabe had to repeat himself twice when he interrupted her. "It's time for dinner."

Rho's file sat further down the screen, and Raleigh very much wanted to read it. She wanted to know what his relationship with Sigma was like before they were forced into hiding. She reluctantly slid back from the computer. She could see why G and A called the Designed monsters—at least one of them was.

"I can't eat right now." Raleigh rubbed a hand across her knotted stomach as they left. The video killed her appetite.

"Take a rest then."

Raleigh separated from Gabe, heading towards her cottage. Her mind replayed the video of the island. She had a lot to consider.

LATER, WHEN RALEIGH went to extract, she found only Dale in the room.

"You skipped dinner," he said.

"I saw the video of the massacre." Raleigh sat down and tore off her sweatband. "It was upsetting. I wanted to have some time alone after that."

"Yeah, the Designed are screwed up. They should've made us Modified from the start."

"Do you think it's fair what they've done to you?" If Rho didn't like being used for his Lucidin, how did Dale and Quinn feel?

Dale snorted. "I don't think they did it to be malicious. They need this medicine, and this was how they chose to make it. It's not like they hurt me in any way. And the Designed were given gifts. Beauty. Smarts. They owe Grant and Able."

Raleigh wondered if Dale was infertile. Would he feel the same way if Grant and Able had taken that from him? If they did it to the Designed, then they almost certainly did it to the Modified. They'd want to control who had the drug and how much. It was too bad that the lab brains didn't work yet, or that they hadn't been developed years ago.

Dale leaned back in his chair, the vial in his machine almost full. "I believe in the work Quinn and I are doing here. It's true, I wish that I would've worked in the lab when I first got here. Since you've been here, I fit in better. I guess I needed a push to get involved."

Either that, or they needed a push to involve him. She wondered how accepted he'd be when she entered the field. It would be good if he had someone to make sure he was included when she left.

"Well, I guess you could come running with Adam and me tomorrow. How's that for a push?"

Dale laughed. "No way. That's your problem."

"You should get to know the guys. I'm not going to be here forever. Gabe's already training me for the field, one day I'll be gone."

Running his fingers over his gut he grimaced. "I'm not in great shape. Adam will hate that you invited me."

"No, he won't."

"I guess it would be awesome to go home all ripped."

She wondered if he would ever go home. Would he be so forgiving of G and A if he were trapped? Were the Modified really here for their safety? Or was it because they needed the Lucidin. Either way, they were here for the long haul, and it would be a long time before Dale saw his folks.

"Come running." She wanted to make sure he'd be well taken care of when she was gone. Then she could work on expanding his freedom.

CHAPTER
22

ONE MONTH LATER

DALE COLLAPSED AGAINST the dormitory building. He took
heavy breaths as he rested his head against the wall and stretched
his legs out in the dirt. "Am I ever going to feel like I'm not going
to die after a run?"

Raleigh plopped down next to him, the orange desert dirt plastered to her skin with perspiration. She wiped her brow with the
back of her hand and licked her dry lips, tasting the salty sweat.

It'd been a month since they began running. At first, they took
brisk walks. Now they dashed down the trail, their improvement
evident in their physical transformations. Dale's legs didn't exhaust
like they used to, and muscles appeared on Raleigh's thin body. Dale
was still on the heavy side, but his face had thinned. He looked older,
part of that might have been his newfound sense of confidence.

Raleigh's body wasn't the only thing that changed. The relationships she formed with Adam and the other Receps had strength-
ened. In her spare time, they did extra training, played cards, and

swapped stories of home. Over the last few weeks, the Receps had started referring to her as a Recep, and so did she.

"You're both doing well." Adam's shadow blocked out the sunlight as he stood over them. With his hands on his hips, he nodded his head. Their success was his. Gabe had mentioned that Adam might make a good instructor, and that comment prodded Adam to push them harder.

Dale lifted himself from the ground, dusting his hands against his shorts. "Thanks, Adam, I should get back and extract."

Raleigh wanted to stay tethered to the ground, but a full day lay ahead, and she'd rather not stink for all of it. "I need to clean up."

"See you in training." Adam waved and then stopped. "Hey, Dale, you should come, too."

"No way. Having you two watch me run is bad enough."

"We only practice with Lucidin part of the time since the rationing," said Adam. "Most of the time we do sports and team building. You should come along."

Raleigh's stomach tightened. Dale with the Receps? "Did you clear that with Gabe?"

Adam shrugged. "He won't care. It'll be fun. The guys respect Dale and what he does for them. They aren't going to tease him the same way they do us lower Receps. Dale, haven't you been complaining about how boring the labs are?"

Dale had been vocal about the tedious work. Once the initial creepiness of the brains wore off, he was a little bored. "Okay, why not? What should I wear?"

"I'll find you some clothes." Adam patted Dale on the back.

Raleigh followed Dale to the main building, she considered how much happier he was than when they met. Still, she didn't like the idea of him training. "Dale, I think this is a bad idea."

"Aren't you the one who wanted me to make friends with them?

You insisted on it, we've been running for a month, and now you're telling me not to? They've all been really nice, not inclusive until you came, but nice."

The Receps trained with Lucidin every third day, and Raleigh felt a nervous shift in them. The competition was downright brutal at times. Dustin pummeled her during a touch football game, and she had a large black-and-blue bruise on her hip as proof.

"The rationing is hitting them hard," she said.

"That's not my fault. I've upped my extractions to three a day."

"It isn't going to be enough."

"No, but it's a start. Soon you'll be out in the field getting us another Designed."

Gabe scheduled Raleigh to go out in two weeks. Her official mission would be assigned after a benefactors' dinner in Virginia later in the week. She couldn't believe how fast the last month had flown by. Life here had become routine. Dale and Adam were her friends, and she was happy.

Mu and Tau remained hidden, and she would never find them. That was clear. Information about the boat remained highly guarded, and Gabe didn't seem to know any more about it than she did. Going back to Rho seemed foolish. Even if he still wanted to run and hide, he'd eventually be caught. She registered for school in the spring. College and life as a doctor were on the horizon. All she had to do was repress the uneasy feeling she had thinking that some of the good Designed would be captured. There were good Designed. The files showed that not all of them were as cruel as Sigma. Gabe and the others realized it, too. That's why there was a capture list.

Trevor had texted her two weeks ago with updates. She'd stared at his vague message for a long time. She wanted to inform him that she'd sided with Grant and Able and to assure him that she wouldn't give them Rho. Instead, she told him she'd made no progress. If she'd never met Sabine and had just gone to Grant and Able in the first place, she wouldn't have her guilt about Rho. She dreamed of him every night. Sometimes Gabe killed him. Other times she helped him escape.

"You worry too much." Dale punched her shoulder. "So, I can see you in training?"

"Just wait until the Lucidin isn't rationed. The Receps are too unsettled."

Part of her wondered if the Receps's edge was due to her Lucidin. They cut Dale's with the synthetic and hers. Some of the Receps mentioned that the hit was a little different. They assumed, wrongly, that it was an adjustment to the synthetic. Brent's comment about addicts preferring her Lucid echoed in her mind, making her cringe. She should've asked Brent if he thought hers would be more addicting.

"It doesn't matter to me if they're unsettled."

"I don't like that they're dependent on you."

Dale scrunched his nose. "Is that why you still haven't told them that you extract?"

"That, and I'm worried that they'll be upset that I'm not affected by rationing. It's made all of them cranky. It's bad enough that Gabe favors me and that I'm going out into the field so quickly. Knowing that I extract would just make them hate me more."

"I guess it's too late now. It's the kind of thing you should've told them from the start."

They ducked into the extraction room and started making their donations. Quinn was there, and he went on about one of his online groups. Raleigh hadn't helped him the way she had Dale. Not that Quinn seemed upset. Raleigh listened to him prattle on for the duration of her extraction.

Returning to her cottage, she hopped in the shower and

washed the grime from her hair. She didn't usually shower after a run on training days, but today she felt too filthy not to. Fortunately, she wasn't a prim girl. Being surrounded by guys brought out her tomboy side, which she liked. More than once she'd considered lopping off all her hair. Instead, it lived in a ponytail.

When she arrived at the cafeteria, she found a long line. Oatmeal was her go-to breakfast these days, and she had her eyes on the raisins at the back of the case.

"You dosed up again." Dustin grabbed Brandon's bicep. They were two people ahead of her in line.

Brandon was in the ninety-seventh percentile, which meant that he often ate with Adam. Recently, he'd done better in training, making Gabe take notice.

That made ninety-niners like Dustin wary.

Brandon tugged his arm free. "No, I haven't."

Raleigh couldn't help overhearing them, but she didn't want to get involved in the politics around rationing. Dustin, and some of the others preparing to go into the field, had insisted that they deserved to get more Lucidin in training.

"Then how come you're always so calm?" asked Dustin.

Everyone noticed the increase in ticks and fidgeting. She remembered that Collin could never sit still, and the rationing made the Receps behave the same. Over the last two weeks some of the guys had bitten their nails down so short that their fingers bled. Others bounced on the balls of their feet, as if preparing for an unseen tennis match. One of the guys, Carter, liked to crack his knuckles. Gabe had told them all to scale it back. Otherwise, the small quirks were accepted as a part of life.

"I didn't." Brandon grabbed his tray and plowed ahead.

Brandon lied. Dustin was right. The unrest that seemed to plague the lot of them didn't affect Brandon.

"You and the girl are getting hits on the side because you're some of Gabe's favorites," Dustin yelled after him.

The last thing Raleigh needed was for him to know that she was a source of Lucid. Let them draw their own conclusions. Some of them thought it was because she was a girl, and others assumed that Gabe was playing favorites. None of them had confronted her. Raleigh was curious though—if Gabe hadn't given him any extra— why was he holding up better? Maybe he made a small amount himself and that soothed his need?

All of it made Raleigh wish that Dale wasn't going to training. The Receps weren't in the best state of mind. She collected her raisins and oatmeal, then searched the tables for Dale. She didn't see him, so she ate with Adam.

CHAPTER
23

RALEIGH HEADED TO the gym. She couldn't decide if it was a good or bad thing that it was a ration day. If they didn't dose, Dale would be on level ground. But with the dose, the Receps were kinder.

As Raleigh entered the meditation room, she could feel the relief the Lucidin brought them. She wondered how the healers were holding up. They didn't have the same competitive atmosphere, or testosterone fueling their cravings. They also weren't forced to scale back. Raleigh'd met them over the phone so she couldn't sense how Lucidin affected their bodies. She hoped that this was a temporary problem.

"Raleigh." Gabe signaled her over when the meditation ended. Gabe had already taught her everything he could about Lucidin. She now served as a dummy for others to practice on. She also helped Gabe ascertain who needed to work on what. "Did you invite Dale to training?"

"No. Adam did. I think it's a mistake."

"You couldn't talk him out of it?"

"Nope. Are you going to tell him no?"

Gabe shook his head. "You know how important the Modified are. Dale and Quinn are a vital aspect of our team, even if all they do is provide Lucidin. Agatha's worried that he'll slip back into the slump he was in before you arrived. She thinks it's a good idea for him to be more involved."

"That's because she doesn't realize how restless the Receps have become since the rationing. Do you still think that they aren't addicted?" It was a brazen thing to say. As a mole, she never would've made waves like this. But as a Recep it was her duty. Her commitment to G and A had formed, and now she had to do her best to make it a moral company.

"This isn't the time to discuss it."

"It never is."

"How well do you think Dale will do today?"

"He's becoming more confident, which is good. Tell the guys to go easy on him."

"I don't think that will help. I'm sure they'll behave. The problem is more about him not keeping up down the road."

"At least we won't have to worry about it today. Maybe we can find a sport he's good at." Raleigh considered asking Adam to scrimmage them in basketball some mornings.

They followed the others to the basketball courts. Their bodies reveled because of the Lucid. The drug whispered through them, easing the constant yearning they had in its absence. Bittersweet, they knew that tomorrow they wouldn't get Lucidin, and their bodies braced for it.

Dale arrived dressed in Recep black. He sheepishly waved to them as he approached. A nervous flutter filled his stomach.

Raleigh hoped that they'd be playing basketball—because Dale was fairly tall. No. There were ten green balls on the half-court line. Dodgeball. She'd seen the tail end of a game a week ago. It conjured up fun memories of playing in the field behind their development complex when she was younger. The game rewarded agility and aim rather than height and size. She might have a good chance, but Dale was going to be at a disadvantage. The rubber from the balls gave the room a whiff of elementary school. Squeaking sneakers drove the memory home.

Gabe straddled the center line with a foot planted on each side. "Hunter, Dustin, you're team captains."

Hunter, a quiet kid in the ninety-eighth percentile, didn't waste any time. "Carlos."

Dustin gave him a sneer. "Isaac."

"Adam." Hunter gave Adam a fist bump as he came over.

From the first picks it was clear what the stratagems were. Carlos was a shorter, slim guy. Adam, too, was on the slender side. When Raleigh was picked, it was obvious that Hunter was going for hard-to-hit targets. Dustin, on the other hand, chose the beefier guys, hoping for strong throwers. It surprised no one.

"Don't leave Dale last," Adam whispered to Hunter when it got down to the last two.

Hunter glanced over his shoulder at Adam. Reluctantly he turned back. "Dale."

Raleigh could tell that Dale knew he would've been selected last. Instead of showing any sign of disgrace, he jogged over and nodded his head to the team. "This is going to be fun."

Hunter gave a short head bob back. "We should be faster than them. Our best chance at winning is to take the first shots, so get to the middle and get there fast. Try not to get hit, or it's going to hurt."

Gabe's whistle sliced the air silencing them. "Listen up! You should all know the rules, but I'll recap. If you hit someone with a ball, they're out. If they catch it, you're out. Stay on your side of the court. Good luck!"

The teams backed up to the free throw lines, their attention focused on the ten balls. Raleigh sensed the muscles in their legs tighten, like springs ready to be sprung. Their ears waited for Gabe to signal to start, not wanting to waste a precious second. Gabe let the whistle hang on the rim of his thin lips, prolonging the wait until it was uncomfortable. The shrill whistle sounded, and everyone took off for the middle. All the morning runs with Adam paid off. Echoing squeaks of sneakers filled the air as twenty-two players shot toward the balls.

Raleigh lunged through the air, catching a ball. The guy across the way, realizing he'd been beat, retreated. Raleigh, too, scuttled back, knowing from enough elementary school games that the middle was not the place to be. She lobbed the ball and it touched the foot of her opponent.

"Isaac, you're out!" Gabe yelled.

As soon as Isaac left the court, one of the green balls hit her arm with enough force to propel her backward. Hands out, she braced her fall. Pain shot up her wrists and jolted her arms. Getting up, her face flushed in anger.

"Raleigh, you're out!" Gabe didn't show her sympathy, over the past month he'd learned to let her hold her own. She was one of them now. He showed her the indifference he showed the rest.

Raleigh rubbed her shoulder, noticing Dustin smiling across the way. This had the promise of matching the bruise he'd given her on her hip last week. Jealousy hung ugly on him. Raleigh used her Lucidin to numb her own pain, denying him the satisfaction. She rarely barricaded because she didn't want them to know how powerful she was.

The first round ended soon enough. Her side lost. But there

was little time to coddle their egos as they were once again out on the court. The second game was similar to the first, with the exception of Raleigh's shot falling short and Dustin hitting her in the leg. This time she left the game with a welt on her thigh and a fire in her belly.

"Next time, don't go for the center," Hunter ordered her. "Dustin is gunning for you, and you'll stay in longer if we get him out first. Hang back."

Raleigh didn't want to be benched, which this felt like. All month Dustin had targeted her. He was an immature bully, and she had grown tired of him.

Dale, winded, stood next to her. "Dustin's a jerk."

"I don't think anyone here's going to argue with you." Raleigh focused on Dustin across the way.

At the start of the next game, Raleigh crouched down in a sprinter's pose, like the others. The whistle sounded but Raleigh moved back, planting her legs apart and readying her hands. If a ball came her way, she was going to catch it regardless of how hard it came at her.

As the others shot to the middle, Dale, just shy of getting a ball, retreated. Even with Adam's help, he wasn't up to snuff. But Raleigh admired how he tried anyway. Running back, Dale's legs stopped, the muscles no longer under his control. Across the way, Dustin gripped a ball tightly in his hands. He breathed slowly, a telltale sign of influencing.

"Dustin's influencing." She waved her arms over her head to get Gabe's attention.

Gabe didn't take her side. "It's not against the rules."

The ball hit Dale in the shoulder, and he fell over like a statue. Dustin laughed, and Raleigh fumed.

"Dale, you're out!" Gabe shouted, his face filled with indecision. It was unfair that Dale couldn't retaliate. At the same time, the point of this exercise was to hone skills.

Raleigh marched forward. "Screw this! You think you're tough? Picking on someone who can't influence, you lowly ninety-nine?"

Dustin grinned.

Seething, Raleigh threw up her barricade and froze Dustin's entire team. Using the phone analogy, it was a conference call, and she was in charge. Their side stood inanimate. Raleigh grabbed a ball and ran to the middle. She slammed the ball into Dustin's gut, knocking the air out of him. Then she prevented him from doubling over.

"Dustin out!" A smile glimmered in Gabe's words. From the first day, this was what he'd wanted.

Raleigh grabbed another ball and turned to her teammates. "Are you going to help me?"

They stood silent, fear of her written in their expressions. Raleigh's abilities dwarfed theirs.

Adam picked up a ball. "Yeah, we'll help."

One by one, they took out their opponents.

Gabe was entertained. "A win for Hunter's team. No more influencing. Raleigh, release them."

Raleigh gave Dustin a wicked smirk before letting them go. Then she turned to Dale who whooped loudly on the sideline. Half the guys cheered, the other half unsure of what a display like that meant. Gabe could only influence one of them at a time. This wasn't as grisly a demonstration as the Designed had given on the island, but all of them understood the power she had.

Dale patted Raleigh on the back, and Dustin ran across the line, plowing into her. They landed on the ground together, her head hitting the floor with a smack. Dazed, she righted herself a moment before his fist connected with her cheek. Pain erupted across her eye.

"Dustin!" Gabe shouted.

Dustin barricaded, and it was pretty strong, but Raleigh pushed through it like a bullet through paper. She halted his arm as it wound back for another blow. His weight pinned her, and she didn't doubt that the moment she let his arm go it would be connecting with her face. Her best chance was to incapacitate him. Focusing, she could feel the smallest part of his lungs, his bronchioles, hungrily taking up oxygen. She stopped them with little prompting. Dustin's good arm grasped at his neck, as if that was going to do anything.

"Raleigh! You'll kill him!" Gabe yanked Dustin, who turned purple, off of her.

She stood up, watching Dustin flounder on the floor. Rho was right. Some people didn't deserve Lucidin, and Dustin was one of them. She released him, and he sucked down the air in gulps. Coughing, Dustin got his color back.

"She's been training outside of us," one of the guys said. "She's been getting extra doses like Brandon!"

"I don't need doses." Raleigh tore the sweatband from her arm to display her port. "I extract twice a day."

Silence permeated the room, everyone speechless but Gabe. "Dustin, next time, I won't stop her."

"You didn't *make me* stop." The adrenaline wracked Raleigh.

Gabe pointed to the door. "Raleigh, let's get that eye fixed. You're each down a player. Captains are now refs. No influencing. We'll be back."

Gabe walked with Raleigh to the makeshift infirmary. She hopped onto one of the tables, and Gabe pulled a cold compress from the freezer. He wrapped it in a towel and pressed it against her temple.

He asked, "Is this your first black eye?"

"Of course, it is."

"Well, It's going to be swollen shut for a few days. Then it will go down."

"Dustin's an ass."

"His behavior is unacceptable." Gabe's hands cradled her face, his mind elsewhere.

The goofy look wasn't romantic. He'd never given any indication of liking her like that. Awkwardness still crept up her spine. She took the compress. "I can hold it."

Gabe stepped back quickly, leaving a good distance between them. "I'm going to suspend him for a week. I knew they'd discover what you're capable of. But I certainly didn't think it would come out like this. You're as good as them, Raleigh."

"I'm way better."

"I don't mean the Receps. The Designed. Back there, freezing them all, that was something they'd be able to do. You're ready to go out. You're ready to face them. I'm going to get you into the field and let you head the team. You can take Adam if you want."

"I have the benefactors' dinner."

"After that. Next week."

She was ready for the field, the goal of all this training. Like Gabe, she could be a leader. Better than that, she could be the Recep to follow. Screw their percentiles. She set a new precedent. She would get Sigma, and she would make sure Rho could hide.

CHAPTER
24

RALEIGH RETURNED TO her cottage with an icepack clutched to her eye. It swelled and throbbed with pain. Prodding the skin, she wondered if this made her tougher or weaker. Maybe in addition to running, she could practice boxing in the mornings before training, not that she was going to be training much longer.

After giving her parents a call, she decided to eat dinner in her room. When she headed out for her evening extraction, she made sure no one saw her.

"It's all true!" Quinn marveled at her eye. "Does it hurt?"

"What do you think?" Raleigh sat down and attached herself to the extraction machine.

"Makes you wonder if the Receps aren't the ones we should be worried about."

"That's what I've been saying." Or at least that's what she'd been thinking since the rationing.

"They say it still isn't safe for us to go home."

"Do you really want to go home because of this? I'm sure you're not in any danger."

Quinn lifted up his chin. "I'm going to be an uncle."

Raleigh didn't expect to hear that. Quinn rarely discussed anything besides his online gaming. The impression he gave her was that he'd floundered back home and Grant and Able was a welcome relief—a job he could do without really doing anything. Unlike Dale, he didn't want to work in the labs.

"An uncle?"

"I'm much younger than my sister. She's thirty and will be giving birth in a few months. My parents had an easy time getting pregnant with her, but it took years of trying to have me. They had to do IVF." Of course they had, that's how the scientists had access to Quinn's embryo in the first place, to make the modifications. "My sister also had issues, but she's having a healthy baby as far as they can tell. I want to meet it. Agatha said it's going to be tough. But she might let me go as long as I take a bunch of Receps."

"Better safe than sorry."

"Yeah, but I want to go home and help now. My sister's on bed rest. Do you know much about that?"

"No, sorry."

"Anyhow, Agatha said that I could see the baby, but she can't spare me before it's born. My sister could really use the help, and my online courses would be fine to take from home. But I guess that doesn't matter."

Things here suddenly didn't seem so good to Quinn. It was inevitable. Raleigh said, "I'm sorry that you can't go home."

"You've got to catch the Designed quickly." Quinn frowned at his arm port.

Raleigh didn't have the heart to tell him it was unlikely that the Designed would be caught anytime soon. Even if they were, the synthetic sellers would remain a threat. They knew about the Designed, and they'd probably find out about the Modified, if they didn't already know. Defusing that threat would be a challenge. The large board in the intelligence room with the faces and names of the Designed came to Raleigh's mind. She knew Quinn wasn't going to be a part of his niece's or nephew's life until they were much older.

"Is it a boy or a girl?" she asked.

"She wants it to be a surprise. But my mom said she thinks it's a boy, from the ultrasound."

"Congratulations."

"Gabe is taking me into Phoenix tomorrow to pick out a baby outfit as a gift."

"Sounds fun." Raleigh couldn't picture tough Gabe wading through tiny baby clothes. But she knew he was the best person to handle any danger that might arise.

Quinn finished extracting and unhooked himself from the machine. He gave Raleigh a smile as he left holding the door open for Dale, who had just arrived.

Dale rushed over, crouching down to see her face. "Your eye looks horrible! Is that why you missed dinner?"

"Yeah, and I wanted to call home when my sister would be around. I also wanted to avoid all the gossip—well, as much as possible, anyway."

"There's a lot of talk. I've been swamped by the Receps asking questions. Thanks for letting me field those." He sat down in the chair beside her and began his extraction. "They wanted me to sit with them at dinner."

"Which table?"

"I had my pick, zero receptors and all. I guess I'm one of the cool kids now."

"Good for you."

"They all wanted to discuss you, but I was bit tired of it, so I just sat with Quinn."

"Sorry."

"It's fine. I'm glad I was at the famous dodgeball game to see everything for myself. You didn't need to stand up for me. But thanks."

"I wasn't doing it for you. Did you see what Dustin did to my arm and leg?"

Dale smirked. "Now he's scared of you. They all are... a little."

"I'm going out in the field in a week. After today, there's no question. Gabe even offered to let Adam go with me."

The corner of Dale's mouth dipped into a frown. "I'm going to miss you."

"Did you hear that Quinn's going to be an uncle?"

"Did you here that they aren't letting him go home? Maybe once the baby gets out, but it sounds like that will only be for a weekend visit. His sister needs help now."

"I'm sure she'll manage. A lot of people do fine without the help of their little brother. I can't picture Quinn being very good with babies."

"The point is that he can't leave."

"I know. It sounds like you two are going to be here for the long haul."

"If the Designed can do what you did today, the Receps don't stand a chance."

"You're forgetting about the inhibitor."

Dale threw up his arm that wasn't attached to the extraction machine. "Raleigh, we could be here for years. That's if we're lucky. What kind of plan is that? They should've left us at home or explained to us that we'd be signing on for a long time. I thought it would be a year, maybe two. Not forever."

"You could still go home, it just wouldn't be as safe."

"Quinn said he'd risk it and Agatha said no. We're stuck here, Raleigh. I hope you do a good job out in the field."

It was possible that the Designed would never be caught. Rho and the others had strong networks. Yes, G and A were training Receps and developing the inhibitor, but the Designed weren't waiting to be caught. Who knows, if she failed to come back, maybe they'd send in another mole.

Raleigh could tell Agatha about Sigma's house. She knew enough to direct them to the general locale, within about a block. Most of the Designed still hid there, waiting for Raleigh to sound the alarm, and so they could rescue Mu and Tau. Maybe with Sigma and a few of the others gone, G and A would be able to relax a little. The problem was there was no way to get Rho and Kappa out without letting everyone know something was up.

Dale squinted at her. "What are you thinking?"

"Nothing. It's just that there are eight Designed out there. Even if we catch one or two a year, it'll take five to ten years to get them all. That's a substantial chunk of your life."

The number walloped Dale, his mouth flapping open. "Raleigh, I don't know what I'm going to do."

"I'm not sure there's a lot you can do."

Frustrated, Dale pounded his head against the soft leather of the chair three times. How much of him staying was for safety versus G and A's growing need for Lucidin? The Designed weren't people to G and A, and Raleigh hoped that they'd never take that view of the Modified. People shouldn't be made to produce a drug, receptors or not. Raleigh pondered this as the hungry machine filtered the Lucid from her veins.

———

THINGS WEREN'T THE same between Raleigh and the Receps, but she knew they wouldn't be. She was now revered by some, feared by others, and disliked by a few. Never again would she just be the quiet girl who hung around Adam.

As they played basketball the next day, Raleigh was acutely aware of each player. She felt their eyes following her every move. Gabe noticed as well. He'd admitted to her that it was good that she'd kept her secret for so long. In two days she'd be attending the benefactors' dinner in Virginia, and they decided that she should spend more time in the lab until she left.

Dale hadn't been in any of his usual places, and with the Receps loafing around, Raleigh didn't feel like being out and about. It was midday, and the September air was much more forgiving than the August heat. With the window open, the smell of flowers drifted into her bedroom. She found a deck of cards and dealt a game of solitaire.

"You've got to come with me," a voice begged.

It took Raleigh a moment to identify the voice's owner. It was Brandon, one of the Receps. He was a tall young man with broad shoulders and the militant qualities all Receps shared. It was odd to hear him pleading with anyone.

"I'm not going with you," said Dale. Raleigh knew his voice right away.

"Everyone important will be gone in two days. That's when we'll make our escape."

The back of her cottage faced onto a small communal area and beyond into the arid landscape. No one hung out back there, at most, they passed through. Midday most of the cottages sat empty. The urgency in Brandon's voice—and the worry in Dale's—troubled her.

She slunk off her bed and crept to the window, ducking to keep out of sight. From the feel of them, Dale and Brandon moved closer. Both were cagey, their heartbeats faster than they'd be during a normal conversation.

"You said you loved me," Brandon said.

Dale was in love with Brandon? That put a new spin on things. It wasn't as though there were a lot of dating options at G and A—at least not options that Raleigh had thought of. But she and Dale had never talked about it. Relationships with the Receps were forbidden. Her mind swept back almost two months to the meeting with Marcel. Kissing was a source of Lucid. Rho had told her not to date guys with receptors. The story of Mu's girlfriend came to the front of her mind. She regretted not telling Dale about it. Dustin had insisted that Brandon was getting extra Lucidin. And he was—but his doses clearly didn't come in vials. Everything clicked into place.

Dale's heart skipped in his chest, Raleigh knew his answer before he said it. "I do love you. It's just... we can't leave. Agatha says it's not safe."

"And she's never going to let us be together."

"You don't even have a plan. Where are we supposed to go?"

"We'll figure it out." Brandon's voice became more aggressive and less pleading. His muscles tensed, and his head ached slightly.

"I'm sorry, Brandon. The answer is no."

"You're mine. You told me you were mine!"

Raleigh briefly peeked out the window. They argued near a tree about fifteen feet away. She didn't want to intrude or intervene. Hopefully, Brandon would back away. That seemed less likely with each passing moment. Rho had been concerned about this very thing happening to her.

Fingers dug into Dale's arm, the pain making Raleigh rub her own. "Let go of my arm," said Dale.

"I'm not even gay!" Brandon's revelation caused the air to leave Dale's lungs. "You're never going to get a guy like me again. If I'm able to stomach all this, you should be willing to leave."

"Then... why be with me?" Dale's words spat out in a sob.

"Because you're mine! Quit crying. Someone's going to see or hear. We need to be quiet. No one can suspect that we're leaving. Do you understand? You *owe* me."

"No."

Raleigh heard a slap, and pain exploded across Dale's face. Moments later his arms hurt, then his back. She didn't have to peer over the sill to know exactly what happened. Brandon had Dale pressed up against the tree. Enough. Things weren't going to scale down, and there was only so much she could listen to. Brandon didn't barricade, leaving him defenseless against her. Unlike during the dodgeball game, she simply made Brandon go slack. He crumpled to the ground in a heap.

"Brandon!" Dale didn't make an effort to help him.

"Dale?" Raleigh grabbed her phone, pushed the screen out of the window, and crawled over the ledge. "What's going on?"

"Why aren't you in the lab?" A red handprint lit up the side of his face, dangerously close to his puffy eyes.

"I was playing solitaire."

"What did you do to him? Is he dead?"

"No, he's breathing. I just made his muscles relax."

"Are you hurting him?"

"No, he's fine. But he was going to hurt you." She looked at the marks on Dale's arms. "He *did* hurt you."

"How much did you hear?"

Raleigh flipped open her phone. "Enough."

"Who are you texting?"

"Gabe."

"We can't tell Gabe!"

"Brandon is going to come after you again."

"It's my fault. I seduced him." Dale's eyes fell on the boy at his feet unable to speak or move.

Raleigh didn't think seduce was the right word. Brandon wasn't in it for the reason Dale assumed.

"There's Lucidin in our saliva," Raleigh said.

"What?"

"He gets a small dose of Lucidin when he kisses you. That's what Dustin was sensing. He suspected that Brandon was getting extra vials, but it turns out it was you."

"What?"

"Brandon's addicted to Lucidin."

"It isn't addictive."

"You can't sense, so you don't know. They're all addicted. Trust me. Brandon isn't thinking clearly. Rationing has made them all jittery. That's the reason I'm not allowed to fraternize with them."

"All this time, he's only been with me for the Lucidin?"

"I don't think we can say that for sure. But there's a good chance that it played a part."

"I feel so disgusting." Dale crossed his arms and stepped away from them both.

Gabe dashed around the back of the cottage, his phone in hand. "Raleigh, what happened?"

"Brandon's been seeing Dale. I overheard him trying to convince Dale to run away with him. Dale refused. Brandon became violent. Then I did this." If nothing else, she was succinct. She didn't want to detain Brandon any longer than necessary, so it seemed like sticking to the facts was somehow kinder than delving into the details.

"What? What do you mean they've been seeing each other?" Gabe clearly hadn't suspected anything.

"I'm gay," Dale said unabashedly. "We fell in love... or at least I *thought* we did."

"Brandon's been getting extra Lucidin from Dale." She assumed that Gabe knew how it worked. She hoped she wouldn't have to spell it out.

Understanding flickered in Gabe's eyes. He must have known about assault on Gamma on the island—and what could happen to the Designed, her, and the Modified.

Gabe furrowed his brow. "Unacceptable. Raleigh, let him up."

Brandon sprung to life and immediately scrambled to his feet. "Gabe, I can explain."

"You're out, Brandon."

"You can't do that!" Brandon gestured wildly. "You can't do that!"

"I'm escorting you to your room now, where you will pack your bag."

Raleigh snorted. "From the way he was talking, he's probably already packed."

"I can't go." Brandon was at a loss. "What will I do?"

"That's your problem." Gabe put his arm firmly around Brandon's shoulders and began leading him away. "Raleigh, you stay with Dale while I get this straightened out."

"Dale!" Brandon yelled. "Don't let them do this! I'm sorry. Don't let them make me leave."

Dale opened his mouth to say something. Raleigh shot him a look and he shut it. "I have an icepack in my room for my eye. We can use it on your cheek."

Dale stood motionless, tears running down his face before falling to the dry Arizona dirt. He'd been slapped in the face, but a strong pain burned in his chest. "I'm such a fool. I should've known something was up."

Raleigh led him to the front door of her cottage. "Why didn't you tell me? I mean I know that I'm not the most gossipy girl, but I thought we were friends."

"We are friends, and I wanted to tell you. Brandon insisted that we keep it a secret. He said that if you found out you'd tell Agatha, and he'd be gone."

"I would've told her." Raleigh held the door open. "Sit down. You're not feeling well."

Dale sat on the edge of the small sofa. "I'm so stupid. A guy like Brandon would never have gone for a guy like me."

"You mean a straight one?"

"I didn't know he was straight. I was thinking I'd never have a chance with a guy as confident as him. I was shocked to find out he was gay. And I guess that's because he isn't."

"How long have you been together?"

Dale rubbed the back of his neck. "A month, ever since we started running with Adam. One day after dropping Adam off he caught up with me. It wasn't romantic, we talked about running and Arizona. A day or two later we bumped into each other after dinner. It was friendly. Things were going so well with the lab, Adam, and you. To me, he was one more friend to make here. A week later we were playing cards in my room. A few days after that I kissed him."

"You kissed him first?"

"Yeah. I don't know where I got the confidence. I've never been that bold." Dale blushed. "He said that he normally didn't find guys attractive, seemed really split about it. That night he left in a hurry. For two days we pretended not to know each other. Then one night he tapped on my window. He said that he didn't care if I was a guy or what the others might say, he was into me."

"And that's when you started dating?"

"We snuck moments here and there. Brandon was sure Agatha

would be against it, that they all would. He said that he wasn't supposed to have anyone like me distracting him from training. It made everything more exciting. I've never been with anyone before. It felt forbidden and star-crossed."

"It was. But not for the reasons you thought." Raleigh sensed Dale push a lump of regret down in his throat. She fetched him a glass of water.

"I'm such a fool. Brandon started hinting that if we wanted to be together, we'd have to run away. He knew you and Gabe would be gone on your trip. It would've been the ideal time for us to leave."

"That I heard."

"Now he's gone. What's going to happen to him?"

"I have no idea."

"I kissed him first. It isn't his fault."

"He was violent with you."

"I'm not saying I want to stay with him. He's been getting more and more possessive. But that doesn't mean he should leave. This is everything to him."

Raleigh remembered that Rho'd told her it would've been better for the Receps to have gone home. Collin would probably have been healthier if he left, but Rho couldn't do that to his friend. Rho was right about the Receps. The idea turned her stomach. "Grant and Able are ruining these men. I can guess that the healers are the same."

There was a knock on the door, and Raleigh went to open it.

Gabe waited on the other side, entering when Raleigh stepped out of the way. "Brandon's on his way to Phoenix. He'll be gone from the state by the end of the night. Dale, I'm going to have Adam keep an eye on you while we're gone. You're not seeing Adam, are you?"

"What? No." Dale began to go pink around the ears, either from indignation or embarrassment.a

"I'm sorry. I didn't expect this." Gabe twisted the fingers of his hand. "Raleigh, are you seeing any of them?"

"Of course not." The idea sickened her. "Dale has to come with us to Virginia."

The concern on Gabe's face turned to disapproval. "This is a very important dinner. And we already have a lot to worry about, safety-wise."

"Dale isn't safe here. I'm not leaving without him. Agatha will agree. We should probably bring Quinn, too."

"Quinn's fine," Gabe said. "He doesn't associate with the Receps. Bringing Dale will take some arranging."

"Then arrange it."

CHAPTER
25

TWO DAYS LATER the private jet touched down in Virginia. Raleigh itched with uncertainty. After the dodgeball stunt, she'd cemented her reputation as a powerful Recep. Now she prepared to assume the leadership role Agatha and Gabe saw her in. The part of her that still wanted to be with Rho kept her from betraying the Designed. But, in effect, she'd been turned.

That wasn't to say that the past few days hadn't muddied things. With Quinn unable to go home and Dale mistreated, she worried about the Modified. They were prisoners, and unlike the Designed, couldn't stand up for themselves. She desperately wanted to be a doctor, but not at the cost of their freedom. Agatha also needed to address the growing addiction of the Receps.

Gabe sat across from her on the plane. "You're going to do fine. You're impressive enough without any grand speeches."

Raleigh forced a grin. Gabe mistook her apprehension for concern over the benefactors' dinner. It was true that she hated fancy parties, but her mind was far too occupied with dual alliances and unstable Receps to care.

Agatha, Gabe, Dale, and Raleigh deplaned into the humid climate of the South. Raleigh wondered how much Grant and Able asked their benefactors to shell out. This wasn't some fledgling company trying to get off the ground. She could only imagine the kind of money the benefactors had to play with.

A limo took them from the small airport into an older, upscale neighborhood. The houses grew larger, and the walls scaled higher the farther in they went. Trees that looked like they might've witnessed the country's Founding Fathers draped their long branches over the main road. Raleigh marveled at the spectacular wealth on display.

"Where's the dinner?" Raleigh asked. They weren't near any hotels or venues.

Gabe inclined his head forward. "At a house, just up ahead. Don't worry. There's plenty of room for all of us."

From the size of the houses they passed, Raleigh didn't doubt it.

The limo eventually stopped in front of an old house with a wrap-around porch. With so much history staining its bricks, she could picture generations of people who'd called this place home. Who knew what sort of ghosts lurked in a place owned by the chief benefactor of Grant and Able?

Agatha's delicate hand patted her shoulder. "Be yourself."

That would be easier if Raleigh had a better sense of who she was. As she walked up the front steps with Gabe, she noticed two Receps. They nodded to him with respect and familiarity. She and Gabe could well protect Agatha and Dale. The additional Receps seemed excessive.

She pulled Gabe to the side before they entered. "Are we expecting an attack?"

"Never hurts to be prepared." Gabe smoothed his shirt down and allowed her to enter first.

"You made it!" A man with a Southern accent swept up Agatha's hand and kissed it. With white hair, a light-blue shirt, and neatly pressed black slacks, he looked casual but had the air of money about him.

"Frank, this is Raleigh." Agatha stood between the two, her arms reaching out to both.

Frank took Raleigh's shoulders in his hands and straightened her up. Then he took a step back, inspecting her from her feet up to her head. She half-expected him to tell her to turn around.

"Our white knight." He bowed to her.

"And this is Dale," said Agatha.

"A Modified? I didn't know we were going to make his acquaintance."

Dale uncomfortably held out his hand. "It's nice to meet you."

"It's mutual." Frank clasped Dale's hand between his. "Gabe, good to see you, too. Your men are ecstatic, although you've trained them so well that you'd never know."

"Nice to see you, Frank." Raleigh half expect Gabe to salute, but instead they too shook hands.

Frank's smile disappeared. "Raleigh, it's dinner time, and we have a buffet set up in the dining room. Oliver's already settled in. Would you like to meet your special guests now or later?"

The East Coast humidity made her sweaty, and her casual summer clothes weren't exactly appropriate attire for meeting the financers. In fact, she wasn't up for meeting anyone—let alone someone described as "special."

She pressed her hands to her hair, taming the fly-aways. "I thought we weren't meeting the benefactors until tomorrow?"

"It's not the benefactors," Gabe said. "Are they in the cellar?"

Frank nodded. "Along with two of your men, so I've been told."

"Agatha, why don't you and Dale join Oliver and Frank for dinner. We'll be back soon." Gabe lightly pressed his hand against Raleigh's back and led her down a hallway.

"I'm really not ready to meet anyone." She watched the others go to the casual dinner.

"They won't expect you to be elegant."

"I hope no one does."

Elegance belonged to Agatha, not her. She'd never float a room that way. If anything, her movements had become more aggressive. It was Gabe's fault, but she didn't mention that as they continued through the back hallway. Opening a side door, they entered the kitchen. From there they descended a narrow stairwell.

The musky smell of damp dirt filled her nose. Unlike the rest of the house, the basement wasn't gaudy or clean. Gravel made up the floor, and it didn't really seem like the same house. The stairwell they descended appeared to be the only way in or out.

The racks of wine collected dust, and the dampness was cool, not sweltering. If there were ghosts in the attic, what lurked down here? Raleigh followed behind Gabe as they wound through the vast collection of ancient bottles that had labels tattered with age. Turning a corner, her attention was no longer on the collection of presumably valuable wine.

In the corner loomed two large metal cages with built-in clunky locks that required big metal keys to open them, a primitive sort of cell. A lone toilet sat to the side—no sink and no privacy. Raleigh could make out four men in the dim light, but she could only sense the two Receps standing guard. Her mind couldn't detect the men inside the cages. She held her breath. Only one type of person could barricade that well.

"These are the Designed." Gabe sounded like a zookeeper

showing off his animals. "Mu and Tau are from separate triplets, but all of them look a bit alike in a weird way."

He was right, they didn't look normal. But it wasn't their eerily good looks that caught her attention. It was their tattered clothes, greasy hair, and scarred arms. Their mental barricades were too strong to break, so there had been attempts to do so physically. Even without sensing—with their sunken eyes and bowed backs—she could see the toll the extractions took on them. Raleigh stepped up to the bars, observing them as best she could with the limited light from the small bare bulbs overhead.

Mu looked like Kappa, but his green eyes were dull with exhaustion. He had blue hair that Thalia would've appreciated. His blond roots gave a clue about how long he'd been imprisoned. His shirt hung loose, and tattoos peeked out, the most prominent one being a large Greek "mu" symbol at the base of this throat. He would've been frightening if she couldn't picture Kappa's smile on his identical lips.

"Who is she?" Tau put his hands on the bar and inspected her.

He was the first of his triplet set that she'd met. According to the files, Chi was a recluse, and Beta was dead. Like Mu, Tau had a menacing expression. But his large blue eyes with long dark lashes softened his face, and the scruffy beard along his strong jaw helped.

"This is Raleigh." Gabe didn't elaborate.

Mu arched his eyebrows. "Gabe, you can't hurt her."

"If he does, the blood is on his hands." Tau released the bars. "We aren't going to give up anything. If you stoop low enough to hurt a girl, that's your decision. We aren't telling you a thing."

Raleigh's heart twisted. They didn't expect her to be a danger. Instead they worried for her, implying Gabe would harm her in an attempt to draw information from them. What had he done to make them think he was that ruthless?

"Are they on the inhibitor?" she asked. The bars were thick, but they couldn't keep out the abilities of the Designed mind.

"They can't hurt you," said one of the guards. With his dark skin he easily blended into the shadows.

Raleigh's attention returned to the cages. Hating to see anyone imprisoned, she wanted to turn away, but she couldn't go back now. "Will the locks hold?"

The kind Recep held up the keys. "Trust me. They won't open without these."

Gabe rubbed his hands together. "All right, time to get down to business. We think they know where the others are, a meeting location. We want you to break their barricades and do what you have to do to get that information."

"You want me to torture them?"

"What did you think we were training you for?"

That was it. Maybe one day G and A would let her become a healer, but that was contingent on her becoming a weapon first. In that moment she knew that she was going to get Mu and Tau out. No one deserved to live like this, caged like an animal and robbed of their Lucidin. Yes, there'd been a massacre that these two had failed to stop, but if they were evil, they would've been killed not captured. The pain of their captivity reminded her of the way she felt when she had blackouts—trapped, lonely, scared. They were in a real prison, and hers was due to what she mistook as an illness, but she could draw the parallels.

The weary expression on Tau's face mirrored the desperation she had after so many inconclusive doctor appointments. It represented a life stunted, denied the right to grow in a normal way. Seeing Rho on the cusp of death had been scary. Seeing these two trapped like feral animals infuriated her. She could no longer stay with Grant and Able. She would find another way to become a doctor.

Raleigh studied Mu. Curiosity and animosity warred in his eyes. She wished that she could somehow let him know she was on his side. If it were a movie, she would've had a password or something to let him know. As it was, she had nothing.

"Where are the others?" Raleigh voice came out frail.

"This isn't going to work, Gabe," the second guard said. He was beefier than the first guard, and Raleigh noticed bruising on his hands. He'd clearly taken a shot at getting them to confess.

Tau spat on the ground. "Go to hell."

Mu turned to his brother, then to Raleigh. "Leave us alone. We aren't talking."

"Raleigh, you're going to have to be a bit more forceful." Gabe put a hand on her shoulder. "You're strong enough. Apply a little pain. Just a bit."

"The inhibitor doesn't stop their barricades."

Gabe removed his hand and stepped back. "You can break them."

"Which one knows more?" There was a chance that neither knew anything.

"Tau, probably," the kinder, smaller guard said.

Raleigh took two steps over until she was directly in front of Tau. "Can you tell me where your brothers are?"

Gabe rubbed his nose between his eyes. "If asking sweetly worked, we wouldn't need you."

She closed her eyes. Reaching out her mind, she sensed a few feet away, where Tau's mind should've been. Probing, she tried to establish some sort of line of communication. The phone rang, but he refused to pick up. It wouldn't be as easy as breaking a Recep's barricade. Their barriers were like tissue paper compared to Tau's stone.

Raleigh pressed his mind and winced at its sturdiness. "I can't do it." What she neglected to say was that she didn't want to break it. She could picture Rho being trapped behind those bars. He wouldn't be, though. They would have killed him on sight.

Gabe crossed his arms. "We can stay down here as long as you need us to."

Raleigh's eyes flitted to the cracked ceiling. It was odd to think that Dale was up there eating a buffet dinner, unaware that she was grappling with the largest moral dilemma of her life. The worst thing she'd ever done was punch a kid in kindergarten. It was a skirmish over the water fountain. The boy pulled her hair, and she walloped him across the face. Their parents were called, and they both got a pink slip in their file. Her mother, unsurprisingly, made a huge deal about it, insisting that Raleigh compose a letter of apology. Thalia decorated it with stickers. That was for one hit. If she did what Gabe asked, no words, stickers, glitter, or guilt would be able to undo it.

Maybe she should break them out now. She knew where the keys were. Three Receps, including Gabe, would be easier to manage than breaking Tau's barricade. But what would they do if she broke them out? How far could they realistically get? Two Receps waited upstairs, presumably ready with the inhibitor. The place was already on high alert. She had her phone in her back pocket. She could call Trevor, but he wouldn't be in Virginia. A good spy would've given him the heads up that she was on the move. But since she'd given up on being a mole, she'd let the communication slack. No. She couldn't break them out tonight. There were too many unknowns, and they'd be running away on foot.

"I know you can do it." Gabe mistook her pause for inability.

Yes, she could. It would be hard, but she knew that in Tau's depleted state he didn't stand much of a chance. Raleigh needed to keep Gabe's trust a little longer. It had to be done. She closed her eyes. All her other senses went silent. She barely heard Mu ask

Gabe if Grant and Able made her. The cold air ceased to annoy her. The world was one thing—Raleigh's mind. She pressed up against Tau's barricade. It was an impenetrable wall of silence. Slowly the Lucidin pooled in her. Then, all at once, it surged, cracking Tau's mental wall in two. Now she sensed two things—her and him.

Concentrating, she raised her eyelids and took in the world she'd forced out. On the other side of the bars stood Tau. His blue eyes widened with fear and contempt. She couldn't face those eyes. Lowering her head, she shut hers.

Hunger churned Tau's stomach. He hadn't eaten much that day, and the water he'd drank sloshed around. Next, she experienced the exhaustion that comes with extraction—the bone-deep kind she'd endured all those months ago when she saved Rho. Lastly, she felt his heart. It was strong and beating with the accuracy of a clock.

She chose to focus on his head because she didn't want to touch any of his organs, and it seemed like the most effective way to get what she needed. The pain started off dull, like a foggy headache. Then she ramped it up to a throbbing sensation that threatened to knock him out.

Tau screamed.

Awareness of her surroundings flooded back, her eyes flashing open in time to see him fall to the floor. The pain made Raleigh sick as Tau heaved up water.

"What is she doing?" yelled Mu.

Gabe remained calm. "Getting information. Raleigh, you're going to have to do worse than that."

She pictured the sharp pain of a hornet's sting. Focusing on the sensitive skin on his arms, she prompted the pain receptors to shoot stinging burns up and down the length of the limbs. Writhing on the ground, his hands grasped his arms in an attempt to extinguish the pain.

"Stop it! *Stop it!* Northern California!" Mu confessed as he grabbed the bars between their cages. "That's all we know!"

Raleigh stopped. Tau's barricade went back up, and she allowed it because they had what they wanted. Gabe said something, Tau moaned, and Mu fumed as Raleigh ran back through the wine racks. She dashed up the steps to the kitchen and ran over to the sink. The nausea she'd found in Tau washed over her. It was a bitter cocktail of disgust, pain, and guilt. She vomited in the sink.

"Raleigh?" The kind Recep hung back steps behind her.

Lifting her head, she noticed that the soap dish was shaped like a frog with an open mouth. It was an unexpected quaint thing for a house with such secrets in the basement.

Raleigh turned, straightening. "I'm not going back down."

"Let's go upstairs. You can get settled in. I'm sure that was hard on you."

Raleigh nodded and followed him out of the kitchen. As they walked past the dining room, she heard polite conversation before they went up the grand staircase that led to the bedrooms. He opened the door to a room with a four-poster bed and a doily on the nightstand.

"I think you're in this one. I'm Darius, if you need anything. I know what happened back there was difficult. They look like people."

That was the problem. They all thought they were something else. "What makes them less than human? Their brutality when they escaped from the island? Since when are humans always kind? We're all capable of that evil. I've just proven that."

Darius's face faltered. "It's for the greater good."

Raleigh pulled herself together. More than ever, she owed it to Mu and Tau to get them out. It was time to put on her spy face. "I know. I've read their files. It's hard to feel pain in someone else and know that you're the cause of it."

"Gabe says that when this mess is cleaned up, you'll be a healer."

"Will I have to see them again?"

"If you're up to it. They should be here for a day or two. But tomorrow you should focus on the dinner. The day after we'll see if Gabe thinks there's anything else you might be able to get out of them."

"Would you tell Agatha to save some food for me? I need a bit of time to rest."

"Sure. I'll see you later." Darius stepped out of the doorway and into the hall.

Raleigh stopped the door from closing. "Is it safe holding them here? There are only a handful of Receps."

"There are ten of us and a camera in the basement. Don't worry. If their brothers come, we have a trick up our sleeve." Darius nodded to her and headed down the hall.

Raleigh shut the door. A trick. They assumed the brothers might come. They were definitely planning for it. The real question was, were they planning on it? Raleigh wouldn't be able to get them out herself. She needed the Designed, and it was going to be messier than she'd anticipated.

Pulling out her phone, she knew she had to let Trevor know that she was in Virginia and the guys were here, too. This had to be done strategically. She didn't want Trevor to know too much or the Designed to jump the gun. The ideal time for them to arrive would be during the party. The Receps would be focusing on keeping the guests safe as well as watching Mu and Tau.

She decided to send a text.

If you call Arizona, I won't answer, sorry. I'm in Virginia the next few days. Wish you were here. The weather is beautiful.

Raleigh clicked both Thalia and Trevor and pushed *send*. If anyone from G and A asked, she'd say she added Trevor by accident. Hopefully Thalia wouldn't notice, and Trevor would get the clue.

Best-case scenario was that the Designed would come to Virginia, and she could hold off bringing them closer until tomorrow.

As she lay on the bed, she knew that while she slept Rho and his brothers would be preparing. Going down to dinner wasn't an option now. She couldn't face Agatha and the others, not moments after betraying them.

CHAPTER
26

"RALEIGH?" AGATHA'S SOFT voice filtered through the bedroom
door. Unlike Raleigh, she hadn't gone to bed early, and her body
was tired.

"Come in." Raleigh sat up on the bed. Daylight streamed in
the curtains. The denim shorts she slept in stiffly rubbed her skin,
and her stomach grumbled angrily because she'd chosen the escape
of slumber over its well-being. Her mother always said troubles
seemed lighter after a good night's rest, but hers held finality. She
sent a text message yesterday. That wasn't a dream.

Agatha slipped in and sat on the bed. For a woman who wasn't
a mother, she was surprisingly maternal. "Gabe said you managed
to get information out of them, but it was hard on you."

"I hope it helped."

"It will. We now know where to focus our attention. We
shouldn't have sprung them on you."

"A heads-up would've been nice."

"We weren't sure if the boat would have time to dock, or if we could even get them here. Luckily, it worked out."

Luckily.

She patted Raleigh's shoulder. "I feel better sending you into the field knowing that you can match them."

"Tau and Mu are weak. You've been draining them. They're worn out. The others won't be the same. But, yes, we are evenly matched."

"You need breakfast, and I have a girls' day planned. We've had you in the trenches with the boys too long. We have the excuse of tonight to get all done-up. I'll meet you in the dining room for some breakfast. Do you want to extract?"

"Yeah, I'll do that first."

Agatha squeezed her hand. "I'll have Gabe put the extraction machine in the dining room, so you can eat something."

As she extracted, Raleigh ate a simple breakfast consisting of an omelet and toast with an obscene amount of butter. She wondered what was on the menu one floor down. She wasn't sure if she could face seeing Gabe, any Recep, or Dale who'd have questions about the Designed. She ate quickly.

Before long she sat beside Agatha in a rented car. The Recep who drove them to the spa waited in the lobby with a book, and the two women embarked on their spa day. The lobby smelled of lavender and oranges, and the employees were eager to help. Raleigh wondered if the workers knew who Agatha was, if they were paid well, or if it was simply Agatha's commanding presence.

This wasn't the makeup counter at the mall and home manicures. The schedule they'd handed her indicated it would take a few hours.

Large marble tubs and various saunas took up a good half of the building. They enjoyed mud baths first. She compared the silky mud to the coarse Arizona dirt that usually covered her skin. They rinsed off and wrapped themselves in large fluffy white robes before heading back to the locker room.

While wrapped in her warm soft robe, her mind wandered to hornets. How could she enjoy the feeling of terrycloth after what she'd done to Tau?

She'd left her phone in her locker. She didn't know Frank's address, but she only had to get Trevor within ten miles to pick up the chip in her shoulder. She undressed and turned on the shower. The noise of water hitting the marble tiles made it hard to hear when Agatha turned on hers. Raleigh soon began to sense the hot water removing the dirt from Agatha's skin. Agatha's muscles relaxed as she languished under the herb-infused water.

Raleigh washed quickly and cracked opened the glass door of the shower. She waited for an older lady to leave before slipping over to her locker. She unlocked it with the small nautical-themed key, grabbed her phone, and typed the message she'd been composing in her head the better part of the morning.

Sorry I sent that last night! It was meant for my sister. I guess maybe it's fate's way of saying we should connect again soon. Just hitting up Alexandria. If my parents wanted to name me after a southern town why couldn't it have been that instead of Raleigh? Tonight I have a party. Remember homecoming and how we danced? Too bad you won't be here to join in. It won't be as fun without you. I've made a couple of new friends. Maybe one of them will share a dance. Talk soon!

Alexandria was near enough for them to pick up the chip. She sent the text. That was it. She went back to the shower. Agatha remained under the stream of water, oblivious.

Minutes later, wrapped in large robes with their hair in blue-and white-striped towels, Raleigh and Agatha headed to the pedicure room. They dipped their feet into the warm wax as a helpful woman laid out nail polish choices before leaving them to soak.

Agatha stretched her toes. "You aren't relaxed. Is there anything you want to talk about?"

Thus far, there'd been no discussion of Receps, Lucidin, or going into the field. Raleigh preferred to keep it that way. "Will there be dancing tonight?"

"Probably."

"Do you think it would be okay if I asked one of the Receps to dance?" Raleigh forced a blush to creep up her cheeks. She had to make it visible because Agatha couldn't sense.

A conspiratorial smile crossed Agatha's face. "Which Recep? Surely not Gabe."

"Yuck. Not Gabe. That would be like dating my brother."

"I'm glad you feel so close to him."

"Training will do that."

"Which one?"

"Darius." Raleigh casted her eyes down. "I know we aren't allowed to fraternize, but he was so nice last night. He's caring... but I don't know. Maybe he's not for me."

"I don't see why you can't have a bit of fun. After all the training, you should dance with him. If you can't let your hair down every now and then, what's the point? But remember, just dancing. Not dating." Agatha smiled.

The text sat heavy on Raleigh as she grinned back. This woman was someone she respected, and Raleigh'd jeopardized everything.

"You're living in a man's world. I'm sorry for that. We employ equal numbers of men and women in our labs, and, of course, the healers are female, but the field is male-dominated."

"I've had Dale and Adam to hang with."

"Yes, but it's not the same as hanging out with other women, is it?"

No. It really wasn't. Back home Raleigh had both male and

female friends. She missed the gossipy conversations she and her friend Emily used to share. Last time they'd spoken, Emily had received her college class assignments and stressed endlessly about her new roommate.

"When you started at Grant and Able, it was mostly men, right?" asked Raleigh.

"*All* men. Except the surrogates for the babies, and they were often in horrible moods. I was used to being around men though. My father took me with him from job to job. My mother and I were never that close. After they divorced, I saw less and less of her."

"I see too much of my mother."

"She seems very invested in your health. You're lucky. Mine wasn't as attentive. I pushed to have the Designed be female. Did you know that?"

"Really?" She attempted to picture Rho's deep-set eyes on a more feminine face. "Why aren't they girls?"

"I was the only one who voted for it. I think each scientist who worked on them mixed a bit of their own hopes and dreams in. They wanted to make men to mirror their own ambitions. I added my own stamp to Sigma, the worst of them. I gave him the coloring of my best friend growing up. He was an Egyptian boy who liked to play in the labs. The first words we had in common were lab supplies. He was fun and happy. I guess I wanted to give Sigma that joy any way I could."

"Did his other two triplets end up as bad? They didn't seem to... going by the files."

"I had hopes for Rho. All three of those triplets were leaders. In the end, he and I argued. He didn't approve of people receiving Lucidin. He thought it was hurting the Receps."

Raleigh shifted in her seat, the wax sliding higher to her ankles. "He is right. They *are* addicted. We need to find something better than the synthetic for them. Even with natural Lucidin, I think they're addicted."

Agatha leaned back in her chair. "Natural Lucidin shouldn't be addictive. Once we capture more Designed, we won't need as many Receps, and we'll use less synthetic."

If the G and A clinics took off in New York and Chicago, the medical demand for Lucidin would increase. Even with Raleigh, all the Designed, and the Modified, they would never have enough. The lab brains might be a solution, but they weren't near ready.

Two pedicurists entered rolling nail polish in their hands. They removed Raleigh and Agatha's feet from the wax, effectively ending any small talk. At least, Raleigh had said her piece about the Lucidin addiction. Hopefully, Agatha would take it to heart, coming from her.

After their toenails and fingernails had been painted, it was time to do their hair and get dressed. Soon they would be confronting the evening.

CHAPTER
27

AGATHA HUMMED A light tune as the mansion came into view. The Recep drove slowly, the windows down. Crickets chirped, and the smell of freshly cut grass lingered in the air. It reminded her of sitting on the back deck with her parents, playing cards and making jokes. She wished she could go home and avoid tonight, but it was time to do what she'd gone undercover for.

Agatha wore a sweeping floor-length emerald gown, and Raleigh donned a light-pink cocktail dress. She'd come a long way from the girl who dressed up at Uncle Patrick's birthday party.

Agatha stopped her as they walked up to the house, pulling her into a brief hug. "I think the two of us are going to be quite the team someday."

Raleigh liked Agatha. She was the type of woman Raleigh herself wanted to be—strong, empowered, and in charge of her future. Raleigh's voice caught in her throat as Agatha pulled away. "Thanks for everything."

Agatha squeezed Raleigh's arm, and together they approached the house. One of the Receps abandoned his post to open the door. Raleigh could've sworn that the chip in her shoulder tingled as they walked in. She'd never been more aware of it.

With only an hour until the party, caterers circled the table making last minute adjustments, and florists positioned large arrangements near the door. The workers moved with a choreographed grace. Raleigh tried her best to stay out of the way.

"All the chaos." Agatha reached out to touch the petal of a rose between her fingers. "I better find Oliver and make sure everything's in order before people start to arrive. See you at dinner."

"Wow! You look great!" Dale arrived as Agatha departed. He wore a slightly dowdy suit that was a bit tight at the waist. "I look like an old man."

"You look fine."

"It was all they could find at the last minute. You look amazing though. I was worried about you. You didn't eat with us last night. Gabe said we shouldn't worry about you—which made me think we should."

"Mu and Tau are in the basement," Raleigh whispered.

Dale stiffened. "I know. They told me. But there's nothing to worry about. The other Designed have no way of knowing that we're here. And even if they did, Gabe says we're ready for them. I'm sticking by you all night. You're strong enough to fight those monsters."

Raleigh diverted her eyes down, noticing how the light reflected off her heels. "I'm not so sure that I'm not a monster too. I hurt Tau last night, getting information."

"It was justified. I don't know what you did, but any harm that befalls them is karma."

"Let's hope karma has a short memory."

"Oh, don't worry about them. Are you ready to go out there and wow the benefactors?"

"Sure, what about you?"

"Let's not pretend that they care about anything other than my Lucidin."

"I do, though, and they should. You're a very good friend."

"Don't get all dopey on me. We still have a few nights before you go into the field."

Raleigh gave him a hug anyway. Over his shoulder she caught Gabe speaking to a Recep. His formal suit was Recep black, he never let his guard down. Security would be on point.

The guests filed in one by one, and they offered compliments and long handshakes. Agatha introduced her to so many people that she hadn't a hope of remembering any of their names. At dinner she positioned herself between Oliver and an older man who asked her the same questions again and again. Across the table Dr. Arthur, the head healer, was answering many of the same questions.

At any moment Raleigh expected the Designed to burst in. She rarely let the smile fall from her lips or her eyes from the door. By nine o'clock she began to consider the possibility that they weren't coming. Trevor hadn't answered either of her texts. There was no evidence that he'd seen them. For a month she'd been quiet. They may've abandoned her. She'd been so caught up worrying about the violence that might occur when the Designed showed up that she hadn't considered what would happen if they didn't.

Should she forget about getting Mu and Tau out? No. She couldn't back down now. No one deserved to be caged like that. Gabe had forced her to torture Tau once. There was no guarantee that she wouldn't have to do it again. She had to take her chances tonight, help or no help.

After dinner the guests began wandering out to the veranda in back. Alcohol contributed to more than one of the partiers engaging in impromptu dances.

Agatha found Raleigh as she stepped out onto the back porch. "If you want to ask Darius to dance, now's the time. I convinced Gabe to spare him for the last hour. Go grab one of the other Receps to take his post. They're on the third floor."

"Thanks." Raleigh had so much she wanted to say. She wanted to explain that Rho had been worried about her safety the morning they met, that there was a goodness in him that Agatha didn't have enough receptors to sense. She wanted to explain that the Receps were being torn apart by the Lucidin addiction and that Dale and Quinn were prisoners of Grant and Able. Instead the words sat heavy in Raleigh's throat.

Agatha shooed her into the house. "You better hurry. An hour won't feel long once you start dancing."

By the time she reached the stairwell, the hubbub of the party was reduced to a mere din. Raleigh ascended the two floors to the camera room. She rapped once on the door and waited.

"Raleigh, how can we help you?" asked one of the Receps with the door cracked open.

"Agatha said I'm supposed to get one of you to relieve Darius... so I can get a dance."

"We need to be less concerned about dancing and more concerned about security."

"There are three of you, right?"

"Four."

With four Receps here and two in the basement, that accounted for six. All the others must be patrolling.

Raleigh steadied the door open with her hand. "Agatha said he could take the last hour off. Can you check with Gabe?"

"He's busy."

"When is he due to check in here?"

"When he has time. Get Dale to dance with you."

Raleigh glanced both ways down the hall and then froze all four men. There was no point in taking out the two in the basement if the ones up here were watching and could sound the alarm. She slipped into the room. The one she'd spoken to stood inside the door, mouth half-open in mid-conversation. Another stared in her direction. The other two hunched over their monitors. She willed the one nearest the door to step back, so she could shut it. She may've been fooled into thinking that she froze time as effectively as their muscles if it weren't for the screens showing the party from various angles—and the prisoners in the basement. She would have to go downstairs, but her influencing couldn't hold up that far. They'd have to be incapacitated before she left.

The narrow closet with folding doors would have to do. She began yanking cords from the computers. Then she bound their hands. It was difficult due to the copper wire making the cords firmer than rope—not that she was used to tying people up with rope. Sliding her hands into the Receps' pockets, she removed their cell phones. Then she marched them into the closet one by one, closed the doors, and tied a cord around the handles using a knot she knew wouldn't hold. With all her might she dragged the heavy desk toward the closet. It required her full attention, which was hard to give since she needed to focus on influencing. Four sets of ears on four frozen bodies listened as she struggled to shift the desk into place. She tallied up how long she had before they escaped their bonds and opened the door. Then she slammed the monitors to the floor and watched them shatter, but she knew it wouldn't buy her that much time. The table had a glass of water on it, in which she gave the phones a damaging bath. They'd have to get help the old-fashioned way.

She'd have to be quick in rescuing Mu and Tau. The knot and closet wouldn't hold them long. She calculated how long she had, and it would be tight. Leaving, she tugged the door shut and whirled around to go down the hall, bumping straight into the broad chest of a Recep. The shock made her slip in holding the frozen Receps for a fraction of a second. Reestablishing the connection, she stepped in front of the guard, making it so he couldn't enter.

"Can I help you?" the Recep asked.

"They just sent me to find Gabe. He's needed on the lawn. It sounds important. They want him out back right away. I'm worried it'll take me too long to find him." She resisted the urge to glance back at the door. Would he sense their frozen bodies?

"I saw him out front."

"Would you let him know to go around back?"

"Why don't they just call him?"

"His phone isn't working." Raleigh attempted to keep the lines of her face smooth. Lying didn't come easy to her.

The Recep huffed, tossing out his arm turning the way he came. "And on a day like this! I'll get him. I'll be faster than you."

"Thanks."

She watched him dash off before she slid out of her heels. Her nylon-covered feet skidded on the steps that she took two at a time. By the time she was one floor down, she lost her influence over the four guards. Hastily, she tucked her feet back into the shoes before entering the kitchen and did her best to calm her large breaths. With her hair falling out of place and sweat forming on her brow, she hoped no one saw her. One guest passed, but he didn't observe her closely enough to suspect anything was wrong.

Raleigh finally reached the door to the basement. She opened it, the smell of earthy cellar wafting up. She took off her shoes as she rushed down the steps, the cold of the gritty ground icing her toes. The difference between the atmosphere at the party above and here below couldn't have been more pronounced.

Winding through the wine she wondered what would happen if she failed. Would she end up in a cage beside them? Would her parents come looking for her? The fear of being imprisoned worsened when she arrived at the cages. Darius, the other guard, Mu, and Tau turned to see her.

Darius rose up from his seat. "Raleigh, you're upset. Are you all right?"

"Darius, do you have the keys?"

Confusion crossed his face. Obediently he removed the heavy keys from a clip on his side, holding them out to her. With the keys dangling within reach, she froze him and the other guard. She untangled the keys from his fingers venturing a glance over her shoulder at the camera above. With any luck, the feed didn't go anywhere other than the control room on the third floor.

She approached Mu's cage holding up the keys. "Which one?"

He got over his shock quickly moving forward to help her single out the key. "This one."

Raleigh jammed the key into the heavy lock. Her awareness of the guards, simmering with anger, made her hand shake as she turned the key. The clasp snapped open and Mu stepped out, taking the keys from her so he could release Tau.

With them both free Raleigh peered through the darkness at the wine racks. "That's the only way out."

"Tau, help me put them in. She won't be able to hold them forever," Mu said. He yanked the first of the two into his cell closing the cage. Tau dragged the second into his former prison. As he fitted the lock onto the door, a fine mist showered down from above and a siren cut the air.

Raleigh's hand shot up to cover her ears, the mist filling her mouth with a bitter taste. She coughed, her mind wondering if it weren't a poison. Before she could ask what it was, her abilities dulled then ended. The inhibitor. Darius and the other guard sprang to life, grabbing the bars and shouting. Raleigh could only barricade now.

"We have to hurry." She ran toward the stairs behind Mu. "They must know I broke you out. I'm not sure how far we'll get."

Tau grabbed her arm and slammed her against one of the shelves of wine. A bottle crashed to the floor and glass sprang up and cut her leg. The blood ran down the back of her ankle and mingled with the Chianti pooling on the floor. She didn't register the pain as her attention was on her throat—which he clutched in his hands. He lifted her up and she gasped for air.

Mu halted on the first step. "Tau, let her go! We don't have time."

"Just until she loses consciousness."

"She saved us!"

"We don't know who she is."

"Rho," she squeaked.

Mu yanked his brother's arm. "Put her down!"

Tau loosened his grip, and Raleigh inhaled. The air came in rough, and she moved her fingers to her throat. "I know Rho! I'm a mole. I'm here to get you out. We have to leave on foot, and we need to make it quick."

"Don't lie!" Tau's fingers cut into her arm.

"Let her go!" a familiar voice demanded. Kappa barreled down the stairs yelling into a walkie-talkie. "They're in the basement! I have them! Stop the search!"

Kappa pushed Tau away from her and swept her into a tight embrace. "You didn't wait for us."

"I wasn't sure you were coming!"

"What's the plan?" Mu stared up the stairwell.

"Front door."

"They have an inhibitor." Raleigh's bare feet struggled to keep up. "We can't influence."

Kappa looped an arm under her shoulder, helping her the last few steps to the kitchen. "That inhibitor mist is all through the house. We have guns."

Those would work. The four ran through the kitchen and into the living room where a clear path lay to the front door and freedom. Mu and Tau left with Kappa. Gamma and Xi came down from upstairs. Raleigh didn't see Rho. She frantically searched. Finally, she spotted him in the dining room, his face as handsome as she remembered, and a great deal more worried. On soft feet she hid behind the arched doorway to the room.

"Sigma, let's go!" Rho moved back, his eyes looking over his shoulder in the direction of the front door.

"We won't get a chance again, brother," Sigma growled. "Everyone stay against the wall!"

All twenty guests gathered against the wall on the other side of the large table. A few of them cried, many of them clutched each other. They stared in shock, Dale's terrified face among them, as Rho, Sigma, and Psi held them at gunpoint. The guests huddled behind Gabe and a Recep. Both of them stood, hands raised in surrender. The inhibitor lingered in the air, Gabe and his man, like her, would be stunted by it.

"Sigma, let's go!" Rho's gun remained raised on the guest, but his head turned to Sigma.

Sigma sneered at Rho then motioned his gun at the crowd. "Agatha, Oliver, Gabe. Step forward. No one else move. If you're lucky, we may let some of you live."

The three separated from the group. Agatha held onto Oliver, who paled beside her. Raleigh's heart twisted in her chest. Not Agatha. It wasn't supposed to happen like this.

"Do the condemned have any last words?" Sigma asked.

He had no interested in hearing them, nothing they said would save their lives. Despite that, Agatha pleaded with him. The dishes from dinner sat piled in the hallway, a steak knife on the side glinted in the light. She reached for it, gauging the weight of it in her hand. Against a gun it wasn't much, but she had surprise on her side. Could she stab him? Gabe had trained her to fight without her Lucid.

"Not good enough, Agatha." Sigma leveled the gun at her heart.

Raleigh thought about all the good times with Agatha, some earlier that day. She remembered the pictures of dead boys on Agatha's wall and replayed the video from the island in her head. She wouldn't stand by and let evil win. Fearlessly, she lunged forward and drove the knife into Sigma's arm. Then she slid it up at an angle as she'd been taught in a self-defense class years ago. The lesson came back to her with a stark clarity, as promised.

Sigma swore as the gun tumbled from his hand. Raleigh kicked it across the floor. Psi aimed his gun at Raleigh and fired. The bullet grazed her shoulder and the sharp pain knocked her to the ground. Without pause, Psi pointed the gun at Gabe, who scrambled to get Sigma's pistol. Psi and Gabe fired at each other simultaneously, neither one having time to aim. Gabe hit Psi in the chest and Psi's bullet hit Gabe in the leg, dropping him to the ground.

Sigma, dripping blood and disarmed, ran toward the front door. Gabe retrained his weapon on Rho who, uninjured, stood ready to shoot Gabe. Psi, unconscious on the ground, was no longer a threat. Without sensing, Raleigh couldn't tell if he was dying.

"Gabe, I don't want to shoot you," said Rho. "We both know that I have the better shot."

Gabe craned his neck to see the others. None of them moved, although a few eyed the gun resting in Psi's open hand.

Kappa rushed in. "Rho, we've got to leave."

Rho motioned his head towards Psi. "We need help to get Psi out of here, and take his gun."

Kappa picked up the firearm and left. He soon returned with Xi and Gamma who lifted their brother. Kappa stayed, not leaving Rho's side.

Rho stepped backward, his eyes and gun still trained on Gabe. "We're leaving. Don't follow us. I have no intention of killing any of you. But I will if I have to."

Gabe tossed his gun to the ground with a clank. "I'm going to take you at your word, because I don't have much choice."

For the first time that evening Rho acknowledged Raleigh. He looked at her, his expression tense. "Kappa, help Raleigh. She's been shot."

Agatha moved forward, and Gabe grabbed out to pull her back. "You can't take her, please don't harm her."

Raleigh shook her head. They didn't know that she led the Designed here or that she'd trapped Receps in the closet and the cells. "I'm sorry, Agatha." She didn't ask for forgiveness. She didn't regret her decision.

Kappa wrapped a strong arm around her. "You're pale."

"I feel foggy." Many times in the past, doctors had asked if she felt lightheaded before her blackouts. The answer was always no. Now she experienced the narrowing vision they'd described. Bracing herself against Kappa, she said, "Rho, take Dale."

Rho scanned the crowd. "Raleigh, we don't have much time."

"Take Dale. If he wants to come. Dale, you want to come, don't you?"

Dale's eyes rose high on his brow. "What?"

"We've got to hurry." Rho motioned over his shoulder for Dale to move.

Raleigh concentrated on her friend, her body shaking. "Dale, you trust me, don't you? Come with me."

Dale looked at Agatha, Oliver, and, lastly, at Gabe before stepping through them, past Rho, and over to Kappa and Raleigh. The three of them left, and Rho kept the rest of the room in line. When he finally joined them outside, he wasn't followed. The four made their way to the helicopter in the open field across the driveway.

Kappa hoisted Raleigh into Gamma's arms, and he rested her inside the helicopter. Kappa jumped in and helped Dale up before moving to give Rho space to enter. Collin manned the controls.

"We don't have Sigma," Xi said.

Rho faced the door, his eyes on the field. "He ran. Collin, go. If he isn't here, he isn't coming."

A few of the others protested, but Collin's fanatical loyalty to Rho, for once, came in handy. With the door shut, Collin took it up.

CHAPTER
28

THE THUMPING OF the spinning propellers echoed through the metal ribcage of the helicopter. Raleigh's stomach dropped as they rose. The motion was less like an airplane and more like the ground being ripped away. The noisy, cramped space and the pitch-black darkness outside disoriented her. They all had to shout to be heard—although they didn't need the excuse.

"We have to get to a hospital, Collin!" Upsilon cradled Psi's head in his lap. "I can keep him from bleeding, but he needs a doctor."

With her legs weakened from the shock, Raleigh sat in the corner, pressing her hand against the floor as the helicopter jostled in the wind. Kappa slid beside her, propping her up.

"How can you influence?" she asked Upsilon.

"I hung back on purpose. I'm the only one who didn't get dosed with the inhibitor."

Xi moved towards Rho. "Where's Sigma? What happened back there?"

Rho's eyes darted to Raleigh for a moment. "Raleigh stabbed Sigma. He was going to kill Agatha, Oliver, and Gabe."

Raleigh heard the collective intake of breath. Bolstering herself she faced them. "I promised to get Mu and Tau out, not help you kill your enemies."

"Then Psi shot Raleigh," Rho continued, "and turned his gun on Gabe, who by that point had Sigma's. They both fired, and Psi ended up like this. Sigma ran out. We left shortly after."

"She's one of them!" Xi yelled.

"She got us out." Mu eyed her curiously, as he moved closer to her and Kappa. "If it weren't for her, I would still be in that cage."

Xi didn't let it drop. "Because of her, Psi is dying. She chose them over us."

"She didn't know it was going to happen." Rho challenged Xi, staring him down as the helicopter dipped and swayed.

"It doesn't matter. It's her fault." Xi pointed at Raleigh, his lips snarled.

Rho shook his head. "We all knew it was dangerous."

Raleigh met Xi's eyes. "I'd do it again. Sigma was going to slaughter them. I didn't sign up for that."

"Oh, yeah? And just what the hell *did* you think you were signing up for?"

Gamma restrained him. "Calm down, Xi."

"She's *out!*"

"No, she's not. You wanted her to prove herself by getting Mu and Tau out, and she did. She's done as you asked, and she's in." Rho sat back down beside her and Kappa. He cupped her cheek in his hand.

Xi tugged free of Gamma. "I'm not allying with her."

"Then you're not with me," Rho said.

Kappa exhaled. "Is this really the time to be splitting up?"

"I'm not spending any more time around her." Xi glanced at Psi again. "Psi would agree with me, and so would Sigma. The rest of you have to choose."

"Raleigh." Kappa held her a little tighter in his arms, she only had to peer up to see the commitment in his eyes. He could've said Rho, but he chose her name instead.

"Raleigh." Mu leaned down and extended his hand. "Thank you for getting me out. Tau?"

Tau's stern eyes studied them through his lashes. "I'm with Rho."

"Then you're with Raleigh," Rho said.

Tau's face twisted, but he didn't change his mind. She closed her eyes, picturing the hornet stings.

Yes, she'd gotten him out and got herself shot in the process, but he didn't owe her.

Kappa looked at Gamma. "Gamma?"

Gamma and Upsilon faced each other, their dark eyes in an unspoken conversation.

"We're with Rho," Gamma said, turning to Rho.

Upsilon nodded.

The Designed had ended their alliance to one another. Rho and Raleigh won the loyalty of all but Sigma, Psi, and Xi. Raleigh could easily live without the three, but she didn't know how this would affect the others.

"I'm landing at the hospital," Collin said. "It's going to be quick."

The blue and red lights of the hospital helipad shot in the dark windows coloring the shadows.

Rho kneeled down. "Raleigh, can you wait to see a doctor? I'd rather we just drop off Psi."

Despite her spinning head she wanted to be far from here. "Yeah, I can manage."

Collin landed, and the guys unloaded Psi and Xi. Most patients weren't delivered by unannounced helicopters, never mind those with near-fatal gunshot wounds.

"How will they explain themselves?" Raleigh clung to Kappa as the helicopter returned to the sky.

"Not our problem," Upsilon said, looking out the window.

Dale coughed in the corner. In all the commotion, she'd all but forgotten him. He'd tucked himself in the front, holding on tightly to the seat, his face contorted with worry. Raleigh'd had time to think about what she wanted to do when they saved Mu and Tau. Dale had less than a minute. Hopefully he wouldn't regret it....

"She's not doing well," Upsilon said, his voice sounding like it was in a tunnel.

That was the last thing Raleigh heard.

THE SKEPTICAL DOCTOR peered over his clipboard at Raleigh. "All right, Alice, you need to take one of these twice a day. Normally, with your type of injury, I'd call in a social worker or the police."

They had cleaned and wrapped Raleigh's wound. She didn't tell the doctor that she knew a lot about dressing wounds as he handed her a leaflet about proper wound care and how often to change her bandages. Instead, she looked over the information and asked questions.

"I was holding the gun when it fell and went off." Raleigh had repeated this lie enough times that she herself was in danger of believing it.

Dr. Young didn't buy it. "Usually I'd keep you longer than a few hours."

A few hours were already too many. Kappa and Rho camped out in her room, only leaving when the doctor requested them to.

"I feel great." Raleigh got off the exam table folding the papers. The cocktail dress had no pockets, so she crumpled the papers in her right hand. The bullet had grazed her left arm. Once the inhibitor wore off Rho and Kappa influenced the cut to bleed less.

Dr. Moore inspected the bandage. "I've never seen anyone heal the way you do. Are you sure I can't call your parents?"

"No, my friends will take me home."

"I have no doubt about that. They've been very attentive. I'm going to give you the card of a women's shelter and therapist."

"It was an accident."

"In case you change your mind about what happened." Dr. Young correctly assumed that something was off. Thankfully, the truth was so obscure that she wasn't worried about him guessing it.

The fake license Marcel had provided came in handy, and the nurse bought her story about not having insurance. Kappa told Raleigh not to worry about the bill, but she was worrying about everything right now. With a prescription for pain meds and a bottle of antibiotics, she said her farewells. Rho and Kappa escorted her from the building, her arm in a sling.

Rho held open the front door of the car, and Raleigh sat down, wondering where'd they gotten it on such short notice. "Where are we headed?"

"My house." Kappa drove through the short buildings of Washington DC. "It's safe. Well, as safe as anywhere."

"How's Dale?" Raleigh asked. Rho had insisted that only he and Kappa should accompany her to the hospital.

Rho leaned forward his mouth inches from her ear. "He's fine. What's the deal with him?"

"I'm going to let him tell you why he's here." She leaned back in her seat. If she could draw the parallels between the Modified and Designed, surely, they would as well.

CHAPTER
29

RALEIGH OPENED HER eyes and rolled onto her left side, the pain where she'd been shot nipping at her. Sitting up quickly, she almost bumped her drug-muddled head on the bunk above her, the sheets twisted uncomfortably around her legs.

Rho, Raleigh, and Kappa had arrived at Kappa's house in the very early hours of the morning. The other Designed and Dale slept, affording her another few hours before she had to explain everything. Kappa had led her to a room with twin bunk beds, and after taking one of the bottom bunks, she quickly drifted off. Now, awake, she would have to face the day.

"You're up." Dale spoke loudly enough to ensure that she wouldn't be going back to sleep. He was perched across the way, on the edge of the made bunk.

Raleigh unwound the blankets with her right arm and swung her legs over the side of the mattress, her feet padding onto the beige carpet. "I'm glad to see you're all right."

"They're all downstairs."

"Have you been watching me sleep?" She reached her hand up to her forehead and brushed back the hairs that clung to her face.

"What was I supposed to do? Rho invited me to join them for breakfast and then lunch, but I didn't want to. Why are we here?"

Raleigh let out a loud yawn, unintentionally mocking Dale's turmoil. "Sorry. These pain meds make me groggy."

"One of them shot you."

Raleigh didn't need the reminder, the pain in her arm didn't let her forget. "I went undercover with Grant and Able to get Mu and Tau out."

Dale jumped up with his hands out. "Obviously! I figured that out. How could you do this to Agatha? To Gabe? To Adam?"

"I didn't know them when I set out to betray them." There was no sense in not owning it.

"How could you?"

"Because they were wrong. Wrong to capture Mu and Tau. Wrong to get Adam and the other Receps addicted to Lucidin. Wrong to capture you and Quinn."

"I wouldn't call it being captured." He sat back down. Raleigh sensed the weariness that came with uncertainty and too little sleep.

"Then why did you leave with us?"

"Because you're my friend, and I trust you."

"Then trust me when I tell you that the Designed are as human as you and me. Grant and Able used them, too. Only they were never fed the promise that they'd get out one day when it was safe. Because Grant and Able isn't making the world safer. They've unleashed something very unsafe, and it isn't the Designed."

Dale leaned forward on his knees. "Lucidin? You're talking about *Lucidin.*"

"You saw what it did to Brandon."

"But Lucidin is good. It cures cancer."

"It's not black and white."

"The Designed are evil."

Raleigh rubbed the bridge of her nose with her right hand. "Dale, they aren't. I met Rho weeks before I went to Grant and Able. He was near death from what the synthetic dealers had done to him. Do you know who he was most concerned about? Me. Sigma and some of the others might be nasty, but, as a whole, they're like everyone else—a mixed bag."

"So now we're on their side, just like that?"

"I'm sorry that you didn't have time to think about your decision and had to make it in the middle of that mess. I never dreamed I'd get you out. Hell, I didn't think I was ever going to get the chance to see Mu and Tau. I'd given up on the whole thing."

"You were going to stay with Grant and Able. No one is that good an actor. You were going to become a healer."

"I was. I bought into it all. The idea of being a healer down the road and going to college was enticing. I thought the added synthetic was to blame for the addiction. The longer I was there, the more abstract the Designed became."

"You were about to go out in the field to catch them."

"I was going to help get Sigma and Psi. But I was going to do a crummy job on the rest, get sent home, and start college."

"But instead you did this!"

"Let's go downstairs and talk with the Designed. They need to know about who you are. It was kind of them to take you no questions asked, but we're going to have to give them those answers now."

"We don't have any other choice, do we?"

"I could try to get you back to Grant and Able if you want?"

Dale rose and stared at the carpet for a moment. "No."

"Then let's go downstairs, and you can meet them. But I stink, I have to clean up first." Raleigh wore some of Kappa's clothes and desperately needed a shower. She stepped into the bathroom as Dale hesitantly went down the steps. The bathroom had a tub, toilet, and two sinks. Underneath one she found a package of toothbrushes. Kappa must've predicted that his home would be used as a safe house. Brushing her teeth, she wished that the events of the last day could be as easily scrubbed away. In the end they weren't, but at least her breath smelled minty.

Right-handed, Raleigh was fortunate that her left arm had been shot. Regardless, using one hand made everything slowgoing. The bobby pins and hair tie wound tightly into her hair proving difficult to remove.

For a split second she considered finding scissors and cutting it all off. If there'd been any chance of her doing a decent job, she would have.

There was a rapping on the bathroom door.

With her hand entwined in her knotted hair, she reluctantly said, "Come in."

Rho entered closing the door slowly behind him. "You look better, and Dale seems less terrified of us. I wasn't able to get him to leave your bedside."

"He's a good friend."

"I've been worried about you, too."

"I'm fine. But if you could find me some scissors...."

Rho flipped down the lid of the toilet with a loud *clunk*.

Raleigh sat.

"Brent would be better at this." He hunched over her inspecting the knot on her head.

If he was Brent, she wouldn't have been this nervous. His fingers grazed her scalp as he delicately pulled out one bobby pin and then another. She wondered if Rho'd thought about her as much as she'd thought about him over the last month.

"I didn't think I was ever going to see you again," she said.

"There's a reason I didn't want you to go. I'm glad you're back." He crouched down, leveling his face to hers. "Don't ever volunteer for something like that again."

Raleigh couldn't make that promise. Who knew what the future held? The mission to rescue Mu and Tau hadn't gone exactly to plan—not that there had been a real solid one—but it had been successful.

"Raleigh, promise me you won't do that again."

Raleigh gazed into his ocean-colored eyes. She didn't want to lie. As a spy, it became a necessity. As a friend, it wasn't. Instead, she reached out her hand, touched his cheek, and reveled in his presence. Then she leaned in and kissed him.

It wasn't like any kiss she'd ever had, partly because his lips were softer, but mainly because his Lucid laced it. Rho didn't stop her, even though the passion was one-sided. She sat back, her lips leaving his. Her eyes searched his as the rejection sobered her groggy mind.

"Raleigh." His voice worried her as much as his lack of participation. "I don't think we should go there."

The rejection cut her, making the gunshot wound trivial. Regret coaxed her away, her hands matting down her hair. She wanted him to leave. "Of course, you don't want me." Before Grant and Able, she never would've been so forward. The training had bolstered her confidence a little too much.

"No, no, no." Rho delicately lifted her chin with his fingertips. "The timing isn't right. I'm not sure that it's a good idea. It has nothing to do with you."

Only it did. They both were aware of it. He was right. The timing was off. The odds would've been better if she'd stayed with him in California instead of leaving.

"Let's forget it." Raleigh moved him out of the way with her good arm so she could stand. What she meant was for him to forget it, because something like this she never could. "I'll finish my hair. Thanks for getting out the tough ones." She yanked the other pins from the knot.

"You should really let me help you." He reached out, but she ducked away.

"I'm good. I'll see you downstairs. Make sure the others are being nice to Dale, would you?"

Rho knitted his eyebrows together. His charisma had failed.

"I'm not the first girl you've turned down. I can't be. It'll be fine." Now she was comforting him.... Unbelievable.

"The other girls didn't mean as much to me as you do, and you do, very much. You have to know that."

"I do. Check on Dale."

Reluctantly, he left the bathroom. The moment the door shut Raleigh grasped the counter and sucked back a sob. This was no time to wallow in embarrassment. She had a lot to discuss with the Designed. Her romantic dalliances, or lack thereof, weren't on the list.

Twenty minutes and a sponge bath later, she exited the bathroom. In Kappa's clothes she looked like a teenage boy who'd seen better days. Not that any of it mattered. Her appearance wasn't as important as getting the Designed to accept Dale—and for Dale to accept them.

She bumped into Tau as she walked to the stairwell. Raleigh never realized just how much she relied on sensing people until they barricaded.

"Watch out," he said.

Yes, Raleigh had rescued Tau. But from the look on his face, he didn't consider her his champion. The torture sat thick between them, the ends not compensating for the means.

"Tau." The tone of her voice poured an apology into his name. "I wanted to say that I'm sorry for what happened."

"Your boyfriend was very proud of you."

"Gabe? You know it's condescending to think that just because I was working with him, we were dating." This wasn't usually how she handed out apologies. Normally she wasn't so defensive, the wound and rejection made her disagreeable. Now wasn't the time to be talking to Tau.

"No, it plays a part. You look like the helpless little girl."

"I'm not helpless."

"Don't worry, I know that. I've got your number. I'm not going to dote on you like my brothers. Don't think that I'm going to let my guard down around you."

"We're on the same side."

"We have common allies. That's it. But trust me, we *aren't* on the same side. Not even close."

"You know, I got you out."

"My *brothers* got me out. You simply told them where to go."

Raleigh had done more than that. She infiltrated Grant and Able, made friends, and forged bonds only to break them. It cost her.

"I didn't enjoy torturing you," she said.

"Could've fooled me."

"I had to make it realistic, or Gabe wouldn't have bought it. He knew that I was strong enough to break you."

"About that." Tau said stepped close to her, his lips as near to her as Rho's had been moments before. But she didn't mistake this for intimacy. "I'm stronger now. You won't break my barricade again."

"I'm not out to break your barricade. I only did it before to get you out. It's not like I wanted to, but it had to be done. If I didn't, you'd still be stuck there. Now, if you'd get out of my way, we can go downstairs and discuss what to do next."

"*We?*"

"That's right. You chose Rho. If you don't like it, go find Sigma."

"You're something. You know that?"

She'd been called something before—usually after saving someone's life with sensing. Raleigh reminded herself that he was right. He just didn't know it. She was something, and that something was strong and resilient.

By the time Raleigh opened her mouth to respond, Tau was on his way down the steps. She guessed they'd be splitting up, and she assumed she'd see little of him. Nearing the living room, she found the Designed grouped around a coffee table. They simultaneously looked up. The weight of their gazes and the expectations that came with them bore down on her. Throwing her shoulders back, she took a seat. It was time to formulate a plan—and prove to herself and Dale that they'd made the right decision.